20 December

Mark Hebden is the author o:
was a sailor, an airman, a j(
cartoonist and a history teach
writing, Hebden created a sequence of crime novels,
inventing the well-known character of Inspector Pel.

MARK HEBDEN

HOUSE OF
STRATUS

This edition published in 2001 by House of Stratus, an imprint of Stratus Holdings plc, 24c Old Burlington Street, London, W1X 1RL, UK.

www.houseofstratus.com

Typeset, printed and bound by House of Stratus.

A catalogue record for this book is available from the British Library.

ISBN 1-84232-896-4

*Though Burgundians might decide they have recognised it –
and certainly many of its street names are the same – in fact,
the city in these pages is intended to be fictitious.*

one

'Have you ever been in love, sir?' Didier Darras asked.

Inspector Evariste Clovis Désiré Pel lifted his head. Sitting among the long grass on the bank of the River Orche, he had been holding his fishing rod with slack fingers, drowsily watching his float as it moved in the ripples just beyond the reeds. There was a dragonfly hovering above it and the thundery air was filled with the drone of insects. He looked at the line of fishermen along the bank nearby then at the boy alongside him.

'Many times, mon brave,' he said.

Mostly, however, he remembered sadly, without much success. With the names he bore, you could hardly expect to be a wow with the girls. The minute they learned them, they either registered shock or fell about laughing. One, he remembered bitterly, had actually fallen out of bed. Even as a child, he recalled, he had felt he had more than his fair share of the sort of labels that would arouse mirth in a schoolyard.

Fortunately for people like Pel, the world also had its quota of those who recognised that names, like relatives, were something you didn't choose but had wished on you and – Pel smiled at the thought – Madame Geneviève Faivre-Perret, who ran a beauty salon in the Rue de la Liberté in the city where he worked, was one of them, so that he was led to expect – believe – think – hope, anyway – that one day he might make her his wife.

He gave a mental shrug. Unhappily, the affair had had so many ups and downs it could hardly, even at this late stage, be regarded as a certainty. Police work had a habit of intruding into his private life – so much so, he often thought, it might almost be wiser to wait until he retired. On the other hand, Madame Faivre-Perret – he still found it difficult to think of her as Geneviève – was a widow, like Pel past the first flush of youth and, despite her undoubted charm and what was a clear if – to Pel, anyway – surprising fondness for Pel, even inclined to be short-sighted. It was quite possible, Pel had to concede, that she didn't see him as other people saw him – a small dark man with sharp eyes and an intense manner, rapidly going bald so that his sparse hair, combed flat across his head, looked a little like seaweed left draped across a rock by the receding tide. Under the circumstances, it might be better to push his suit before she took to wearing stronger reading glasses.

Busy with his thoughts, Pel stared at his float. An unexpectedly free afternoon had brought him out into the countryside. Much as he enjoyed Didier's company, he had to admit it would have been pleasanter with Madame Faivre-Perret alongside him, offering him dainty sandwiches and glasses of wine. But Madame Faivre-Perret had a business to run and probably couldn't stand fishing, anyway. Judging by her normal elegance, in fact, she probably didn't go much on flies and fresh air.

Pel made himself more comfortable. He didn't expect to catch a fish. Judging by the number of people who were always trying to catch them, French fish had to be the cleverest in the world. But, sitting on the bank of a river with the air heavy with heat and loud with the hum of bees, angling was one of the joys of Pel's life.

As he browsed, Didier snatched at his rod and began to reel in.

'How is it,' Pel asked aggrievedly, 'that you always catch fish and I never do?'

Didier shrugged. 'I work at it,' he said.

Pel accepted the fact. To him fishing was an excuse to sit in the sunshine doing nothing. Catching a fish was a bonus.

'Besides,' Didier went on, tossing a handful of white pellets on to the water, 'I prepare better.'

'The crumbs, of course.'

'They aren't crumbs. They're small pieces of bread. I roll them specially. Between my fingers. Then I dry them. They open up in the water. Like those things you used to get at kids' parties.' Pel noticed the 'used to.' At fourteen, Didier obviously considered he had put childhood behind him. 'You put these little green and red things in a saucer of water while everybody's sitting at the table, and they open up and become flowers. It's the same principle with ground bait.' He grinned at Pel. He didn't think much of him as a fisherman.

He was a sturdy youngster who had brought a lot of happiness into Pel's bachelor life. He was the nephew of Pel's housekeeper, Madame Routy, and turned up at Pel's house from time to time when his mother disappeared to care for an ailing father-in-law. To Pel he was an ally against Madame Routy, who not only cooked bad food but also made Pel's life a misery with her addiction to the worst offerings of television.

He looked at the boy affectionately. He had a sly sense of mischief that made him always willing to fall in with any of Pel's schemes to irritate his aunt. It was sad, Pel thought, that if he ever brought himself to the point of marriage – and the idea grew daily more interesting – Madame Routy would inevitably have to go and that, he feared, would mean the disappearance of Didier, too.

He was considering the possibility when the boy spoke again. 'I think I'm in love,' he said. The enthusiastic way he had unhooked the fish he had caught, studied it, then dropped it into the net that lay in the water by his feet made nonsense of the statement and Pel ignored it. He sniffed the air and cocked his head as he heard a growl of thunder. There had been rumbles rolling round the Burgundian hills for a few days now and he had a feeling they were building up to what would be quite a storm when it came.

'I think it's time we left,' he said.

Didier nodded and began to pack his fishing bag. Taking out of the net the fish he had caught, he tossed them back into the water.

'We can always catch them again,' he pointed out.

'*You* can, mon brave. I can't.'

Didier grinned. 'Are we eating out?'

Pel smiled conspiratorially. Madame Routy, they both agreed, was perhaps the only bad cook in a province which, in a nation of excellent cooks, claimed to have the best of them all, and it always gave them a malicious pleasure to eat out unexpectedly so that she had to polish off her repulsive dishes herself.

'Doubtless we can find somewhere,' he said. 'Then I'll look in the office.'

'You're always looking in your office,' Didier said. 'Are you busy?'

Pel's eyebrows rose. It made no difference whether he was busy or not. He just couldn't imagine the Police Judiciaire functioning without him.

'Not particularly,' he said. 'Garage hold-up at Regnon off the N7. Got away with the takings. Assault case at Auray-sur-Tille. Minor riot at Castel. Somebody threw a petrol bomb. But these things are all in a day's work.'

As they walked towards Pel's car, Didier lifted his head. 'Louise Bray,' he said.

'What about Louise Bray?'

'She's the one.'

'Which one?'

'The one I'm in love with. She lives next door. She used to hit me over the head with her dolls.'

'But now she doesn't?'

'Oh, no. She's all right. I decided last week. She had a party. We danced together all the time.'

'Having your arms round them always makes a difference, I've found.'

Didier gazed at Pel. 'You don't dance that way these days,' he said contemptuously. 'She had a disco. She always has good parties. Always novelties. Those flowers you put in water I told you about. That sort of thing. Have you ever seen them?'

'They had them,' Pel informed him dryly, 'when I was a boy.'

Didier frowned. 'I shan't be seeing her when I go home,' he said gloomily. 'We're going to Brittany for August. Think she'll wait?'

'I'd say it was more than likely.'

'When are you seeing yours again?'

'My what?'

'The one you always wear your best suit for.'

Not much slipped past young eyes, Pel reflected. He smiled. His affair with Madame Faivre-Perret had become a joke between them. 'Soon,' he said. 'I thought I'd arrange dinner somewhere. Make it an occasion. Impress her a bit. Don't you agree?'

Didier shrugged. 'Always dangerous, trying to impress them,' he said. 'Something always goes wrong.'

He didn't know how right he was.

Gilbert Lamorieux, the night watchman at the quarry on the eastern boundary of the village of St Blaize, was a small man no longer young. It didn't worry him much, though, because there wasn't much you could steal from a quarry. The site contained only an ugly huddle of buildings thickly coated with the dust of the diggings; a set of old-fashioned steam engines driving the rollers that crushed the clay and rock; a string of lorries, none of them new; an office full of dusty papers; and a little ready cash in a locked drawer. And that was all. Except, of course, for the explosives store, which was a steel bunker, situated for safety away from the main buildings.

Lamorieux could see the bunker from the window of the room where he made his coffee and ate his sandwiches and only went near it if he heard something suspicious. Children sometimes got into the quarry, and it was his job to keep them out. But the old steam engines seemed to intrigue them, and once he had even found a group of teenagers with a rat gun and had had to chase them away.

As he opened his sandwiches and poured himself a mug of coffee, the dog which helped him guard the premises sat up expectantly. It was young and he didn't like it because it had once wolfed his supper when he wasn't looking, and he gestured at it angrily so that it turned away, its tail between its legs. As it did so, however, it cocked its head suddenly and began to bark.

Lamorieux sighed. Kids, he thought. He picked up a torch and a heavy stick and signed to the dog to follow him. As he moved among the delapidated dusty buildings, he was thinking sourly of his coffee going cold and was just working himself up into a monumental bad temper when he realised that, for the first time in his experience, he actually had genuine intruders to deal with. Just ahead of him the beam of a torch was moving near the hut where the detonators for the explosives were kept.

'Hé!'

As he raised his voice, he saw a blur of white faces turned towards him, and, gesturing to the dog to move into the attack, he began to run. As he did so, the torch flashed in his direction again then, to his surprise, he heard a shot and a bullet whacked over his head to whine away into the distance. As he dived for the grass and pulled himself as close to the earth as he could get, he noticed that the dog had turned tail at the bang and bolted for the shelter of the office.

At just about the time Lamorieux was first spotting the light at the quarry at St Blaize, Madame Marie Colbrun, of Porsigny-le-Grand, was on her way home from her mother's house on the western boundary of the neighbouring village of Porsigny-le-Petit. Her mother, who lived alone, was over eighty and growing frail and it was Madame Colbrun's habit to visit her at least once a day to make sure she was all right.

On this particular day, Madame Colbrun had been into the city. Porsigny-le-Grand was a long way from civilisation and trips to the shops came round only occasionally, but she'd been offered a lift by a neighbour and, snatching at the chance, had begged money from her husband and disappeared soon after breakfast.

She was not used to spending money and had bought nothing but a new underslip but, since her husband was no more than a farmworker, an underslip was a luxury she didn't often afford. Above all, she had eaten a lunch prepared by someone else and gossiped over her coffee, something she rarely had time to do, and her mind was still full of her day out as she pushed at the pedals of her bicycle. She was a sturdy countrywoman with no fear of the dark. Nothing much bothered her and she was not even afraid of the rats that came after the grain she kept for her chickens, because her eldest son, who was fourteen and an expert with a rat gun, liked to sit and wait for them to poke their noses out. But he was a responsible boy and a good shot, which was more than could be said for some. It was not unusual in those parts for a youngster to help himself to his father's gun and take to the fields without much thought. She had once been peppered – fortunately at extreme range – by pellets from a twelve bore, and once a boy after rabbits had shot out her mother's kitchen window with a .22 from over a kilometre away.

She thought happily about her new underslip. Admiring herself in the mirror, she had suddenly remembered that she still had to check on her mother, and had decided to keep it on because her mother was inclined to be cantankerous and she had hoped it would take her mind off her woes for a while.

Her mother had been in a disgruntled mood and Madame Colbrun had sat down with her to have a glass of wine. After a lot of talk, she had finally persuaded the old woman that she was not being neglected and that everybody had her welfare at heart, and now, satisfied that her mother was content once more, she was cycling leisurely homewards. She had no light, which was against the law, but since you never saw any traffic in those parts after six o'clock at night and not very much before, she had no fear that the law would worry her.

Happy after her day out, she began to hum to herself and had almost reached home when something struck her thigh a blow as if it had been hit by a hammer. It jerked her foot from the pedal, so that she lost her balance, spun round and fell from the bicycle. Sitting on the roadside, her ample behind in the damp grass, she wondered what had happened. She had seen no assailant. Could it have been some animal she hadn't noticed which had collided with her?

Then she noticed a small spreading red stain on her dress and, lifting her skirt, saw that the new underslip was marked, too. Raising the underslip itself, she stared disbelievingly at her plump white thigh.

'Mon Dieu,' she said. 'I've been shot!'

Sergeant Jean-Luc Nosjean, of Pel's squad, was sitting in the Texas Bar of the Hôtel Central. The Hôtel Central was the best hotel in the city, as was obvious from the number of American tourists who used it. As everybody knew, American tourists were fabulously wealthy and lived in houses and apartments as big as the Parc des Princes, and the Hôtel Central was careful to make them feel at home. The Texas Bar lay on the right of the entrance hall. The New York Grill lay on the left. The Manhattan Cocktail Lounge lay directly ahead with, just beyond, the dining room – known throughout the city as Le Hamburger from its habit of including even that doubtful delicacy among its courses. Nosjean was all for catering for tourists, even for making them feel at home, but, considering how many French people also ate and drank in the hotel – especially out of season when there were no Americans – he felt the management had let their enthusiasm run away with them a little.

He was low in spirits. To his hurt surprise, his girl, Odile Chenandier, whom he had considered his personal property for two years now, had just informed him that she was getting married to someone else. To Nosjean it seemed an act of basest treachery. He had always assumed she was unable to live without him and wasn't sure whether to be bitter, angry or sad.

He stared at his drink gloomily. It wasn't every day a man got himself thrown over by the girl he had expected to marry – the fact that he had persistently ignored her for other girls was conveniently overlooked – and he decided that getting drunk might be a good idea. Unfortunately, it wasn't possible at that moment because officially he was engaged on enquiries about the garage hold-up at Regnon.

The Hôtel Central wasn't Nosjean's usual stamping ground, but in his present mood he was feeling reckless and was half-hoping to bump into a librarian who looked like Charlotte Rampling, whom he'd once met in the Texas Bar. As he brooded, the telephone on the reception desk rang. The clerk answered it, looked at Nosjean and held up the instrument. The voice that came to him was that of Inspector Daniel Darcy, Pel's deputy and Nosjean's immediate senior.

'You doing anything at the moment?' Darcy asked.

Bitterly Nosjean wondered what he could possibly be doing, with Odile Chenandier in the arms of another man. 'What's on?' he asked.

'We're pretty busy here,' Darcy said. 'There's been another break-in at the supermarket at Talant. That damned place ought to get guard dogs. De Troquereau's on that, and Lagé's investigating an indecent assault at Roën.'

'There's always Misset,' Nosjean pointed out.

'Misset went to Paris this morning on some business for the Chief. Something to do with some missing gelignite at Dom. He should have been back by this time but he hasn't reported in. I expect he's at home and keeping quiet.' Misset wasn't among the more ardent members of Pel's team. 'Either way, that only leaves you and me. And since the Old Man's taken the day off for a change, I'm on call here. There's been an attempted break-in at the quarry at St Blaize.'

'How do you break into a quarry?' Nosjean asked.

'There's an explosives store.' Darcy's voice was cold. 'And somebody fired a shot at the watchman.'

Nosjean sighed. Occupying himself with other people's troubles, he decided, would stop him brooding about his own.

'I'll get out there,' he said.

When he reached the quarry, he found Lamorieux in a bad temper but surprisingly unconcerned.

'Kids,' he said as Nosjean climbed out of his small red Renault and fished out his notebook.

'Why do you say that?' Nosjean asked.

'It's always kids. They were at the hut where we keep the detonators. It's separate from the explosives bunker. Safety measure. If it hadn't been kids they'd have gone for the gelignite.'

'You seem pretty certain.'

'Well, they were small, weren't they? It was almost dark but I could tell they were small.'

'What did they take?'

'A tin of detonators.'

'No jelly?'

'No.'

'They could blow their fingers off with detonators.'

'They could. But they won't. They know as much about detonators these days as you do.'

'If it was kids, why did they shoot at you?'

'Not *at* me. Over my head. They did it to frighten me. Panic, I expect.' Lamorieux shrugged. 'I suppose one of them had got hold of his father's .22 and it went off by accident.'

'You seem remarkably calm about it.'

The night watchman stuck out his chest. 'That was nothing,' he pointed out. 'I was under fire a few times in the war. I was taken prisoner in 1940 but I escaped and joined the Resistance.'

Nosjean looked about him. Something seemed to be missing.

'Wouldn't it help,' he asked, 'if you had a dog?'

The night watchman scowled. 'I've got one,' he said. 'It's locked in the lavatory. I'm wondering whether I ought to shoot it. It ate my supper.'

two

Vieilly didn't amount to much as a place – not even on Bastille Night, when most places looked better than normal. Surrounded by thickly wooded hills, it lay in a dip in the land and contained two banks, one or two small shops, four bars, a garage, a police substation, a mairie as solid as a fort, and an ancient church which, with the mairie, occupied the wide main square. It also sported a hotel which at first glance appeared to be far too big for the population but was explained by the fact that it had a splendid dining room well known throughout the district. Vieilly's only real claim to fame, in fact, was that it was the birthplace of Evariste Clovis Désiré Pel, and though that wasn't sufficient to get it in the guide books, it was enough for Pel to make quite a song and dance about it, because alongside him as he strolled along the village street in the last of the light was the woman he hoped to make his wife.

'It means a great deal to me,' he said, showing off a little.

The truth was he hadn't been near Vieilly in years, and his presence there wasn't because of his connection with the place at all, since his parents were dead and his two sisters, both older than he was, had married and left the district. It wasn't even because of any sentimental affection for the place; sentiment claimed only a small part of Pel's make-up. He was there, in fact, for the very simple reason that he had been checking up on a few recent events in the area and, being a little on the mean side, had thought he might kill two birds with one stone.

Following the disappearance of the detonators from the quarry at St Blaize, radio, television and newspaper warnings had been put out appealing for their return. Nothing had happened and it had been assumed that, as usually occurred in these cases, whoever had taken them had not had the courage to own up and they were now at the bottom of the river.

Pel, however – being Pel – was beginning to wonder if they were. It had not escaped his notice that when the gelignite had been stolen a few days before at Dom, as at St Blaize the thieves had been disturbed and detonators had not disappeared with it. It seemed to demand a few more enquiries, especially since in recent weeks there had been a spate of pamphlets, emanating, they knew, from the University, demanding a free Burgundy, whatever that was. As a good Burgundian, Pel entirely sympathised with the idea of an untrammelled and dominant Burgundy – after all, he had never been able to see the point of the rest of France – but the phenomenon troubled him. The world was full of freedom movements whose more enthusiastic supporters had got into the habit of throwing bombs about, so that it was not beyond reason to suspect that the stealing of explosives from Dom and the stealing of detonators from St Blaize could be connected. After all, the country was full of the fag-ends of other people's pogroms and the old colonial empire, and just lately many Africans, driven from their homelands by independence or the dictatorial set-ups that had followed independence, had started turning up in his territory, many of them aggressively hostile. And since he had to visit the district to check the activities of the sous-brigadier who ran the substation at St Blaize, it followed naturally that he should suggest to Madame Faivre-Perret that they should take dinner at the Trois Mousquetaires at Vieilly.

13

The meal was good and Pel was in a mood of euphoric self-satisfaction as he went to fetch his car round to the front door while Madame Faivre-Perret powdered her nose. Across the square a bar was being set up for the Bastille Night celebrations. There was to be dancing in the open air and the band was just erecting its amplifiers. Pel shuddered as they reminded him of life with Madame Routy.

He watched them for a while, memories of Bastille Nights in his youth running through his mind. He drew a deep breath, full of nostalgia, smelling the wood smoke of long-dead fires, hearing the long-gone calls of children and dogs across the sunlit fields and the slow talk of old men playing boules on the dusty footpath near the river.

He was still absorbed with his memories as he turned away and, not looking where he was going, crashed into the young man, also deep in thought and also not looking where he was going, who swung round the corner from the car park to the hotel.

Nosjean was a good policeman – sometimes too ardent for everyone else's comfort – but at least he had ideas and the thoughts that had occurred to Pel about the shooting at St Blaize had occurred to him, too, though they had arrived from an entirely different direction.

Like Pel, Nosjean wasn't satisfied that children had been responsible for the theft of the detonators and, making enquiries, had come up with the information that, on the night of the shooting at St Blaize there had been another incident at Porsigny-le-Petit where it seemed a woman had been slightly wounded. Because St Blaize was a substation of the main police station at Buhans and Porsigny was a substation of the main station at St Yves, the reports that had been made out had not been seen by the same police inspector and it was only by accident that Nosjean had spotted them at the Hôtel de Police.

A few quick enquiries had shown that the woman at Porsigny, who had not been very much hurt, had been hit by a bullet at the end of its trajectory. She had herself picked out the bullet, which was only just below the skin, and had thrown it away, so it had not gone to the forensic science department for assessment as to size and type, and she had not even bothered to go to hospital. But – and this was the point that intrigued Nosjean – it seemed her wound had been inflicted at just about the same time as Lamorieux's 'children' had been taking a pot shot at him at the quarry. Studying a map, Nosjean had worked out that a bullet fired at the quarry could just about have come to earth where Madame Colbrun had been wounded, and it was for this reason that he was in Vieilly. He had had another interview with Lamorieux then, pursuing his idea, had dug out Madame Colbrun.

To his surprise she had taken the same view as Lamorieux.

'Kids,' she said. 'They're always getting hold of guns People should be more careful and keep them locked up.'

'These "kids",' Nosjean pointed out, 'took a pot shot at Lamorieux, the night watchman at the quarry at St Blaize.'

She sniffed. 'Lamorieux's a bit of an old gasbag,' she said. 'To listen to him you'd think he won the war on his own.'

'Did you see anyone?'

Madame Colbrun cast her mind back. While she had been sitting in the shadows at the side of the road beside her bicycle, a car had passed. She had still been sufficiently shocked not to think of stopping it and it was only when it was vanishing from sight that she had come to life and called out.

'There was a car,' she said.

'What sort of car?'

'I didn't see.'

'Going fast?'

'Fairly fast.'

'See the occupants?'

'Not really.'

'Which way was it going?'

'Towards the city.'

'From where?'

'St Blaize direction.'

'It might,' Nosjean said, 'have contained the people who shot at Lamorieux and hit *you*.'

Madame Colbrun looked at him contemptuously. Nosjean was still young and looked even younger than he was. She didn't consider him very experienced.

'That was kids,' she said. 'With a .22. After rabbits. Somebody ought to do something about them.'

Nosjean had thought about the two incidents a lot and it occurred to him that it might be a good idea to have a search made for the bullet Madame Colbrun had taken from her thigh. She had shown it to her family then, with the indifference of a countrywoman to whom guns were not unfamiliar, had tossed it through the kitchen window into the bushes outside. He had a feeling that it would turn out to be something different from the .22 Madame Colbrun thought it was, in which case it would indicate something more than children. Nosjean suspected, in fact, that it had come from a handgun, and country people didn't use pistols or revolvers for shooting rabbits. He decided to do something about it the following day.

It was late when he stopped his car in Vieilly and he was hungry because he had had nothing since breakfast but a beer and a sandwich at the Bar Transvaal opposite the Hôtel de Police. Remembering that the hotel at Vieilly was supposed to run a good kitchen, he had decided to blow part of his wages on a good meal. It might, he thought, take his mind off Odile Chenandier.

He lit a cigarette and was deep in thought as he turned the corner to the hotel entrance. Crashing into the man coming towards him, he reeled backwards and looked up to find himself staring at his superior officer.

Pel glared at him. It didn't please him to bump into members of his team when he was engaged in one of the rare romantic interludes that entered his life. What made it worse was that Nosjean was smoking and Pel had been struggling all evening not to. Pel's struggle with his smoking had reached epic proportions and he was fighting manfully – if not to give it up, at least to cut it down from two million a day to five hundred thousand. He had struggled with twitching nerves all through the meal to avoid lighting up and had managed right to the moment when Madame Faivre-Perret had drawn out her own small case and offered him one. Having snatched at it like a starving man grabbing for a crust, to see Nosjean happily puffing away at what seemed the largest and most vulgar cigarette in the world was no help at all.

Slight, intense, a junior edition of Pel himself, Nosjean had drawn back, his jaw dropped.

'Patron!'

'What's happened?' Pel asked.

'Happened, Patron?'

'Who wants me?'

'Who wants you?' Nosjean was confused. 'Nobody wants you, Patron.'

'Then why did you track me down here?'

'I didn't track you down, Patron.' Nosjean's confusion increased. 'I was making a few enquiries and just stopped here on my way home. It's my night off and I thought – well, I thought I might as well. There's going to be dancing later and a bit of a procession.'

Pel studied him. He had always found Nosjean an honest young man and perhaps the most imaginative member of his

17

team. Nevertheless, Pel had an inbuilt reserve that prevented him wishing to share Madame Faivre-Perret with the rest of his staff. Madame Faivre-Perret had arrived unexpectedly in Pel's life and, for almost the first time, after a great many mistakes and a great deal of interference from his job and her relatives who had a habit of dying just when he had made arrangements to see her, he had got her alone. He preferred to keep it that way.

'It's odd you should come the night I happened to be here,' he said coldly.

Nosjean blushed. Like most of the Hôtel de Police, he had been following Pel's romance with interest. Like everybody else also, he was all for it succeeding, if only for the fact that it might improve Pel's temper.

'It wasn't intentional, Patron,' he insisted. 'I promise you. I was going to have a meal here, that's all. Are you?'

'We've had our meal,' Pel said. 'I was doing a bit of checking on those stolen detonators at St Blaize.'

'I was doing the same thing, Patron,' Nosjean admitted. 'A woman was wounded at Porsigny about the same time.'

'How did you discover that?'

'Accidental, Patron. Porsigny comes under St Yves and St Blaize under Buhans. They weren't on the same report and nobody noticed.'

This, Pel decided, was something that appeared to require his attention. He studied Nosjean, and, accepting that as usual he had been using his brains, he tried to make good his earlier sharp reprimand by smiling. He wasn't used to smiling and it made him look as if he was suffering from indigestion.

'Give my regards to Mademoiselle Chenandier,' he said.

'Odile Chenandier's not with me,' Nosjean said stiffly. 'I'm on my own.'

'Pity to waste such a warm evening.' Pel was feeling almost genial. 'You should have brought her.'

Nosjean gave him a grieving look. 'I can't,' he said. 'She's busy arranging her wedding.'

Pel's smile widened. The Hôtel de Police had been taking bets for some time on Odile Chenandier.

'Congratulations, mon brave,' he said.

'They're not in order, Patron,' Nosjean explained through gritted teeth. 'It's not to me. It's a type in the tax office who works regular hours. I think she might have waited.'

Pel decided Nosjean was asking rather a lot, considering the number of Catherine Deneuves and Charlotte Ramplings who had engaged his attention. He put his hand on Nosjean's shoulder. With his own affairs secure for the first time in his life, he felt he could spare a little sympathy.

'I'll leave it to you, mon brave. I'm off now. Tomorrow, come and see me and we'll compare notes on what we've found out.'

Collecting Madame Faivre-Perret, he moved towards his car and was just about to open the door when a policeman approached him, touching his hand to his képi. Every policeman in Burgundy, to say nothing of a few in other provinces, had got to know Pel. Many of them had had occasion to feel the length of his tongue and this one was trying hard to look alert and on his toes.

'Sir,' he said, 'I wonder if you'd be so kind as to wait just a moment.'

Pel's eyebrows lifted and the policeman stiffened nervously.

'We've just stopped all the traffic,' he explained. 'For the children's procession, you understand.'

Pel frowned. In his view, the only person allowed to make demands was Clovis Evariste Désiré Pel.

'It'll only be for a quarter of an hour or so, sir.' The policeman looked as if he'd been set in plaster of Paris. 'Perhaps you'd care to have drink. I think we could find you one in the substation.'

Pel tried to imagine Madame Faivre-Perret sitting in the substation drinking a quick brandy out of the thick glasses they kept in the cupboard there. 'I think we'll watch the procession,' he said.

Inevitably, the procession took rather longer than the quarter of an hour that had been predicted, and the minute princesses, clowns, pierrots and pierrettes continued to fill the roadway as they jostled and shoved their way towards where the Maire was handing out lollipops. Pel and Madame Faivre-Perret watched, Madame with a maternal smile on her face, Pel with a blank expression because, if there were one thing he didn't like, it was being delayed when he was on his way somewhere.

As the procession finally dispersed, he touched Madame's arm and they headed for the car, only to find it hemmed in by late arrivals. The policeman who was guarding it wore a harassed look.

'We'll get it free, sir,' he announced. Just let me have the keys and I'll attend to it myself. I know who the owners of these other cars are. I'll shift the stupid cons. I'll let you know as soon as you can move.'

The band had started and a few couples were jigging quietly. As the music changed to a waltz, Madame Faivre-Perret looked at Pel. Pel tried to look the other way but it was no good. It was obvious she wanted him to dance with her. He gave her a sickly smile and held out his arms.

'I'm not much of a dancer,' he mumbled as they circled slowly.

Madame Faivre-Perret smiled indulgently. 'So I notice. I won't insist on another.'

As the crowd increased, the band switched to a modern beat and turned up the volume. It seemed to Pel at times that the whole of the younger generation, like Madame Routy, had been stricken with deafness. Someone was bawling a chorus which seemed to consist of the words 'We mounted the stairs, we mounted the stairs' over and over again, and they were just about to turn away when the noise stopped abruptly and Pel heard his name over the loud speaker.

'Monsieur Pel! Monsieur Pel! Will Monsieur Pel please come to the space behind the band at once?'

Pel looked at his companion. 'They've got the car free,' he said.

They pushed through the crowd to an area curtained off with canvas. It was criss-crossed with all the leads and wires that gave the instruments volume. To Pel's surprise, Nosjean was there.

He had already seen more of Nosjean than he had expected to see but he remembered his manners sufficiently to introduce Madame. Then he noticed Soulas, the brigadier of the substation, standing nearby, looking ill at ease.

'What's all this about?' Pel asked. 'Where's my car?'

Nosjean gave him a worried look. 'It's not your car, Patron,' he said. 'It's trouble.'

Pel gritted his teeth. Why, he wondered, did God have it in for him so? One of his dates with Madame had been ruined when he had found himself in Innsbruck in the Austrian Tyrol with two dead men. Another had been spoiled by one of Madame's aunts giving up the ghost at the crucial moment so that Madame had been away for what had seemed years attending to her affairs. It appeared that this sort of ill luck was to pursue him throughout the whole of his courtship.

'I suppose,' he said bitterly, 'that some policeman, in between drinking a bock of beer and making love to his wife, has stumbled on a break-in, and hasn't the wits to handle it himself.'

'It's rather more than that, Patron.' Nosjean drew him a little furthur towards Brigadier Soulas so that Madame Faivre-Perret shouldn't hear. 'A kid's been found dead in the woods. it looks as if he's been murdered.'

three

At just about the time that Pel was trying to inform Madame Faivre-Perret that a pleasant evening out had come to a very abrupt end, events were taking place in the city which were going to involve him even more.

Maurice Rohard, an elderly draper, who lived over his shop in the Rue Ruffot in the oldest part of the city, was standing with his head cocked alongside the wall which separated the back of his premises from the back of the premises next door. He could hear tapping and that, he knew, was not as it should be, because the shop next door, belonging to his friend, Eugène Zimbach, a jeweller, was normally locked up at six o'clock every night, and unlike Rohard, Zimbach did not live on the premises.

Calling his elder sister, Violette, who kept house for him, Rohard directed her to listen.

'It sounds like knocking,' she decided. 'Hammering even.'

'Well, that's odd, isn't it?' Rohard said. 'Because Eugène's been locked up and gone home two hours now. I think I'd better have a look around.'

He donned his hat, and, because he thought it would look less suspicious, called to the surprised dog, which had already been for its evening walk and wasn't in the habit of getting two. He returned half an hour later, having strolled quietly past the jeweller's next door and gazed into the window on the pretence of studying the goods for sale.

'I couldn't see anything wrong,' he said.

'Well,' his sister pointed out, 'they're still at it. Hadn't you better call the police?'

'They'll be busy. It's Bastille Night.'

'There must be one or two available.'

Rohard reached for the telephone and five minutes later the doorbell rang and a young plain clothes policeman appeared. He was from the team of Inspector Goriot who, until a few months before when Pel had been promoted, had been equal in importance and even hoping for promotion because his uncle was a senator and had a great deal of influence in the places where influence mattered. The young policeman's name was Desouches and he was one of Goriot's best men. Rohard called him in and they listened together to the tapping sounds.

'Sounds like drilling now,' Desouches said.

There was another series of taps then a muffled clattering.

'That sounds like someone breaking down the brickwork,' Rohard pointed out.

Desouches frowned. 'What do you think they're after?'

'There's the jeweller's next door,' Rohard said. 'But I've had a look and there doesn't seem to be anything wrong. Of course, they could be trying to get in through the back from the Impasse Tarien.'

'What's in the Impasse Tarien?'

Rohard shrugged. The Impasse Tarien was a shabby cul-de-sac in an area of the city that the city fathers were endeavouring to eradicate. It had no architectural value and insufficient age to be a curiosity – just a group of houses erected in the last century when the city had begun to expand, devoid of beauty and possessing little in the way of amenities.

'Not much,' he admitted. 'It's due to be demolished.'

Desouches listened again. 'Where do you think it's coming from?' he asked.

23

'It seems to be coming from Number Ten or Number Eleven. But it can't be. They've been empty for some time.'

'Does Zimbach keep much on his premises?' Desouches asked.

'He's got a safe in the cellar.'

Desouches made up his mind. 'I'll have a sniff around,' he said.

Walking round to the Impasse Tarien, he knocked on the door of Number Nine and asked if anyone were working in the yard.

'No,' he was told. 'I think you've got the wrong place. It's next door.'

'You can hear them?'

'All the time. I think they're in Number Ten.'

'Isn't Number Ten empty?'

'It's supposed to be. If there's anyone there, they're squatters.'

'What about Number Eleven on the other side? Isn't that supposed to be empty, too?'

'It's supposed to be.'

Desouches nodded and tried Number Ten. The shutters were closed and his suspicions were aroused at once as the doorway was opened no more than a slit. 'I'm looking for Monsieur Rohard,' he said.

All he could see in the dark interior beyond the door was a blur of nose, mouth and eyes. A hand gestured towards the end of the street, then the door shut firmly in his face.

As he turned away, Desouches noticed a man standing in a nearby doorway. He appeared to be watching because, as the policeman turned, he swung away and vanished round the corner. Deciding not to use his radio at once but to go into the next street where he couldn't be seen, by this time Desouches was convinced that something underhand was taking place. Turning the corner, he pressed the switch of his radio and spoke.

'Stay where you are,' he was told. 'We'll have a car round there at once.'

Three minutes later a police car drew quietly to a stop. Desouches knew both the men inside because the driver, Emile Durin, was his cousin and had joined the police after his military service for no other reason than that Desouches had. The brigadier commanding the car was a burly Meridional called Randolfi. Desouches explained what he'd been doing and Randolfi reached for the door handle.

'We'll go together,' he said. 'Did you get a look at them?'

'Not much. Just a blur. It was dark inside. They didn't turn on any lights. I think he was a foreigner.'

'Why do you think that?'

'Because he didn't say anything.'

'He might have had his mouth full,' Randolfi observed dryly. 'It's rude to talk with your mouth full.'

'He could have waited till he'd emptied it,' Desouches retorted. 'But he just gestured and shut the door in my face.'

It didn't take long to find out that Number Eleven had been officially empty for some time and Randolfi decided they ought to have Inspector Goriot in on the affair. Within a few minutes, another car drew up behind the first. Inside were Goriot and two more detectives.

Goriot gestured to them. 'You, Aimedieu, and you, Lemadre,' he said, 'go round into the Rue Ruflot. The yards in the Impasse Tarien back on to the yards there. It's quite obvious it's a break-in and if we appear at the front they'll probably try to go that way. Get over the wall and pick them up as they come out.'

As the two men vanished, Goriot gestured to the others. 'I'll leave it to you, Desouches,' he said. 'It's your case.'

Marching boldly up to Number Ten, with Goriot, Randolfi and his cousin, Durin, just behind, Desouches tapped on the door. As before, it opened slightly and a dark face appeared.

'We've had complaints,' Desouches said. 'About noise. Have you been working or knocking inside there?'

The man behind the door stared.

'Did you hear what I said?' Desouches went on and when the man still didn't answer, he pushed the door further open. 'You a foreigner?' he asked.

There was still no answer and Desouches decided it was time to put on the pressure. 'I'd like to see your papers,' he said.

Immediately, the door was pushed to but Desouches got his foot in the gap.

'Open up,' he shouted. 'Or we'll come in!'

Thrusting the door open, he stepped inside and found he was in a small hall, with a room off to his right. As he looked round him, Goriot pushed in, too. 'Anybody working here?' he asked.

The man spoke at last. 'No,' he said.

'I'd like to have a look,' Goriot said. 'Show us the way.'

The man pointed down a passage to the rear of the building and Goriot glanced at Desouches. The hall was crowded now because Randolfi and Durin had also pushed their way in. As they turned towards the rear of the house a door opened and a man appeared, holding a pistol in each hand. Goriot heard the sound of the shot and felt something tug at his sleeve. Immediately there were more shots and Desouches staggered back and, collapsing against the half open door, fell over the doorstep. Alongside him, Randolfi was hit as he reached for his pistol and, stumbling over Desouches, fell into the street. As he rose and staggered away, he was hit again and as Durin ran to help him a bullet shattered his thigh bone. Struggling with the man who had opened the door, Goriot had also been hit.

As the policemen who had gone into the Rue Ruffot appeared at the other end of the hall, Lemadre was in the lead and as he came through the rear door, the man with the pistol whirled and fired. Lemadre grabbed him but the pistol was against his body and the trigger was being pulled repeatedly so that his legs finally buckled and he fell, dragging with him the man with the pistol. Aimedieu, who had been just behind, was about to grab for the gunman when there was a terrific jolt that seemed to shake the house and he was whirled aside by a hurricane of air. A ball of orange flame swept out of a room on his right and there was the roar of an explosion and a gust of black smoke. A tremendous clamour beat against his ears and his mouth seemed to be full of cinders so that he felt as if he were looking into the muzzle of a gigantic blowlamp. Figures were staggering about in the smoke and flame, then the ceiling fell on him and he went down covered in plaster and laths, while whirling fragments swung about above him like frenzied glittering bats.

For a while he lay still, then, realising he wasn't dead, he lifted his shoulders and straightened up, the plaster, dust and bits of broken wood falling from him to the floor. His face was black with the soot the explosion had brought down the chimney and there were little flecks of blood on his face and hands and small rents in his clothing where flying fragments had caught him.

The shooting had stopped and there was a dead silence. A few dazed people had appeared and a woman in the street started screaming that she'd been wounded, in a harsh nerve-wracking way that spoke of hysteria. Another lay dead.

Desouches was sprawled in the doorway with a wound in his neck. Goriot was lying in the hall, groaning with a bullet in his hip. Maurice Rohard was supporting Brigadier Randolfi, who was clearly dying. Durin sprawled near the stairs and Lemadre was struggling on hands and knees. As Aimedieu pushed through the debris to help him, he heard the wail of a police siren.

At Vieilly Pel was struggling to explain what had happened to Madame Faivre-Perret. She didn't look any too pleased
but was trying hard to put a good face on it. Romance with
Pel was sometimes a little trying.

'I'll arrange for a police car to drive you home,' Pel was
saying.

Madame Faivre-Perret touched his hand. 'My dear
Evariste,' she said. 'I'm quite capable of driving myself. I'll
take your car.'

'There aren't many cars about like my car,' Pel said, faintly
ashamed. It was probably a good job, too, he thought;
nothing on it seemed to work and he had been wondering for
some time how he could afford a new one, because he was
terrified the door would fall off as they went round a corner
and deposit Madame Faivre-Perret in the gutter. 'We'll attend
to it.'

He spoke quietly with Brigadier Soulas and a car – not the
official one but Soulas' own, which, Pel noticed bitterly, was
newer than his – appeared within seconds.

'Perhaps it's better this way.' Madame Faivre-Perret
squeezed his hand. 'It can't be helped,' she said, a trifle
disconsolately. 'Telephone me as soon as you can.'

To Pel's surprise, she kissed him gently on the cheeks and
turned away. A policeman waved the car off and it slipped
through the shadows towards the main road. Pel stared after
it for a moment then drew a deep breath. But he made no
complaint. Crimes committed in his spare time usually raised
a bleat of protest, but children were different. He hated
crimes involving children.

From the other side of the canvas screen the band was still
pounding away, its beat thudding inside Pel's head like a
metronome. Soulas looked worried.

'Should we send everybody home?' he asked.

'What good would that do?' Pel asked. 'No, leave it. But get the names of everybody here.' He turned to Nosjean. 'Have you contacted Darcy yet?' he asked.

'Not Darcy,' Nosjean said. 'I got hold of Misset. He's just got back from Paris.'

Misset was Pel's bête noire, the one man on his team he felt he could never trust.

'I hope he got the message correctly,' he growled. 'Where's Darcy?'

'He's been called out on something.'

'Right,' Pel said. 'Let's go.'

The woods at Vieilly were dark but Brigadier Soulas had rigged up lamps and canvas screens. The body was clad in a red, white and blue jersey and Doctor Minet, who had just appeared, was bent over it, while the lab men prowled around with tape measures, their noses to the ground, looking for anything that might help.

'Who is he?' Pel asked. 'One of the local children? From the procession?'

'Soulas doesn't know him,' Nosjean said. 'And he's been here seven years and reckons he knows them all. I think he's from the city. He's got a membership card in his pocket for a youth gymnasium near the Place Wilson.'

'Check with whoever runs it. Find out where all their members are supposed to be.'

As Nosjean turned away, Pel lit a cigarette. Under the circumstances he felt he could be forgiven and, with a case on his hands, he knew it was a losing battle, anyway. He looked at Doc Minet who had just straightened up and was stretching his back.

'What happened to him?' he asked.

'At first glance – strangled.'

Pel said nothing, conscious of a pulse beating in his head as he thought of the boy's terror.

'I don't think he was killed that way, though,' Minet said in a strained voice. He was a cheerful little man who enjoyed teasing Pel, but the murder of a child changed everybody. 'I've still to make certain – and that'll take time – but I think he died from suffocation.'

'Scarf? Coat?'

'Neither. The ground's soft here. His face was pressed into it. If you look closely you can see the impression it made – nose, chin, mouth, everything. There's soil in his eyes, nostrils and mouth.'

'Sexual? It is a sexual attack?'

'Doesn't look like it. His clothing's not been disarranged, except in the struggle that must have taken place. Nothing else, though. I'll tell you better when I've examined him.'

'Anything in his pockets?'

'A few coins and – ' Minet opened his hand to show three blue and yellow capsules – 'and these.'

'What are they?'

'They look like diazepam.'

'What's that?'

'Tranquillisers. Vallium based. These'll be five-milligram doses.'

'For a boy his age?'

'I've heard of kids taking them. God knows, they're prepared to try anything these days for a kick.'

Pel tossed away his cigarette and fished for another but, because he'd come out that evening intending to cut down his smoking, he found he'd finished what he'd brought. Minet saw his look and pulled out a pack of Gitanes.

'I thought you were trying to stop,' he said.

'This sort of thing doesn't help,' Pel growled.

He prowled about, studying the ground about him. One of the lab men lifted his head.

'Anything?' Pel asked.

'Not much, Patron, beyond a few cigarette ends. None of them particularly new.'

When Nosjean came back, Pel was standing with his hands in his pockets, his shoulders hunched.

'I've contacted the type who runs the gymnasium, Patron,' he said. 'Name of Martinelle – Georges Martinelle. It's only a small one, with about fifty boys. He's an ex-major. Not a fighting man, it seems, but a physical training instructor who ended up in charge of all recruit training at Clermont-Ferrand.'

'What about the boy?'

'He couldn't say. He's promised to take a list of his members round to the Hôtel de Police. I let them know to expect it.'

'Who? Darcy?'

'Cadet Martin was on the desk. He said everybody was out.'

'Everybody?'

'Well, there's no one in Goriot's office and there seems to be nobody in ours.'

'What's happened to Misset?'

'He seems to have disappeared too, now, Patron.'

'He would. What in God's name is Darcy doing? He should be here by this time.'

Leaving Nosjean to look after things, Pel signed to Brigadier Soulas, who drove him to the substation where his car was parked. By this time, the celebrations had a worn look. The band was still thumping out its beat but the bar had run out of drink and only a few youngsters were still dancing. Everybody else had gone home. Pel glanced at his watch. It was past midnight.

'What in the name of God's Darcy up to?' he growled again.

With every policeman in the village suddenly on duty, the telephone was being attended by Madame Soulas.

'I have a message for you,' she said. 'Inspector Darcy rang. Will you ring in at once?'

Pel glared. 'Will *I* ring in?' he growled. 'Who does Darcy think he is?'

He picked up the telephone and dialled the number of the Hôtel de Police. The operator answered at once but it seemed to require a long time to get hold of Darcy. When he finally answered, he sounded breathless and in a hurry.

'I think you'd better get back here, Patron,' he said immediately before Pel could start asking questions.

'What do you mean, I should get back there?' Pel snapped. 'You should be out here. We've got a murder on our hands.'

There was a moment's silence. When Darcy's voice came it sounded tired and deflated. 'So have we, Patron.' He spoke slowly and clearly so there should be no mistake about what he was saying. 'Four! Three of them cops!'

four

By the time Pel reached the Hôtel de Police he was grey with weariness, but if anything Darcy looked even more tired. Darcy was a handsome young man, dark-haired with flashing eyes and a way with women. It had often been in Pel's mind that while he, Pel, didn't spend enough time in other people's beds, Darcy probably spent too much. Nevertheless, he was a good policeman who was always willing to work long hours, and had enough energy, if it could only have been harnessed to the power system, to run a battleship. At that moment, however, he looked jaded in a way that didn't spring entirely from physical weariness.

His ash-tray was filled with half-smoked cigarette stubs and his desk was littered with half-consumed cups of coffee. In the office outside, Claudie Darel, the sole woman member of Pel's team, was talking on the radio and he noticed that Cadet Martin, whose job really consisted of looking after the mail and running errands, was by the telephone despite the hour.

'Everybody else's out,' Darcy said. 'Every damned man we could raise. We've dragged them out of bed and off leave, and left messages when we couldn't find them. Goriot's in hospital with a bullet in his hip and one in the thigh. Desouches is dead. So are Lemadre and Brigadier Randolfi, of Uniformed Branch. Durin's in hospital with Goriot.'

It made Pel's little affair out at Vieilly sound tame. He became calm at once, his temper subsiding as he realised what Darcy had been handling. 'Inform me,' he said.

Darcy did so. 'They were rushed to hospital,' he continued. 'But Randolfi was already dead, shot through the heart, with two other bullets just above the hipbone. Goriot's suffering from shock and loss of blood. Lemadre was brought in with six bullet wounds in him, one just above the right scapula, a second an inch to the right of the tenth dorsal disc, a third in the left side, an inch below the tip of the left rib, a fourth and fifth in the left thigh, and another in the right calf. He was suffering from internal haemorrhage and was operated on at once, but he died within the hour. Desouches was brought in semi-conscious, a bullet in the right shoulder joint, another in the neck. His spinal cord was partially severed and his lower limbs were paralysed. He answered a few questions rationally but we've just heard he's died, too. His wife was expecting a baby. Durin's thigh was smashed. There was also a woman who happened to be just going home. Bullet in the head.'

'What happened?' Pel asked, shocked. 'Did someone declare war?'

'It started as an investigation into a suspected break-in.' Darcy described what had happened. 'They just let go with everything they had. Then the bang came. They obviously had explosives there and one of the shots must have hit the charge and up it went. Or else they'd prepared some mechanism for Zimbach's safe and, when Goriot's people arrived, they forgot it in the panic.'

'Was no one arrested?' Pel asked quietly.

'Patron, every man but one of the group that went to investigate was hit, and that one was buried by the debris of the explosion.'

Pel gestured. 'I wasn't criticising, Daniel,' he said gently and Darcy looked up because he couldn't remember the last time Pel had used his first name.

'We have a witness called Arthur Mattigny,' he went on. 'He says he saw two men helping a third man away and a woman hurrying behind. When Mattigny stared at them, the woman screamed "Go away, go away" at him. He thought the man was drunk and it was only when he got round the corner into the Impasse Tarien that he realised something had happened. Then he saw Randolfi on the pavement and thought the police had put on a raid on a brothel and Randolfi had been shot as they broke in. Whoever they were, they've got plenty of ammunition. Apart from what's been dug out of Goriot, Durin and the dead men, they've already found seven bullets in what's left of the house. There must be more under the debris.'

'And the house?'

'Wrecked.'

'And the people who were seen escaping?'

'They got away, Patron.'

'Car?'

'Nobody's reported seeing them get into a car. When the smoke had gone and we'd cleared our casualties away, there was nobody there. They must have disappeared in the confusion. When I arrived the place was empty. De Troquereau got the witnesses into a bar and started questioning them. He was on the ball at once.'

'Lagé? Misset?'

Darcy managed a small twisted smile. 'Just like Lagé and Misset. They did their job but I wouldn't give either of them top marks for brilliance. We've got Aimedieu working with us, from Goriot's squad. He's only a kid but he's useful. He's also the only one who was there and knows more or less what happened. We've also got Brochard and Debray from Goriot's squad. It looks as though we're going to be busy, because Goriot's squad's been cut to half size.'

'Go on.'

'We've got a search going on now. There's a group of workshops at the end of the street and Misset's going through it with the uniformed branch in case they went in there. Personally, I don't think they did. There was food in the house and I found a pressure gauge, a flexible metal tube and several feet of rubber tube. The windows have been broken by the firing and bullets were found in the ceiling. It was like a Wild West shoot-out.'

Pel listened patiently, saying nothing, and Darcy went on.

'In the back yard there were indications that someone had climbed the wall to get into the house. There was an oxygen cylinder, broken bricks and tungsten-tipped drills, a carpenter's brace, a chisel, crowbars and a metal wrench. A hole had been made in the brickwork, twenty-four inches high and twenty across. In the house there was mortar, sand, pressure lamps and asbestos boarding. The door was locked from inside and jammed so it couldn't be opened. The ammunition all seems to be Browning. There's a safe in Zimbach's place that contains jewellery. It's concreted in and they were either going to chisel it out or break into it.'

'Any ideas who they were?'

'I've got my suspicions.'

'You'd better make them public, mon brave.'

Darcy looked up. 'I think they're terrorists,' he said.

Terrorists! That was something they could do without.

For a moment, Pel sat in silence. Then, as he fished for a cigarette and found he hadn't any, Darcy pushed a packet across and leaned forward with the lighter.

'Can't have this, Patron,' he said gently. 'Smoking mine.'

'I've been smoking yours for years,' Pel growled.

'Not lately, Patron. I'd begun to think you'd deserted to the non-smokers.'

'I wish to God I could,' Pel said.

He huddled in his chair, his head down, still wearing his hat, deep in thought.

'Why do you think they're terrorists?' he asked.

'I don't know, Patron. Just a hunch. We've had a lot of people drift into this area in recent years, accepting low wages that are pushed even further down by their numbers. There was that riot at Castel and that case last month at the glass works near Dôle. Attempted wages snatch. They got away, you'll remember, but not with any money, and when they were holed up in Longeau they shot themselves. They were identified as dissident Algerians. We also know of other groups.' Darcy stopped to draw breath. 'How about yours, Chief?' he asked. 'I gather you've got one, too.'

Pel started. In his absorption with the killing of the policemen, he had almost forgotten Vieilly.

'A child,' he said. 'Nosjean's handling it for the time being.' He rose, his hands in his pockets. 'We'd better do a check,' he said. 'The Maire's diary. The Prefect's. If these people of yours *are* terrorists and were preparing explosives, what were they for? They must have been for something. Get in touch with the Palais des Ducs. There must be something coming up they were hoping to disrupt. Let's have a list of possibilities. And let's have everybody in for a conference first thing in the morning. Uniformed branch can keep an eye on Vieilly and the Impasse Tarien until we've sorted things out. You'd also better get on to the Chief and see if we can have a few men from Uniformed Branch for a while. We'll sure as God need them, because there's going to be an outcry in the press: Three policemen and a woman dead, two more wounded, and a boy dead at Vieilly. Make it early. And tell Misset if he's one second late, he'll be back on traffic.'

'That'd be no help, Patron,' Darcy said wearily. 'We're going to need everybody we can get – even Misset.'

By the following morning the shock was beginning to subside a little. The death of a policeman always sent a wave of anger rippling through a police force. Though they all knew the chances of dying at their job existed, nevertheless when someone did it always came as a blow. And three! Three was a massacre!

Inside the Hôtel de Police the scene was chaotic. Everybody was in a mood of cold anger, stunned by the killing. There was a crowd outside, that grew bigger every minute with children, reporters and television cameramen.

Darcy and Pel had organised their team by this time. Sergeants experienced in murder had been brought in from the districts, and other men had been called in to work behind the scenes, to collate the facts, interview callers, keep records and generally make themselves useful. Extra telephones had been installed, empty cabinets arranged, and filing indexes set up with typewriters and stationery.

Going to the scene of the shootings, Pel found the Impasse Tarien cordoned off by police cars. The newspapers were already carrying banner headlines and the television and radio had put out bulletins. As he moved into the wrecked house, there seemed to be dozens of policemen around – in cars, on motor-cycles, on foot.

As he talked with Darcy a man was brought in. He was small and nervous.

'Gilles Roman,' he introduced himself. 'I might have a clue.'

Pel eyed him hostilely, expecting another of the wild statements they'd been receiving ever since the shootings had taken place. 'Well?' he asked. 'What is it?'

'I saw a car in the Rue Claude-Picard,' Roman said. 'It's only a few hundred metres from here. I couldn't tell what make it was but it was pale blue and it was going fast. I saw it scrape three other cars which were parked there. It didn't stop.'

'Its number?' Pel asked.

'I got some of it.'

Pel could have kissed him. At last they had something to work on. 'Let's have what you got.'

'9701-R – and then I lost it.'

Pel gestured at Darcy. 'Get him down to the Hôtel de Police,' he said. 'Then get hold of traffic and find out everything you can about this incident. Get hold of everybody who had a car parked in Claude-Picard and came back to find it damaged. One of them might just have seen something. And let's find who was driving this blue job. We might have something to report to the conference.'

The lecture room at the Hôtel de Police was crowded. Even the Chief was there. So were Judge Polverari and Judge Brisard, who were watching the two cases separately; Inspector Nadauld, of Uniformed Branch, who was there because he was supplying extra men; and Inspector Pomereu, of Traffic, because road blocks had been set up all round the city; to say nothing of Doc Minet, Leguyader of the Lab, Prélat, of Fingerprints, and Grenier of Photography. Half the city's police seemed to be crowded into the lecture room, their faces bleak with the knowledge of what lay ahead of them.

Pomereu had already found the owners of the damaged cars in the Rue Claude-Picard but they had not been near their cars at the time and had seen nothing and, with Roman the only witness, everything seemed to depend on finding the car which had done the damage.

On the other hand, more people had reported seeing the two men helping a third through the street. Like Arthur Mattigny, who had been the first to see them, they had all assumed they were friends helping home a drunk and hadn't taken much notice. From these sources, however, there had been no mention of the woman and they could only assume she'd gone ahead to warn the driver of the blue car Roman had seen or to prepare some hiding place. If nothing else, they now had descriptions of the wanted men, even if only vague, and they had been immediately put out to all forces.

By this time, every message, however trivial, that came in – and there were hundreds – was being recorded and cross-indexed, an open channel had been set aside for radio transmitting and receiving, and a special radio made available for both cars and subsidiary headquarters, an expert operator handling the Hôtel de Police end.

They all took their places and began to shuffle themselves to some sort of comfort on chairs or leaning against walls and filing cabinets. Everybody was there. Misset – running to fat and good-looking in a way that had once got him the girls but now made him look merely self-indulgent – had managed to arrive on time. Only just, but he'd made it, the last to slip into his chair.

'Sorry I'm late, Patron,' he had panted.

'You're not,' Pel growled. 'But you're only just "not".'

He stared round at his squad. Like Darcy, he was drawn with fatigue. Most of the others had managed to snatch an hour or two's sleep but he and Darcy had been at it all night. Pel had taken a few minutes off to telephone Madame Faivre-Perret and had heard her gasp of horror as he had explained what had happened, then the touch of sorrow in her tones as she had said she understood.

He wondered if she did. Marriage was in the air these days but he wondered if she knew what she was letting herself in for: A lot of loneliness and empty evenings, if nothing else, and a deep involvement with the police that often alienated friends and neighbours. Fortunately, she was a businesswoman with the best hairdressing salon in the city, which would compensate by occupying her when she needed occupying.

He looked again at his squad. His men were as familiar to him as his own two hands. Misset: Lazy, careless, bored with his marriage and always with an eye on the young women secretaries employed about the Hôtel de Police. Pel had several times tried to get rid of Misset, but so far he hadn't managed it. Lagé: Friendly, willing enough – even to do other men's work, usually Misset's – but lacking in imagination and usually wandering around like a dog looking for a bone. Nosjean: Pel looked at him with warmth. Soon they would need to promote someone to take Darcy's place as senior sergeant and Pel had a feeling it would be Nosjean. He was quick, intelligent and eager. Over-earnest for Pel's taste's so that his conscience not only troubled Nosjean but all the rest of the squad too, including Pel. At the moment he looked withdrawn and bleak, his face taut. De Troq': Sergeant Baron Charles Victor de Troquereau Tournay-Turenne. With a handle like that, de Troq' ought to have been an ambassador. Instead he was a member of Pel's team, and a surprisingly good one. Educated, arrogant, handsome, self-confident and keen, the absolute opposite of Misset, he was another in the line of Nosjean and Darcy, never expecting evenings off and managing to slot his private life into the gaps left by his police work.

Pel's eyes roved on. Claudie Darel: Sent to his team from Paris, neat, attractive, dark-haired with the look of a young Mireille Mathieu and disruptive in that she kept every male member of the squad on his toes to compete for her favours. At the moment De Troquereau was leading the field. Régis Martin: Cadet, almost entirely lacking in experience but earnest and eager to be a proper policeman, on Pel's squad to answer telephones, attend to the mail and fetch bottles of beer from the Bar Transvaal across the road.

His eye fell on the remaining members of Inspector Goriot's squad. Aimedieu: Little more than a boy and still shaken by the events of the previous night. The only witness still on his feet, he was a Meridional like the dead Randolfi and a good man by all accounts. Brochard and Debray: Both pale-haired, pale-eyed northerners from the Lille area who had somehow drifted south to Burgundy, they were said to be great friends but were curiously anonymous with their light colouring. So far, they'd achieved little to give them a reputation. Well, Pel thought, they'd now have a chance to show what they were made of.

As for the rest: They had the whole force to call on. The Chief had made that clear at once. When policemen were murdered, all the stops were pulled out, otherwise people got the impression that policemen could be killed with impunity. An extra dozen men had been drafted from Uniformed Branch to work in plain clothes. If they were any good, two of them would find themselves on Goriot's squad, when he was fit enough once more to run a squad. They all looked. incredibly young, mere boys, and Pel could only think it was a sign of his increasing age.

He gestured at Darcy who stood up.

'You know why you're here', Darcy said briskly. 'Three men have been murdered. All colleagues of yours. Randolfi, Desouches and Lemadre. Two others have been wounded. Inspector Goriot and Sergeant Durin. There was also a woman, whom we haven't yet identified. In addition, a boy was murdered at Vieilly and there may well be a connection. Five murders in twenty-four hours. It's our job to deal with them, so you can expect little in the way of rest until we've nailed who did them, and not much in the way of sit-down meals. You'll be snatching your sleep when you can get it, probably even here on camp beds, and most of your meals will be stand-up affairs at bars. So get that clearly into your heads from this moment.'

Misset, whose growing family provided what he considered a splendid reason why he should be treated differently from anyone else, raised his hand slowly.

Pel knew exactly what the question was going to be. 'No,' he said, and Misset flushed and lowered his hand.

'Because of the casualties,' Darcy went on, 'Inspector Goriot's squad will work in conjunction with mine. Nosjean and De Troquereau will be running the show at Vieilly.

Inspector Pel and myself will be running the enquiries in the city. Debray will work with Nosjean and De Troq'. Brochard and Aimedieu – because he's the only one who was at the shooting in the city – will work with Inspector Pel and me, as will Misset and Lagé. Claudie Darel will handle things here with Cadet Martin and keep in touch with both parties. The others will be split as we find necessary. For the moment, two will work with Nosjean and De Troq' and the remainder in the city. We can also count on Uniformed Branch for further help if necessary.'

As he sat down, Pel rose, his eyes still moving over them.

'The police killings,' he said slowly. 'It would seem to me at first glance that we're not dealing with professionals. Professionals would be cleverer than this and would never go to all this trouble to get at Zimbach's safe, because a raid on a bank's a lot easier and getting rid of jewellery's difficult and always pretty unprofitable. I think they're a new group with a grievance. The world's full of people with grievances: Everybody whose wife's nagged at him, everybody whose girlfriend's refused to go to bed with him, everybody whose mother-in-law's being difficult. They all set up a new outfit and plant a new bomb. So we're looking for amateurs, but if we turn up a few professionals, so much the better. Comments?'

There was none and Pel looked at Doc Minet. 'Anything on the boy at Vieilly?'

Doc Minet sighed. 'Cause of death,' he said. 'Asphyxia Condition of lungs confirms it. Manual strangulation had been tried but I don't think he died from that. I think whoever did it became aware that he was still alive after trying strangulation and killed him by pushing his face into the loamy soil. Time of death, around ten-thirty in the evening.'

'*Was* it sexual?'

'We've taken samples and swabs, but I think not. I've also taken fingernail scrapings and all the usual. He hadn't been interfered with. It doesn't look like a sexual attack.' Minet paused. 'On the other hand, that doesn't mean that his attacker didn't *intend* a sexual attack. It's possible he suggested it and the boy rejected him and tried to run away, and his attacker brought him down and killed him in a panic in case he told someone. We have no means of knowing.'

Pel frowned. Most attacks on children were sexual. There had been cases where children had been killed because they'd stumbled on a crime, but even then death was usually accidental – bonds tied too tightly, a gag too large, a blow that was too hard – and most other attacks were by depraved or twisted people bent on satisfying their lusts.

He turned to Nosjean. 'Check all known homosexuals,' he said. 'And all known sexual deviates – rapists, sadists, clothes slashers, exhibitionists, the lot. Check mental health and nursing institutions for new patients or escapees, and evaluations of any patients recently released. Enquire at prisons about new admissions and at dry cleaners about clothes. And let's remember that if our murderer's a psychopath he blends indistinguishably into the normal populace. He has no visible guilt and no evident motive.'

Grenier, of Photography, offered a large pile of pictures. Pel glanced at them and passed them to the Chief, who also glanced at them and passed them on. Leguyader, of the Lab, had nothing new to report. 'Soil in his fingernails,' he announced. 'Also in his eyes, nostrils and mouth. It bears out what Doc Minet says. Somebody held his face down in the soil. There was an imprint. We'll take a cast.'

'Anything else?'

'We have his clothes. I expect we shall find something to indicate where he'd been, but nothing that could identify his attacker. At least, not until we find the attacker. He wasn't clutching a handful of hair or a marked handkerchief.'

The Chief glanced at Pel and frowned. Leguyader's sarcasm was well known but sometimes it was out of place.

Prélat, of Fingerprints, shrugged. 'Nothing,' he said. 'No weapon –' the shrug came again ' – therefore no finger-prints.'

'Nothing on the boy himself?'

'Nothing.'

'How about you, Nosjean? Has he been identified yet?'

Nosjean opened the notebook resting on his knees. The membership card for the gymnasium near the Place Wilson had done the trick. 'De Troq' went to see Georges Martinelle, who runs the place,' he explained.

Pel's eyes switched to De Troquereau, who had also opened a notebook. 'It isn't a big gymnasium, Patron,' he said. 'Used only by children of the well-heeled. Only a few members. Martinelle supplied the names and addresses of them all. I visited them. The boy's called Charles-Bernard Crébert, aged thirteen, son of Paul and Régine Crébert, of 113, Rue Barbisey. That's in the Avenue Victor-Hugo area. They reported him missing this morning.'

'Anything known about him?'

'Wealthy parents. Spoiled child. Martinelle opened the gymnasium when he retired from the army. He said the boy had the makings of a gymnast. It's the thing these days. Martinelle didn't like him much but he can't afford to offend parents and he was giving him extra private lessons. He paid, of course.'

Pel turned to Nosjean again. 'What about the parents? Seen them yet?'

'Only to inform them about their son, Patron.' Nosjean frowned. Jobs like that often came within the compass of a policeman's work and they were never pleasant.

'What did you make of them?'

'Much the same as De Troq' says of the boy, Patron. Wealthy. Bit spoiled themselves, I'd say. I got the impression that the boy was difficult at times.'

'Did you question them?'

'We only established the identity about an hour ago. I'll be going out there shortly. De Troq's going to see Martinelle again.'

'Right, Darcy, let's have it. Tell them what we know so far about the other business.'

Darcy did so, giving them all that was known on what had happened in the Impasse Tarien, what had been found in the wrecked house, and what had been seen afterwards.

'Two men,' Pel said. 'Supporting another. Followed by a woman who was obviously nervous and frightened. It looks very much as though it was an attempt to break into the safe at Zimbach's, the jeweller's. They obviously had explosives but whether these were to blow the safe at Zimbach's we don't know until the experts have finished, though we have to consider they were preparing explosive devices for use in the streets. Certainly nothing was taken from Zimbach's because Inspector Goriot arrived before they could get at the safe. However, we know that the men we're looking for are ruthless and very dangerous.' He turned to Darcy. 'What did you find out at the Palais des Ducs?'

Darcy scanned a piece of paper. 'There are several possibilities, Patron, but none of them important enough for bombs, until next month when the President appears in the city to open an exhibition of Burgundian art at the Palace.'

'Got the date?'

'I have, Patron.' Darcy's face was bleak. 'We have four and a half weeks.'

Pel was silent for a moment then he looked at the assembled men again. 'If that's the reason for the explosives,' he said, 'then we have a time limit. But that doesn't mean carelessness, so tread warily. We want no heroics. This is a team job and we're not expecting anyone to grab the lot on his own. Claudie Darel will be watching everything that comes in and the telephone will be manned twenty-four hours a day. In the meantime, we have one lead. We're looking for a car. Pale blue, make unknown, number beginning 9701-R. We're also looking for a frightened woman and a man who appears to have been injured, probably shot.'

'Who by?' Aimedieu asked quietly, blushing like a choir boy as he did so. 'None of *us* did any shooting. We never got a chance. There were bodies all over the floor before anybody got his gun out. I've checked, Patron. The Inspector didn't use his gun and neither did Durin, and I've looked at the guns of Randolfi, Lemadre and Desouches. They hadn't been fired.'

'Good point,' Pel said. 'I think, then, that we have to assume that the wounded man was hit by accident by a bullet from one of his friends.' He gestured. 'It makes little difference. He'll still be needing a doctor.'

five

Standing once more in the wrecked house in the Impasse
Tarien, Pel stared about him with Darcy. Debris littered the
floor – broken plaster, splintered woodwork, dust and soot
that had accumulated for years in the ancient chimney. What
plaster remained was chipped where bullets had gouged
holes in it and there were blood splashes on the walls and,
where they could be seen beneath the debris, on the bare
floorboards.

As they worked, an army captain, one of the explosives
experts from the barracks in the Rue du Drapeau appeared.
In his hand were several wide-barrelled felt-tipped pens such
as you could buy in plastic packets at the Nouvelles Galeries
for a few francs. The ink cores had been removed and the
containers stuffed with explosive. They had been tied
together with wire, with wire wool threaded round their
caps, and a sheet of transistors soldered to a tuft of the wire
wool.

'Good as a steel drum for this kind of explosive,' the army
man said. 'It's not gelignite, of course. It's the home-made
stuff. When they're sealed, the pressure built up inside when
it goes off is tremendous. I think they were assembling them
here.'

'What for?' Darcy asked. 'To blow somebody up?'

'Normally they'd use a drum filled with jelly in a sewer for
that. Or a couple of kilos strapped to the exhaust of a car.'

'They'd have a job getting a bomb like that close to the President,' Pel said. 'Perhaps they had alternative plans. Perhaps it won't be explosives, and these things were to be set off just to create confusion.'

They moved about the wrecked building, staring sombrely at the places where Randolfi, Lemadre and Desouches had died. It was a sordid little place of cracked plaster, peeling paint and broken floorboards. Shelves and cupboards had collapsed and the empty bottles which had littered the kitchen lay about in broken shards. The windows had gone and the shutters hung crookedly from broken hinges.

'They must have been mad to think they could get away with hammering without being heard,' Pel growled.

'Some of these people,' Darcy pointed out, 'don't have much grip on reality. They got into Number Eleven, which is the last house in the cul-de-sac, and started living there. Then they knocked a hole through the back wall into the yard and through the wall of the yard of Number Ten. They'd just started on Zimbach's wall when Desouches turned up.'

In Number Eleven the kitchen table was set for a meal, with a coffee pot, a plastic bottle of stale milk, and dirty mugs. An open tin of meat was going bad in the heat.

As they studied them, Prélat of Fingerprints appeared from upstairs. 'I expect the place was full of fingerprints,' he said, stretching his shoulders. 'But we'll not find much after the explosion.'

Studying the tools that had been left behind, Pel picked up a hammer. 'What about this?' he asked, gazing at the varnished handle. 'It would give good prints.'

'There's nothing, Patron,' Prélat said. 'I don't think it's been used and if it was, it was used by someone wearing gloves – workman's gloves, I'd say.'

Pel frowned. He was studying a pale oval mark on the handle where a label had been removed. 'Let's have a check on it, all the same,' he said to Darcy. 'Misset can do it. It'll keep him out of mischief. It looks brand new and the label probably gave the name of the supplier and was taken off in case we found it after they'd finished with Zimbach's and asked who bought it. After all, people don't often buy hammers. We might get an identification.'

While Pel and Darcy were studying the wrecked house, the police were deploying their forces about the city. The garage hold-up at Regnon had been sorted out quickly and a man was in for questioning about the assault at Auray-sur-Tille, and now police had been brought in from Dôle, Chatillon, Auxerre and Avallon – because there was a chance that the local men were too well-known – and they were out in the streets in a variety of disguises, their ears to the ground, haunting the bars and cafés, their heads cocked and listening. Police were also at barriers on every road out of the city, stopping motorists and checking their cars. Others were digging into all known corners, looking for the missing car, or checking up on anybody who might have been involved and quite a lot who might not, in case they'd heard anything in the shady underworld they inhabited.

Nobody had, of course, and there was a great deal of indignation at the killers. 'As far as I'm concerned,' one man told Lagé, 'you can shut up shop at the Hôtel de Police. There'll be no crime here until this lot's sorted out. There are too many Flics about.'

The experts soon came up with proof of Darcy's theory that the criminals were after Zimbach's safe, and one of the bullets dug out of the plaster matched several of the bullets taken out of the dead policemen and the dead woman, who had finally been identified as a Madame Héloïse Lenotre, from Lyons, who had been visiting her brother in that part of the city where the shooting had taken place. She was in no way connected with the crime.

The following day Madame Colbrun, from Porsigny, found the bullet she had dug out of her thigh and brought it in to the Hôtel de Police. With what had been happening in the city, Nosjean had never been able to organise the search he'd intended, so Madame Colbrun had done it for him. It matched the bullets dug out of the wreckage of Number Ten, Impasse Tarien, and the bullets dug out of Madame Lenotre and the dead and wounded policemen, and confirmed what they'd believed all along – that the detonators from St Blaize had been stolen for no other reason than to set off the gelignite stolen from Dom.

The obvious first calls were on known dissidents and Darcy set up visits to them all. For the most part they were desperately poor, unhappy and maladjusted.

There were plenty of refugees who had arrived penniless in France who had made a new life for themselves. One or two of them were actually doing very well, thank you, but, honest or not, on the whole, *their* attitude was not one of defeatism. The bitter, the angry, the sad, were all victims of their own temperaments, and Darcy rejected them as suspects.

He was well aware of methods. Terrorism these days was transnational with respect to communication and a few other things, and it didn't matter a damn what each individual terrorist organisation was after, at bottom they were all after the breakdown of law and order. The British had the Irish problem. The French had believers in Breton, Basque, Corsican and now Burgundian freedom. The Italians and the Germans had their own particular burdens in the form of the Red Brigade and the Baader Meinhof. The Turks, the Iranians and the African countries also contributed a few, and most of those in Darcy's diocese, who weren't so defeated as to be lethargic, belonged to one or another of them.

Out of the whole lot, however, there was only one who really meant much to Darcy – one Tadeuz Kiczmyrczik, a Pole who had arrived in France during World War II with a bitter hatred for Russia, which over the years had changed course and was now for any form of government which seemed sane and non-anarchic. He lived with a Czech woman by the name of Anna Ripka, in a narrow-gutted flat near the Industrial Zone, that was filled with ugly furniture piled with books by Marx, Lenin, and a few others. Darcy was shown in by a small round-faced young man with glasses and a broad smile. 'Come in,' he said. 'I'm Jaroslav Tyl. Anna's out doing the shopping. The old man's resting. He isn't well.'

'That's a pity,' Darcy growled. 'Because I'd like to see him. Get him up.'

'Can't you leave him alone?' Tyl asked. 'He's got a lot on his mind.'

'Not half as much as I've got on mine. Fetch him.'

Kiczmyrczik's bitterness was clearly written on his face. He was gaunt, the lines cut deeply into his features. He was in no mood to be helpful.

'Why should I help you?' he demanded. 'France has done nothing for me.'

Darcy didn't bother to point out that there were a lot of Poles in France – as there were a lot of Russians, Czechs, Letts, Lithuanians, Esthonians and others – to whom France had given little but shelter but who had shown their gratitude by living useful lives within her boundaries. He came straight to the point.

'Where were you last night?' he asked.

'I don't have to tell you.'

'I think you do, my friend,' Darcy snapped.

'Then I was here.'

'Anyone with you?'

'Only Anna. She is my wife. Not in the way *you* believe in wives. But she is still my wife.'

'She the only one?'

'Who else would there be?'

'A few of your friends. A few of your disciples. You hold meetings here.'

'There was no meeting last night.'

'All the same, I'd like the names of the people who make a point of attending your meetings.'

'I can't remember them all. There are too many.'

Darcy's eyebrows lifted. To his certain knowledge there were no more than a dozen or so. People like Kiczmyrczik maintained small and very private groups.

'You'd better start thinking.'

'I have no intention. You'd better call your bully-boys and have me put in prison.'

As they talked, Anna Ripka appeared. She wasn't old, half Kiczmyrczik's age, Darcy guessed, a small slender woman with ill-cared-for hair, a complete lack of style, and the same bitter lines on her face that Kiczmyrczik had. Darcy guessed she'd always been ugly and had turned to Kiczmyrczik for no other reason than that no one else had ever looked at her.

'What's he doing here?' she demanded harshly.

'He's part of the fascist police,' Kiczmyrczik said.

She turned on Darcy, her face suffused with hatred. 'Get out,' she snarled. 'Go away, go away!'

The way she spoke made Darcy remember the woman seen following the two men supporting their wounded friend from the shootings in the Impasse Tarien. But Kiczmyrczik gave her an alibi, as she gave him one, and it didn't really mean a thing. As Darcy left, Tyl, who had listened throughout the interview, a smile playing about his lips, grabbed a handful of pamphlets from a chair and thrust them into Darcy's hand. The headlines read 'We need 1789 again, and a new Revolution.' It was pretty dull stuff and also pretty meaningless.

'You don't have to read them,' Tyl said as he showed Darcy out. 'Nobody ever does. Anna burns them in the grate in the winter when they can't afford coal.'

Darcy turned. 'Are you one of them?'

'One of what?'

'Do you have revolutionary ideas, too?'

Tyl grinned. 'Not really. I'm all for the people, of course, but you've only to look at me to see *I'm* not active. I'm the wrong shape and too good-natured.'

'You could still have revolutionary ideas.'

'Oh, sure!' Tyl beamed. 'I'm out of work, so it would be normal enough, wouldn't it? Only *I'm* an optimist, which they aren't. The revolution'll come all right, and it's our job to help it on by spreading the message, but it'll come in its own good time and doesn't need bombs to push it. In any case, I'm too ugly to have any influence. You have to look like the Old Man for that. Bit like an eagle, with lines of suffering on your face. That's where the appeal lies.'

'Does he make bombs?'

Tyl shrugged. 'He's getting a bit old for it but I wouldn't put it past him.'

'What about the other members of his group?'

'I'm one. Jaroslav Tyl, Apartment 3, 79, Rue Georges-Fyot. I live with my sister. She keeps house for me. Our parents died when we were kids. We're Czechs like Anna. My sister got married but her husband knocked her about a lot and it left her a bit nervous. When he was killed in a car accident – he was drunk – she came to look after me.'

'What about the rest?'

'Come and see me tonight and I'll give you a full list.'

'Are they active?'

'Mostly they just talk. Most revolutionaries just talk, of course. What they do usually varies in inverse proportion to what they have to say. It's the ones who don't talk you have to look out for.'

'You do plenty. Where were *you* last night?'

'Home. With my sister. We can't afford to go out much. We've got no money. But we've got a television. Black and white, of course. We had it given. A type in the same block who was going in for colour and couldn't get anything for his old one. My sister's an addict. I'd rather read a book but – ' Tyl shrugged ' – you know how it is. You've got to let them have their way, haven't you?'

As the few facts that were available were brought in, the press started clamouring for a statement. Fiabon, of *France Dimanche,* Sarrazin, a freelance who represented anybody who'd use his material, and Henriot, of *Le Bien Public,* were waiting by Pel's office. Outside, there were a few others, men from Paris who had come screaming down the motorway as soon as the flash messages from Sarrazin, who acted as their contact in the city, had reached their offices. One or two of them were big names and Pel regarded them with distrust because the Press' habit of giving things which were best kept quiet, as often as not put criminals on their guard and sent them to ground. With terrorists, it was even more tricky because of the Press' habit of giving facts which were best encouragement to the men who made them. And terrorists loved publicity and every word that appeared helped them, to say nothing of providing information for the hosts of eager imitators who still hadn't discovered how to set about things.

He gave them what he could – nothing but the bare facts, but there appeared to be plenty of those for them to get their teeth into. It wasn't every day that three policemen, a woman and a boy were murdered, to say nothing of a house being blown inside out. Despite this, they seemed to feel he was short-changing them.

'Is that all?' Fiabon asked.

'Isn't it enough?' Pel said. 'It's all we know at the moment. You have the names of the dead and wounded men and the injured civilians.'

'We could use more.' Sarrazin was one of the more ardent and vociferous critics of the police. 'The big television boys will be here soon. They'll want more than this.'

Pel didn't look forward to the big television names with their over-publicised commentators. Half the time their strident utterances became clarion calls summoning the faithful to war. 'Doubtless by that time,' he said, 'we'll know more.'

As the pressmen vanished, Cadet Martin appeared. 'There's a type called Andoche to see you, Patron.'

Pel frowned. 'Can't Inspector Darcy see him?' he asked.

'He insists on you, Patron.'

Andoche was a young man in his early thirties, wearing jeans, sneakers, a shirt stamped UNIVERSITY OF CALIFORNIA, and a great deal more hair than seemed to be necessary for a comfortable existence.

'Robert Andoche,' he introduced himself. 'Mature student. President of the Free Burgundy Movement.'

He held out his hand to shake Pel's. Pel regarded it coldly.

A little disconcerted, Andoche frowned and went on more uncertainly. 'Just wanted to let you know we weren't responsible for the death of the Fuzz,' he said.

'For the death of *what*?' Pel growled.

'The – well, you know – ' Andoche gestured ' – it's just a name, isn't it?'

'It's not one we use here.'

'Well, you wouldn't, would you? Anyway, we just wanted you to know, so you don't start making life uncomfortable for us.'

Pel recalled a few occasions when a Free Burgundian meeting, asked to move on because it was obstructing the pavement, had degenerated into a brawl and stones had been thrown. He considered Andoche had a nerve.

He stared at him. He didn't look particularly clean or hard-working. 'You've made life uncomfortable often enough for what you choose to call the Fuzz,' he snapped.

Andoche gestured. 'Well, that's what you're for, isn't it?'

'My impression was that the police existed not so much to be targets for you and your friends but to keep law and order.'

'Within fascist rules, of course.'

'This is a republic,' Pel snapped. 'With great socialistic ideals, whatever government is in power. It was the first true democracy of the people, by the people, for the people, no matter what our friends in Britain or the United States might say.'

Andoche could see he was getting nowhere. 'Well,' he said 'Just wanted to let you know. We wouldn't go in for that kind of violence.'

'But you wouldn't say no to others?'

Andoche grinned. 'Well, anything's allowed in politics, isn't it? I thought you'd be pleased. Thought I'd like to help your investigations and all that.'

Pel reached across his desk and pressed the bell. When Darcy appeared he gestured at Andoche.

'Shove him in a cell,' he said.

Andoche's face reddened. 'I came to help you!' he yelled.

'You probably will,' Pel snapped. 'Give him a going over, Daniel. See who his friends are. They might be interesting.'

six

The flat occupied by Paul and Régine Crébert was as
different from the one occupied by Tadeuz Kiczymrczik and
Anna Ripka as it was possible to be. It was on the ground
floor of a block in one of the most expensive areas of the city,
and it was elegantly furnished with expensive fittings. The
walls were covered with paintings, there was a grand piano,
a large television and a host of potted plants which, with the
light coming into the room through the enormous windows,
made Nosjean feel a bit like a newt swimming among sunlit
reeds.

Madame Crébert was sitting on the settee, in tears, but
still, Nosjean noticed, managing to look elegant. She was tall,
well-made and beautiful and, despite her misery, had dressed
carefully, every hair in place. Some people, Nosjean told
himself, put on the right clothes as automatically as washing
themselves. To Madame Crébert, it would have been bad
behaviour to appear badly dressed, whatever had happened.
Her husband stood by the window, his hands in his pockets,
staring out at the street, his face bleak, his eyes empty.

'He went out after school,' Madame Crébert was saying
slowly, as if picking her way through her thoughts. 'He had
just done his homework. He was inclined to be lazy at school
and was sometimes difficult and he'd been given extra to do.'

'Was he clever?' Nosjean asked.

'Yes.' The father turned and spoke over his shoulder. 'But
he wouldn't work. He wouldn't get down to it.'

'Neither would you,' his wife observed bitterly. 'Never. You could have made something of him but you never bothered.'

Her husband gave her a look which seemed to indicate that he thought much the same of her. Nosjean coughed and brought their thoughts back to where they had been.

'Was he a well-behaved boy?'

'He'd been properly brought up,' Crébert said.

His wife enlarged. 'He had excellent manners.'

'When he chose to use them,' her husband added.

'What do you mean by that, Monsieur?' Nosjean asked.

Crébert drew a deep breath like a sigh. 'He was like most children these days. He could be pleasant enough with other people but with his parents he was difficult. He answered us back, was often sullen, refused to do things, often went days without speaking to us.'

'It wasn't always like that,' his wife said.

Her husband sighed again. 'No,' he agreed. 'Not always.'

'Can you tell me more about when you last saw him?'

Madame Crébert dabbed at her eyes and steeled herself. 'He finished his homework,' she said. 'Then he went out. Shortly afterwards, I had occasion to go to my handbag and I realised a fifty-franc note was missing. I'd got it especially to pay my daily help and it had gone. Then I remembered that Charles-Bernard had been in the hall just before he left the house. I'd thought he was just sulking and thought no more about it. When I realised the money was missing, I realised what he'd been doing.'

Nosjean waited quietly as she dabbed at her eyes again. 'I feel so guilty,' she said, her voice rising to a wail. 'I feel it was my fault.'

For a while she was unable to speak and her husband spoke for her. 'When the boy came in,' he said, 'she accused him of taking the money. He admitted that he had and she told him what she thought of him.'

'But then – ' Madame Crébert's voice was a moan ' – he produced a bunch of flowers and said he'd taken the money to buy them for me because it had been my birthday the day before and he'd forgotten it. I felt so awful. I apologised and said how wonderful he was. But he'd already taken offence and went off in a huff. That was the last I – ' she looked at Nosjean with tragic eyes. 'It was my fault. I know it was my fault. I worried all evening about where he'd gone.'

'Were you here?'

'All evening.'

'Alone?'

'My husband was away on business. My brother came to see me. He sometimes does when my husband's away. He's always kind. We think the world of him. Charles-Bernard was upset because I'd been angry with him, but how was I to know?'

'You weren't,' her husband muttered. He crossed the room to place a hand on her shoulder and looked at Nosjean. 'Sometimes you didn't know where you were with him. When you tried to be kind he rejected you. If you tried to be strict, he sulked. He'd been spoiled all his life.'

'By you,' Madame Crébert said.

Crébert stared at her for a moment, then he snatched his hand away and went back to the window.

'I didn't realise he hadn't come in again,' Madame Crébert said. 'He had his own key and he had to go out that night, anyway, to his gymnastic club. When I went in to wake him for school the next morning his bed hadn't been slept in. At first I thought he'd run away again – '

'Had he done it before?'

'Once he got as far as Vézelay. The second time he didn't go beyond the city boundaries. He did it to make us angry. He was always doing things to make us feel guilty. I rang his school. They hadn't seen him so I thought I'd better let the police know. You have to, don't you? And I wanted him back.'

Nosjean leaned forward. They had already checked all the known homosexuals in the city, the perverts and the men with records of indecency towards children. 'Why do you think he was at Vieilly?' he asked quietly.

The Créberts looked at each other.

'Is there anyone at Vieilly to whom he'd turn if he were in trouble at home? An aunt? Someone like that?'

'We have no relations at Vieilly.'

'Has he ever been there before?'

Crébert frowned. 'Not that I'm aware of.'

Remembering the wounded woman at Porsigny and the shot at the watchman at St Blaize, Nosjean tried a new line.

'Was he interested in guns?'

'Not to my knowledge.'

Nosjean paused. 'Explosives?'

Crébert stared. 'Explosives? What are you suggesting?'

'Nothing in particular. But many boys experiment with making explosives. A lot of them know how. Especially those who're good at chemistry.'

'He was *not* good at chemistry,' Crébert said stiffly. 'His subjects were literary. Languages, mostly. Why do you ask?'

Nosjean drew their attention to what had happened in the Impasse Tarien and mentioned the wounding of the woman at Porsigny and the theft of the detonators at St Blaize.

Madame Crébert covered her face with her hands. 'Oh, God, Paul,' she moaned, 'what had he got himself involved in?'

Nosjean hastened to set her mind at rest. 'We're not suggesting that he was involved in anything,' he said. 'It might not be connected, but we have to enquire.'

'He was a good boy.'

Crébert frowned and seemed to steel himself. 'No,' he said firmly. 'He *wasn't* a good boy. He was spoiled and self-willed and he had a habit of wandering about the streets late at night when he should have been at home. But he knew nothing of explosives and little of chemistry. I'm sure of that. On the other hand, in his roamings, it's possible he may have seen something.'

Madame Crébert's lips tightened. 'He was a lonely boy,' she said. 'Sad. He kept to himself. His father didn't like him.'

'Régine, for God's sake, stop talking like that – !'

'Doctor Nisard said so.'

'Doctor Nisard said nothing of the kind.'

'Who's Doctor Nisard?' Nosjean asked.

'The family doctor,' Crébert said. 'He knew the boy well, of course. He'd treated him since birth.'

'He suffered from depressions,' Madame Crébert put in. 'His father always said he'd come between us. He never really liked him.'

Crébert threw up his hands. 'Oh, mon Dieu!' he said. 'He *did* come between us. But only because he was allowed his own way too much. But to say I never really liked him – in the name of God, Régine – !'

As Nosjean reached the street, a small red Renault like his own drew up in front of the house and a young man climbed out. He saw Nosjean and immediately approached.

'You the police?' he asked.

Nosjean was wary at once. 'Yes,' he said. 'You the press?'

The young man looked startled. 'Mon Dieu, no!' he said. 'I'm part of the family.' He gestured at the house. 'I thought I'd better call round and see how they were. How are they?'

'How would any parents be when they'd just learned their son's dead?'

The young man nodded soberly. 'Yes, of course. Silly question. I'm his uncle. Régine Crébert's my sister. Name of Delacolonge. Robert Delacolonge.'

Nosjean studied him. He had the same features as Madame Crébert, he saw now, the same blond good looks, the same weakness about the mouth. He was immaculately dressed with a touch of the dandy about him, and Nosjean wondered if he were a homosexual.

'Did you know the boy well?' he asked.

'Of course. I'm much younger than my sister and we were very good friends.'

'So you know the things he did?'

'Most of them.'

'Had he ever made fireworks? We think there might be a connection between his death and the theft of explosives at St Blaize.'

Delacolonge considered for a moment. 'Well, a lot of youngsters fancy making fireworks, don't they? But you don't think he stole gelignite, do you?'

'I didn't say it was gelignite,' Nosjean pointed out immediately. 'Why did you think it was gelignite?'

'Isn't that what they use for blasting?' When Nosjean didn't answer Delacolonge went on quickly. 'I always thought it was. In any case, I doubt if he'd know what to do with it if he did steal it. More than likely blow himself up. And that wasn't what happened, was it?'

'No.' Nosjean eyed Delacolonge. 'I wasn't thinking that he stole the stuff. I wondered if he knew anyone who *might* steal it.'

Delacolonge shrugged and Nosjean closed his notebook.

'Mind if I come and have a chat with you in the next day or two?' he asked.

Delacolonge looked startled. 'Why me?'

Nosjean gestured. 'Parents are a little confused and distraught at a time like this,' he said. 'It'd be nice to talk to someone who knows what goes on but isn't too involved. Did the boy talk to you much?'

'Often. Always round at my place when he was in trouble. Came to get things off his chest.'

'Ever stay the night?'

'He has done.'

Nosjean felt he was on to a scent at last. Dandified young uncles who had a place of their own where young nephews often spent the night – it seemed to suggest all sorts of things.

'I'll call round and see you,' he said.

Delacolonge nodded. 'Any time. Number 19, Apartments Sagnier, Rue Mulhouse. Ring up first in case I'm working, though.'

'What do you do?'

Delacolonge hesitated. 'I'm a poet.'

'I wouldn't have thought there was a lot of future in poetry these days.'

Delacolonge managed a twisted smile. 'You're quite right, of course,' he said. 'I have to work for a living, too. I'm a male nurse at St Saviour's.'

'What's St Saviour's?'

'It's a nuthouse.' Delacolonge gave a small deprecatory smile. 'They call it a nursing home, but that's what it is. For disturbed people. They've got some funny types there, believe me. Some of them a bit homicidal. They should never let them out.'

Nosjean's eyes narrowed. '*Do* they let them out?'

'People come and fetch them. Sometimes for a week-end or a public holiday like Bastille Day.'

It put a new idea into Nosjean's head. But there was the other one, too, that featured Delacolonge himself. Nosjean had a marked distrust of people who called themselves poets.

'This poetry of yours,' he said. 'Had anything published?'

Delacolonge gave a sad smile. 'Isn't much demand for poetry these days,' he said. 'Just one slim volume. I paid for it. We gave most of the edition away to friends. They were quite polite about them.'

'You said "we." Who's "we"?'

Delacolonge looked blank. 'Delphine and I,' he said. 'Delphine's my wife. She's looking after the baby.'

'And that, Nosjean thought as Delacolonge waved and ran up the steps to the Créberts' house, seemed to shatter *that* theory.

Still unsatisfied, Nosjean decided to try Doctor Nisard. There had been something about Madame Crébert that had worried him. She seemed strained in a way that went beyond the death of her son, and there seemed to be a distinct division of loyalties, as if she were the sort of person who took sides firmly and found it impossible to change even when the evidence suggested she should. The way she had set herself against her husband was clear proof of it.

Doctor Nisard seemed to think the same. He was an old man with grey hair and a wise, strong face.

'Well, they're an odd lot, aren't they?' he said.

'In what way, doctor? Is there insanity in the family?'

Nisard hesitated. 'Well – certainly, the boy's elder brother isn't normal. Huge chap. Must be eighteen or so now. Beetle-browed. Strong as an ox. He once beat up Charles-Bernard when he upset him. Almost killed him. Judge demanded a psychiatrist's report. Result was that when he did it again two years later, the parents were told he had to have treatment. He went into St Saviour's and he's never been out since.'

'They never mentioned this to me.'

Doctor Nisard managed a thin smile. 'It's not something you make a lot of song and dance about, is it? It's probably what made the mother a little odd.'

'Is *she* abnormal, too?'

Nisard shrugged. 'Subject to depression.' Suicidal at times. I suppose it's natural with your elder son in a place like St

Saviour's. It'll be worse still now that the younger son's been murdered.'

'What's the younger son like? Was *he* unbalanced, too?'

'I wouldn't say so, but he *was* given to fits of fury. She leaned a lot on her brother, of course – young Delacolonge. He was surprisingly good with her, as a matter of fact, and was about the only one who could get her out of her depressions. All the same –' Nisard shrugged '– there's certainly an odd strain running through the family. Her mother committed suicide and her grandmother was found dead – in circumstances that suggested her grandfather had pushed her down the cellar steps. Nevertheless –' Nisard paused '– Madame Crébert is a woman of warmth when she's not under strain. She's law-abiding, unobtrusive, kind and serious – too serious, in fact.'

'What do you mean by that, Doctor?'

'She takes remarks to heart when they're often uttered only lightly. Then she's motivated by resentment or imagined grievances, and tends to be unstable, flitting from one idea to another. She's self-centred and easily moved by hate or love. She's a patient of mine.'

'*Does* she hate?'

The doctor frowned. 'Let me put it this way: When she married, she was very much in love. I've known the family for some time and that was patently obvious. But her husband's a businessman who's often away and then she feels forgotten. When she's low in spirits or tired or unwell, she actively hates him for what she considers his neglect of her. In fact, he's never neglected her. He's a good husband in his own way and she's no worse off than the wife of any other busy man.'

'This hatred,' Nosjean asked. 'Could it turn to hatred of her own son?'

The doctor sighed. 'Well, her condition's certainly become worse in recent years and nowadays she's in a more or less depressed state a lot of the time. She now even has a tendency to unbalanced opinions and morbid and delusive projects.' He raised his hands in a defeated gesture. 'I would have said that any hostility she felt would be towards the husband not the son. Nevertheless in her misery she *could* feel the boy was coming between her and her husband.'

'But he was thirteen years old. A good athlete, too, I understand, and well muscled for his age.'

The doctor gestured again. 'She's a large woman,' he said quietly.

'And the diazepam capsules that were found?'

Nisard shrugged. 'I recommended them for the mother,' he said.

seven

While Nosjean was busy with the Créberts, De Troquereau was talking to Major Georges Martinelle.

The major wasn't unlike De Troquereau in appearance. He was small and slight and carried himself erect, clearly enjoying the fact that he looked a little like Napoleon. Indeed, there were several pictures of the Great Emperor about his gymnasium and he seemed all the time to be holding his face to the light so that visitors could see the resemblance.

For a while he tried to bully De Troquereau with his military manners and commission. 'I don't have to like the sort of people who come here to learn gymnastics,' he said. 'Any more than I have to like you, Sergeant Troquereau.'

De Troquereau was unmoved. He'd grown up knowing how to deal with people like Major Martinelle. '*De* Troquereau actually,' he said mildly. 'Charles-Victor de Troquereau. In fact, if you want the full treatment, Baron de Troquereau Tournay-Turenne.'

Martinelle's eyebrows shot up and De Troq' smiled inwardly. His parents were as poor as church mice and he'd joined the police force because he couldn't afford to do anything else, but it was still sometimes pleasant to use his background to put ill-mannered people in their place.

Martinelle was silent for a moment then he drew a deep breath. 'I once knew a Colonel de Troquereau Tournay-Turenne,' he said. '12th Cuirassiers.'

'Uncle,' De Troq' said cheerfully. In fact he'd never even heard of the man Martinelle mentioned, though he *had* to be a relative of some sort.

The possibility seemed to subdue Martinelle a little, so that he answered with considerably more circumspection and, when they got down to facts, it was De Troq' who had the upper hand because Martinelle even began to fall over himself to oblige.

'The boy had the makings of a good gymnast,' he said. 'It seemed worth taking trouble with him. Besides, I gathered he was always in trouble with his parents. They thought he was clever but other boys from the same school who came here said he wasn't. He was also inclined to bully, and from my experience, when people are bullies, it's because they lack something – usually praise – and take it out on others. When I discovered he was good at gymnastics – he had the perfect build for it – I made a lot of it and I gathered later from his teacher that he'd stopped his bullying. He needed something he could do well. He found it here.'

'Did he ever come on his own?' De Troq' asked.

'Certainly. With a prize pupil, you have to give them extra attention. And, let's face it, I was paid for the lessons.'

'Any friends?'

'I gather he wasn't popular. Most of his real friends were older.'

'Know any of them?'

'Boy named Fesch. Arnold Fesch. Alsatian family. Lives in the Rue d'Albert. He might know something.'

De Troq' paused. 'Did he have any friends out Vieilly way?'

Martinelle shook his head. 'I never heard him mention anybody.'

De Troq' nodded. 'Did he come here the night he disappeared? He was supposed to.'

There was a slight pause and Martinelle looked shifty for a moment. 'The place was closed,' he said. 'I wasn't here.'

'Where were you?'

'At home, with my wife.'

'Will she verify that?'

'Surely you're not suggesting I – '

'I'm not suggesting anything. I'm just trying to eliminate people.'

Martinelle considered for a moment. 'Then, no,' he said. 'I doubt if – ' he stopped. 'Just a minute. That was the night I went to the library reading room. I sometimes go to read the military magazines.'

'Until as late as ten o'clock? That's the time the boy died.'

Martinelle frowned. 'I went for a drink afterwards. In fact I had one or two.' He paused. 'Things aren't quite as they should be between me and my wife and sometimes I don't hurry home.'

'Would they know you at this bar you went to? Could they vouch for you?'

Martinelle shrugged. 'Doubt it. Not exactly a personality. Just an old soldier. Besides, I visited several.'

'It would help if someone *could* vouch for you.'

Martinelle frowned. 'I don't think they can.'

'That,' De Troquereau said, 'is a pity.'

Arnold Fesch was a tall strong boy with full red lips and pimples and a thatch of blond hair that stood up on his head like the bristles of a yard broom.

'Well, he *was* a friend, and he wasn't,' he said. 'Mostly it was on *his* side, if you know what I mean. He seemed to have a crush on me. Little boys do get them on bigger ones, you know.'

'Nothing more than that?'

'Such as what?'

De Troq' paused then brought it out bluntly. 'Sexual?'

Fesch looked startled. 'You mean, between him and me?'
'Yes.'
'Name of God, no! I don't go in for that sort of thing.'
'Did *he*?'
'How would I know? He made no suggestions to me. But I wouldn't know. It's not my line, anyway. I've got a girl. She and I – er – well – '
Fesch managed to blush and De Troq' suspected that he and his girl had already begun to taste the delights of growing up.
'You could ask her,' Fesch offered.
'Would she tell me?' De Troq' smiled. 'Had he any other friends you know about? From Vieilly, for instance?'
Fesch shook his head.
'Ever hear him mention Vieilly?'
'I believe his father used to shoot there a bit.'
'Did you know of *any* of his friends outside school?'
Fesch frowned. 'Well, there was one. I think he was older than Charles-Bernard. He had a car – he mentioned it – so he must have been.'
'Know of any way we could identify him?'
'No. He was a bit secretive about him. He was that sort. Liked to pretend there was more going for him than there was. He was a bit dreary, really, you know, and used to make up stories about himself to make himself seem important. He – well – he learned about me and my girl – you know how it is – and he tried to tell me *he*'d had a girl, too. I didn't believe him. Not for a minute. I know when people are – well, when they've – you know.'
'You can tell?'
Fesch gestured airily. 'I can always tell.'
'You're lucky,' De Troq' said. 'I can't.'

Doctor Anatole Bazin, the director of St Saviour's Nursing Home, was inclined to be guarded. The place was run for profit and he had no wish to put off prospective customers.

'Yes,' he admitted to Nosjean. 'We do have a boy here called Crébert.'

'Son of Paul and Régine Crébert?'

'That's correct.'

'Can you tell me anything about him, doctor?'

'I have no right to. He came here to be cured, that's all.'

'*Will* he be cured?'

'We hope so.'

'I'd like to know more about him.'

'I can't tell you.'

'This is a police enquiry, doctor. His brother's been murdered. We're trying to find who did it.'

Bazin frowned, then he gestured. 'What do you wish to know?'

'Something about him. We know his history.'

'He's a strong boy. He's inclined to fits of rage and has to be watched carefully.'

'Are your patients allowed out?'

'Of course. Our patients aren't mad. They're people with mental problems and they have families and friends who wish to see them and are willing to be responsible for them.'

'Are you certain that this responsibility is always *really* responsible?'

'We have to accept that it is.'

'But it might not be?'

'There's that possibility.'

'On the night of the 14th – Bastille Night – were any of them out?'

'Two women. With their families. Both sound families.'

'What about patients who weren't out? Are there any who might possibly have done this thing?'

'There is certainly one. But he's always carefully watched. He doesn't go out.'

'Name?'

Bazin hesitated then he shrugged. 'Young Crébert.'

'Human beings aren't infallible,' Nosjean said. 'Could someone at some time have neglected their duty so that he became free to wander for an hour or two?'

'No.' The answer was sharp and brisk.

'Can you be absolutely certain of that? Remember, we're talking of murder.'

There was a long pause. This time the answer was not so sharp or so brisk. 'No. I can't be absolutely certain.'

When Nosjean left he was in a thoughtful mood. He had learned a lot about Charles-Bernard Crébert but not, he felt, enough. He needed to know what made him tick, and if you want to know something about a child, he thought, why ask his mother and father when his schoolteacher probably knows him best of all?

The director of Charles-Bernard's school suggested the boy's form-mistress. Normally, at Charles-Bernard's age, he said, a boy had a form-*master*, but the man who normally had the class had been injured in a car accident and a Mademoiselle Solange Caillaux had agreed to look after it. 'I thought there would be trouble,' the director continued, 'because they're at the age when they *can* be troublesome. But –' he smiled ' – Mademoiselle Caillaux is extraordinarily pretty and instead of causing trouble for her, they all fell in love with her and the only trouble they cause is over who's going to carry her books to her car at the end of the day.'

The director was right. Solange Caillaux *was* pretty. Prettier, Nosjean had to admit, than Odile Chenandier. She looked like a young Brigitte Bardot, which was a change from the Catherine Deneuves and Charlotte Ramplings in his life. Nosjean could quite understand why her pupils fought for the pleasure of carrying her books. He decided to enter the fray himself by suggesting a meeting for a drink.

'So I can get to know something about the boy,' he lied.

As a pleasant evening out, the meeting was a great success. Most of the time, self-interest was wrestling with Nosjean's job, and on the whole self-interest won hands down, so that as an exercise in detection it got them nowhere. Mademoiselle Caillaux hadn't been with Charles-Bernard Crébert's class long enough to know any of them much, though she had already formed the opinion that Charles-Bernard wasn't one of those who were likely to take up the cudgels on her behalf.

'He didn't seem interested,' she said. 'He was a sullen boy, not a particularly nice boy, in fact, though that seems a dreadful thing to say now he's dead. The other boys seemed to think there was something odd about him.'

'What sort of odd?'

'Well,' she paused, troubled ' – they seemed to think he wasn't – well – wasn't like normal boys.'

'A latent homosexual?'

'I suppose that's what they felt. But that again's something one ought not to accuse the dead of.'

'It's not a crime these days,' Nosjean pointed out. 'Besides, it's cropped up already.'

'Well – ' she shrugged ' – there may be something in it. On the other hand, there may be not. They're hardly of an age to be experienced in these things.'

'They're aware of them, all the same.'

'I suppose they are. But if Charles-Bernard had been up to something that day, I'm sure somebody would have noticed it. In fact – ' she dazzled Nosjean with a smile ' – why don't I get them to write an essay on anything unusual they noticed that day. It would be a good exercise for them and it might help you.'

Nosjean frowned. 'They'd make things up.'

'I don't think so. And one or two might have noticed what young Crébert was up to.'

'Will they do it?'

She smiled again. It made Nosjean's heart slide about beneath his shirt like aspic on a hot plate. 'For me they will,' she said. 'They'll do anything for me.'

Nosjean wasn't surprised. He would have, too.

eight

Inevitably, every newspaper in France had got in on the act by this time. Every one of them had a man in the city or at Vieilly or even both.

The headlines were as they'd expected. TERRORIST ATTACK IN CITY. THREE POLICEMEN MURDERED. – *Le Bien Public's* headlines were startling but sane. After all, you couldn't much play down what had happened. *France-Soir's* sub-editors had done rather better: THREE POLICE KILLED. BUTCHERY IN EXPLODED HOUSE. *France Dimanche* had come off best: FIVE KILLED IN HOLO-CAUST. POLICE SLAUGHTER. Pel tossed it aside. The impression was that the butchery had been done by the police and the affair out at Vieilly had hardly been noticed, just a paragraph lower down – on the same page so that it would be clear to readers what a violent world they lived in – BOY FOUND DEAD. MURDER SUSPECTED. Whoever did it, Pel thought sourly, would be understandably bitter that he hadn't had a better press.

Television tackled the affair from a different angle. Since nothing had yet been turned up, the big television names were wanting to know why it was that policemen had been killed in such large numbers and were suggesting that it was the fault of the men at the top for not being on the ball. It was all part of the game, and the procedure with television was less to give news than to make comments and stir things up.

There were still crowds outside the Hôtel de Police. Information was pouring in – people who thought they'd seen the car they were seeking, people with tips about men who were known to use guns – and the police were combing the city for anyone known to have used violence on other occasions. But clues were sadly lacking.

Nobody had slept for days but at least, little by little, they kept adding to the descriptions – odd words and half forgotten fragments from the memory of those who'd seen the murderers escaping – and an appeal had gone out. To hotel keepers and people who let rooms, asking about strangers, especially those who had no luggage; to householders asking them to try to remember if a neighbour had gone out unexpectedly at the appropriate times; to hairdressers asking for men who wanted their hair dyed.

Meanwhile, the police had suddenly found themselves popular. It was a phenomenon which didn't occur very often and Pel was prepared to use it to the limit. People were even coming forward with money for the families of the dead men, and local café and bar owners were rallying round to send in drinks and food for anyone working overtime in the Hôtel de Police.

When the funerals were held, half the city turned out. The thing had been well organised and the three cortèges met near the Place Wilson and headed slowly down the Cours de Gaulle towards the cemetery. The three hearses, followed by the limousines containing the family mourners, were watched by an enormous crowd which lined the grass verges five deep. How many of the watchers were mourners, how many there to register their protest at the killings, and how many merely morbid sightseers, Pel couldn't say. He rode with the Chief, his face grim, his eyes on the crowd. It was an old trick – watching the spectators in the hope of spotting someone who could well have done it – but, of course, it never led to anything and it didn't now.

The city had not been mean about the ceremony. There was a sung Mass and the funeral cars were decorated with black and silver drapings, with more round the door of the church inside the cemetery where the priest waited, a red-faced young man who looked almost as if he could have been a policeman himself with his strong features, large hands and the stout boots that showed beneath his cassock.

The weather had changed unexpectedly and the heavy clouds made the hundreds of memorials to bourgeois dead a drab stretch of marble reaching away in the mist. In front of the plastic flowers inside the dirty glass domes and the stones inset with glass-covered photographs, the road was lined with more people. All morning men had been unloading wreaths, and the chapel entrance was patched with damp where the rain had blown in, its interior full of the intoxicating smell of the flowers piled against the altar steps.

Among the trees policemen in plain clothes stood in groups, their eyes expressionless, missing nothing. As Pel moved inside, the only illumination came from the long flames of the candles near the coffins standing in the body of the chapel, watched over by nuns reciting the rosary as the mourners filed past, dipping their fingers in the holy water to cross themselves.

Randolfi's parents stood with his wife, their faces frozen and bleak. Desouches' father supported his mother, propping her up with a hand on her elbow. Lemadre's widow was hard to distinguish beneath the black veil, but Pel could see the handkerchief balled in her hand and hear the occasional sniff as she fought with her tears. Behind them, people pushed quietly to their places as pall bearers, led by the master of ceremonies, quietly laid the late wreaths down.

The choir sang a Requiem Pel had once heard on the radio. The church was full of officials and behind him he could hear occasional bouts of coughing and the creaking of chairs. A child started sobbing and its mother took it out, her

heels ringing on the stone flags. The De Profundis was
played, then the choir started. The strong smell of incense
swept over everybody as the procession moved outside, the
coffins in front, followed by a choirboy carrying a silver
cross and the priest with his head down over his prayer book.
From among the family vaults, more people watched as they
passed, then quietly moved forward to join on the end of the
procession as it moved to the open graves where the clods of
earth lay like wounds on the green turf.

The pressure was kept up. Information continued to come in
but it was never the information they wanted and there was
nothing positive to go on. Tracker dogs and men with
walkie-talkies were still out searching and a large reward had
been offered, supplemented by more offers from city
businessmen who believed in law and order.

The whole area was being turned upside-down. Messages
were sent out to all forces to investigate anyone who had
been brought in for theft, because the men they wanted
might have gone into hiding and been forced to steal to stay
alive, and to all employers to check new employees. Then De
Troquereau spotted a man fitting one of the descriptions they
had, who seemed to be acting suspiciously. As De Troq'
approached, the man realised he was being followed and
jumped on a bus heading up the Rue de la Liberté. Failing to
catch the bus, De Troq' had to grab a taxi, but the taxi
became stuck in the traffic, so he got the driver to pass a
message by his radio to his base, which passed it on to the
police, and as the man dropped off the bus at Talant, he was
met by a police car.

But even as hands reached out for him, he wriggled free
and ran, and in no time reinforcements were pouring into the
area where he had disappeared and every road was guarded.
A police cordon was thrown round the district and every
man on the streets was stopped to prove his identity. The

local children enjoyed it all immensely and had to be shooed away as they tried to climb into the radio van that was working with the men on their two flat feet. Dogs arrived to search the district and, as expectant crowds waited outside, even pushed through the Church of Ste Marie as Mass was being said. Eventually the wanted man was traced to a block of flats at Fontaine and there the hunt was called off when they became certain he wasn't the man they wanted and that, anyway, he was no longer in the area.

The reward was increased again and more information came in, together with a variety of theories: The killers must surely be hiding in a hotel, protected by a woman; they must be in Paris, which because of its size was always the best place to disappear. Hairdressers were checked, especially when one of them became suspicious as a manly-looking woman asked to have her hair cropped short and dyed. Though she matched the description of one of the men they wanted, she turned out to be a perfectly respectable matron.

While the enquiry was going on, three bright young gentlemen at Chenove decided it might be a good time to turn to crime because the police would be too busy to worry about them. But a small boy, standing in a doorway, saw them pulling stockings over their heads and, as they vanished into the offices of Fabrications Métaux Français, he telephoned the police. The three men were picked up as they reappeared and the small boy became a hero for a day or two.

By this time the wanted posters were resulting in hoaxes. Suspects were reported everywhere in the city. Most of the sightings were made in good faith, but a few were from drunks or practical jokers who found themselves very quickly inside 72, Rue d'Auxonne, which was the name given to the local prison. A clairvoyant claimed to have seen the body of one of the suspects in a wood, and when they searched a body was there all right but it was that of a man too old to have been one of the wanted men, and he had cut his throat.

'All the same,' Darcy asked, 'how the hell did she know he was there?'

A pilot leaving the airport alerted the police about one of his passengers but when the aeroplane was met in Paris the passenger turned out to be a German businessman, while three men reported to be behaving oddly as they climbed on to a train turned out to be a group of young executives who had drunk too much at a business lunch.

Then a woman claimed to have seen one of the wanted men in a woman's lavatory and the red-faced police officer sent in to check discovered it was truly a woman. Another woman, who turned out to be slightly round the bend, said the suspects were in her bedroom. They had to investigate but, as they'd suspected, they weren't, while a man spotted wearing a comic mask proved to be the proprietor of a toy shop testing his wares. Finally a railwayman joined the practical jokers at 72, Rue d'Auxonne, when he terrified a taxi driver by claiming to be one of the suspects.

Every postbag brought letters – typewritten, handwritten, badly spelled or perfectly phrased, on stiff parchment-like paper or pages torn from exercise books. Someone had to go through them all. Most of them concerned the police shootings but there was one indignant one – 'Why is there so little in the newspapers about the murder at Vieilly?' It seemed as if someone considered the police victims were getting too much publicity. There were others suggesting that the shootings were a set-up by the Ministry of the Interior as a means of proving the police were needed, which everybody knew was a lie; that they had been committed by a variety of neighbours who appeared to be on bad terms with the writers; one even suggesting that they should look into the President of the Republic, who was a politician and therefore not to be trusted any further than he could be thrown. Most of them were clearly the work of crackpots.

Still the information came in. The suspects were reported to have stolen sandwiches off picknickers in a layby on the N7, to be drinking beer in a bar at Sémur. A man sleeping in a parked car was ringed by armed policemen only to turn out to be waiting for his wife. Every call on the telephone was acted on and each incident was marked on a giant map. There were still no signs of the guns which had been used to do the killings but many illicit weapons were returned to the Hôtel de Police by scared owners, some even left anonymously in parcels on the doorstep. A tip led to a reservoir which was searched by frogmen without success and on another occasion police boarded a train on which two men had jumped at the last moment as it left the city. It was stopped en route and searched without revealing anything, while four naked ladies in a strip club operating illegally at Nancy were surprised by detectives acting on a tip that the men they wanted were hiding above it.

All the time, Pel had his eye on the date. The days were slipping past and he was beginning to grow worried. It had been suggested that the President's visit to the city should be put off but the idea had been firmly rejected by the Elysée Palace in Paris. The President of France didn't expect to be assassinated and it was up to the police to see he wasn't. Which was fair enough but didn't really help much.

Pel left the office feeling old. By this time he had hardly been out of the Hôtel de Police for days and he needed a break. He had smoked so many cigarettes he felt his inside was charred, he had been home only to change his clothes and take a bath, and his feet ached with standing. Cautiously, half-expecting a rebuff, he telephoned Madame Faivre-Perret and suggested they should meet for a meal at the Relais St

Armand, which lay roughly between her premises and the Hôtel de Police.

'I just feel I need to talk to someone about something other than murder,' he said heavily.

She seemed pleased to see him and waited for him to kiss her cheeks. Managing it without disturbing her hair or knocking her eye out, he reflected he was becoming good at it.

'I could be called away,' he warned.

'It's something I've come to expect,' she admitted. 'It's a sick world.'

True enough. Even their own province, Pel decided bitterly, hadn't been behind the door where terrorism was concerned. It wasn't really a new phenomenon, anyway, and the Dukes of Burgundy, never exactly saints, had often been involved in sudden death. Despite his record for courage, Philip the Bold had not been much filled with fellow feeling, while Philip the Good, for all his splendid achievements, had had an ability to strike dismay into his neighbours' hearts – if only with his thirty-three mistresses and twenty-six bastards. Even the holy St Bernard, who liked to remind popes and kings of their duties, must have been a bit terrifying with his aptitude for calling a spade a bloody shovel.

They ate almost in silence because there were few plans they could make and Pel's mind was too full of the killings. Madame didn't seem to mind and sat quietly beside him in a way that he found surprisingly comforting.

When he reached his home in the Rue Martin-de-Noinville it was late and he was feeling depressed. For once it wasn't because his car had started making curious noises in the engine room, that his house looked like a pile of old doors and windows just dumped down and left to erect themselves, or that his front lawn looked like the stubble of a not very well cared for wheat field. It wasn't that he knew that

Madame Routy would be just watching the end of something on the television, with the volume control turned up as far as it would go. It wasn't even that the room would be shabby and ill-cared for, or that Madame Routy would have done as little as possible for her money, because all these problems had changed since Pel and Madame Faivre-Perret had reached an understanding about their future. At least, he could see an end to his discomfort. It was rather the load of work that had fallen on his shoulders and the thought of three dead policemen and the evil people who could see no way to obtain their ends except by violence. That, and the fact that in the mortuary was the cold body of a young boy, murdered at an age when he was probably just beginning to find life exciting.

As he expected, the television was roaring away so that the very foundations of the house were shaking.

'Turn that thing off,' Pel growled.

Madame Routy ignored him. She was absorbed in what was happening on the screen and she had grown accustomed to ignoring Pel.

'Turn it off,' he said more loudly.

She stirred herself enough to answer him. 'I'm just watching the end of this,' she said. 'It's a play.'

'Turn it off!' Pel roared.

She glared at him. 'I have a right to a little entertainment when my work is finished,' she said.

But she turned the switch. 'If I'm not allowed a little pleasure at my age – ' she began.

'I'm not interested in your pleasure,' Pel snarled. 'Three policemen and a woman are dead and two others seriously wounded, and a boy's been strangled at Vieilly. I need peace to think.'

As she disappeared, he realised with amazement that for the first time since she had arrived in his sphere of influence – or was it since he had arrived in hers? – he had had the nerve to lay down the law. It must be Madame Faivre-Perret's encouragement, he decided. Then he shook his head. No, it was just that he had too much on his mind. Murders didn't usually come five at a time.

He poured himself a brandy, noting as he did so that Madame Routy had been at it again, and sat down facing the blank screen of the television. Upstairs, he could hear Madame Routy throwing things around in a monumental huff.

He tossed back the brandy without tasting it then stared at the glass, wondering where it had gone to. Pouring himself another, he sat down again and tried to put his tired thoughts in order. The road blocks, the searches, the questioning had produced nothing. The descriptions they had were vague because the terrorists had been careful to keep their faces hidden, but it had been noticed by a number of witnesses that the wounded man had a mandarin moustache and a thick mop of hair, and that the woman who hurried behind was young, blonde and not very good-looking.

'She was shapeless,' one witness had said fastidiously. He was a smartly-dressed young man who clearly knew what the shape of a young woman ought to be and had probably run his hands over a few in his time.

Pel slept badly and the following morning he opened his eyes warily, as usual half-expecting the day to attack him. Nothing happened, however, except that the meal the night before had given him indigestion. He popped a bismuth tablet into his mouth and regarded himself in the mirror. Nothing seemed to have dropped off him during the night, but he didn't look any better than the previous day. He couldn't see what Madame Faivre-Perret saw in him. If it had been up to him, he felt, he wouldn't have given him house room.

Madame Routy handed him his breakfast in a sullen silence but he was in no mood to worry about her. He had no

85

appetite, however, and did no more than drink a cup of coffee, then he climbed into his car and drove to the city. Claudie Darel, who was dozing in a chair by the telephone, looked up tiredly as he appeared.

'Up all night?' he asked.

'Yes, Patron. But Régis Martin's due in half an hour. I shall get some sleep then.'

There was nothing on his desk so he slipped across to the Bar Transvaal and joined the people at the zinc who were making a breakfast of coffee and croissants. On his return he called on the Chief to discuss things.

Darcy was waiting in his office when he reappeared. 'Watch television last night?' he asked.

Pel frowned. 'There's quite enough television in my house without me at it,' he said.

'You might have seen something that would interest you.'

'Such as?'

'Robert Démon's programme – "France Asks." He's here in the city.'

'I've heard of him. Doesn't like the police. Inclined to stir things up, isn't he? Where's he staying?'

'At the Central. I rang up. He's still in bed.'

'While our people stay up all night so he can sleep soundly.'

'He had the bright idea of making a documentary,' Darcy went on. 'He found three actors from Paris who resembled our wanted men, dressed them up and got them to walk about looking like the suspects – standing in bars, leaning on walls and generally looking suspicious while his cameras worked them over.'

Pel shrugged. 'Helps to jog memories,' he said.

'It also made it seem as if our lot were just hanging around waiting to be arrested and we were too dim to notice. It didn't stop there either. He went on to deliver a diatribe against us.' Darcy laid a sheet of paper on the desk. 'Young Martin taped him and typed out the result. That's it.'

Pel picked up the paper and, sitting down, was about to take a cigarette when he remembered he was trying to give them up. As he thrust the thought away, however, Darcy lit two and offered him one. Sighing, Pel took it, dragged the smoke down to his socks and began to read.

There were the usual interviews with the relatives of the dead, who were trying to be helpful while still barely able to contain their grief, and he decided it was a sad commentary on the human race that people should want to see the manifestation of tragedy in the strained faces and wet eyes of bereaved mothers and wives.

Then the commentary changed.

'Did the police err,' Démon asked, 'in not capturing these men earlier? Great dissatisfaction has been felt that they were allowed to escape. Did someone miss some clues? Was there carelessness? Was someone badly misinformed or did the police merely ignore warnings? Three men are dead and two more are wounded. Was the operation clumsily prepared? Why wasn't the house properly surrounded? People living in the area of the Impasse Tarien have said that they knew there was something very odd going on. Why didn't the police know? It's being said that questions are to be asked in the House of Representatives and that the President has ex-pressed his extreme dissatisfaction. And very rightly, too, because a woman was also killed and if the police had taken greater care she would be alive at this moment…'

Pel flung the paper down. 'I notice he gives no names,' he growled. 'Who says questions are being asked in the House of Representatives? And who says the President's dissatisfied? I've just come from the Chief and he's not been complaining. Who is this damned man, Démon?'

'Real name's Degarron.' Darcy said. 'Jean Degarron. Also writes for *Véracité*. It's a new journal. Considers its stories crusades and Démon its most crusading writer.'

Pel scowled. 'I think we'd better keep an eye on Monsieur Démon,' he observed.

Darcy shrugged. 'It might be a good idea,' he agreed, 'because he's sure as hell keeping an eye on us.'

nine

It was Aimedieu who turned up the owner of the missing
blue car that had done so much damage in the Rue Claude-
Picard. He was a man called Jean-Jacques Hogue, whose
name cropped up as the questioning around the bars inten-
sified. It didn't take long to find him and Aimedieu immediately decided that the safest thing to do with him was to take
him down to the Hôtel de Police and let Pel get at him.

Hogue claimed he had sold the car in question the day
before the shooting and there was nothing to prove he
hadn't, though his description of the new owner was
surprisingly vague, considering he had just done business to
the extent of several thousand francs with him.

'He called himself Araba,' he said. 'Tall chap. Thin. Dark
hair. Might have been North African. He said he'd heard the
car was for sale and just turned up on the doorstep.'

'Where did he live?' Pel demanded.

'He didn't say.'

They checked on the car's registration but either Hogue
was lying or the new owner hadn't registered it because the
change of ownership hadn't been reported and it seemed
safer to keep Hogue at the Hôtel de Police as long as they
could.

Another car of similar make and colour, with what they
knew of the number of the wanted car superimposed, was
televised and that evening a man called Ferry appeared at the
Hôtel de Police, saying he remembered seeing a car like the

89

one they were seeking being driven up a cul-de-sac in the industrial area of the city on Bastille Night.

'It was going so damned fast,' he said, 'it scraped the wall as it went in. It set up a screech that made my hair stand on end.'

Aimedieu found the cul-de-sac without much trouble. At the end of it there was a row of rented garages, all of them shabby and clearly used from time to time as workshops. The doors were old and ill-fitting and Aimedieu went along them, peering through the broken glass panes and warped wood-work. At the end one he stopped. Through a break in the panelling he was able to make out in the beam of his torch a pale blue car whose registration number was obscured by a couple of tyres that were leaning against it. Since the tyres seemed to have been strategically placed to hide the number, Aimedieu decided to break in.

Forcing the lock, he moved the tyres and saw the car's number was 9701-RD-75. It was the one they were seeking. Closing the doors, he headed round the corner for the nearest bar, and asked for the telephone.

Within minutes Prélat and the Fingerprint boys had arrived with the photographers and the other specialists. It didn't take Aimedieu long to discover that the man who had rented the garage was Hogue whom they were still interview-ing as the owner of the car.

'Odd, isn't it?' Pel observed dryly to Hogue, 'that it's still in your garage if it's been sold.'

There were fingerprints everywhere on the car, spare number plates, three recently fired 9 mm cartridge cases – which were soon shown to be from the same gun as the bullets found in the plaster, the dead policemen, Madame Lenotre and Madame Colbrun – overalls, and, above all, nylon stockings which were always useful for making masks.

By this time, Hogue, who'd been found to have a record, had been answering questions for a whole day and he was still insisting he'd sold the car.

'Don't be a clot,' Darcy said contemptuously. 'Do you expect us to believe that?'

'Yes,' Hogue yelled. 'It's the truth! I don't know anything about the shootings!'

'You must be the only person in the city who doesn't. Everybody else does. Are you deaf or something?'

'Well, yes. A bit. Perhaps that's why.'

'Didn't you read about it?'

'I never read the papers.'

'Where were you at the time?'

'I was alone in this bar – '

'Which bar?'

'The Bar du Traffic. In the Rue Henri-Mauray. There was this tobacco salesman in there. I can prove it.'

Finding the Bar du Traffic, Aimedieu soon confirmed that the tobacco salesman had been there at the same time as Hogue but that the time didn't coincide with the shootings. In addition, Hogue had not been alone but with two other men, and had been seen reading a newspaper containing the report of the murders and was looking distinctly ill-at-ease.

'Charge him,' Pel said as Aimedieu laid the facts before him.

At least they'd got one man and, when faced with it, Hogue admitted that he'd driven three men away after the shootings in the Impasse Tarien and that one of them had been injured.

'Why you?' Pel demanded. 'Were you waiting?'

Hogue began to cry. 'I'd waited every night for a week. They were up to something and I was there in case something went wrong and they had to make a quick getaway. They said nothing was going to happen for some time.'

'But it did, didn't it?' Darcy pointed out. 'It turned out a nasty business all round. Where did you drive these men?'

'I dropped them in the Place Auty. They said they'd better change cars in case we'd been seen. They said they had another car there.'

'What were their names?'

'I don't know. One of them came to see me and offered me money to do the driving. That's all I know.'

'We have a truth serum. Would you like a shot? They say it shrivels your balls a bit but it's good for the truth.'

Hogue looked terrified. 'I'm telling the truth!' he yelled. 'I swear it! Would I lie to you?'

'I'm sure you would,' Darcy said. 'If it were worth it.'

It was impossible to shake Hogue. Since he'd been involved in more than one robbery, it began to look as if someone had heard of him and knew he was prepared to accept money to drive in incidents that weren't quite honest. He continued to insist he'd done none of the shooting, however, and Mattigny, the man who'd seen the injured man helped away, studying him in a line-up of suspects, said quite firmly that he hadn't been one of the men he'd seen. Finally, a bar owner remembered seeing him parked just down the street from his premises in the nearby Rue de Genève at the time. Though Hogue had certainly been involved in the getaway, it seemed he hadn't been involved in the shootings.

'What about the woman?' Pel asked.

'I didn't see any woman,' Hogue said. 'There was no woman when they arrived at my car.'

'Couldn't you tell one of them was hurt?'

'I thought he was drunk.'

They got descriptions. Hogue was frightened and this time the descriptions were better.

'I heard their names,' he said. 'One was called Tom and one the Weasel. The other one – the one who seemed drunk – was called Dino or Léo or something like that.'

They were making progress. It was slow but it was progress, though time was steadily growing shorter. Over a week had gone by already and the President's visit to the Palais des Ducs lay only eighteen days away. To be on the safe side, the Chief was already drawing up plans for protecting him, trying to think of every possible contingency from the moment he arrived within their area until the moment he left, and all the houses and apartments along the route from the station to the Palais des Ducs which he was to take on his arrival were being searched. Nobody was taking chances and even the sewers got a going over.

Meanwhile Judge Polverari was giving Hogue another questioning. They didn't expect him to turn up much that they hadn't turned up already. Pel spent the morning studying the reports still coming in like a shower of confetti, then at lunch time he slipped out to the Bar Transvaal for a sandwich and a beer. He was just finishing his second drink when the telephone rang. The proprietor lifted it, listened, then jerked his head at Pel.

'It's you,' he said. 'Better get back.'

Swallowing his beer, Pel hurried across the road. Darcy was in his room, tapping on a typewriter. As he saw Pel he tore the sheet out and handed it to him.

'Typescript of a telephone conversation I've just had, Patron,' he said.

'What about?'

'It was a doctor. At least, he said he was a doctor and he sounded like a doctor. But he wouldn't give his name. He said he went on the night of the shootings to attend a wounded man. He was called to the door soon after midnight. There was a woman there who said her husband had been shot accidentally. She had a car waiting with a man at the wheel. The doc wasn't sure where it was they went because they drove round and round a lot – he thought to confuse him – but it wasn't in any area he knew and he thought it was right across the city. It was a two-storey house and it was in darkness. The woman took him upstairs where he found a man lying on a bed. He was in a bad way and the driver said he'd been shot in the back accidentally. The doc didn't believe him. He made a cursory examination and came to the conclusion that there was a bullet lodged in the man's chest touching the right ventricle. He suggested hospital at once.'

Pel pulled up a chair and sat down, not interrupting.

'Both the man and the woman said no, he couldn't go to hospital. When the doctor asked why, they said the friend who'd used the gun hadn't a licence. He'd been cleaning it and it had gone off by accident. The doctor said that if the woman would come to his surgery, he'd give her drugs and insisted again that the man ought to go to hospital. Again they said no. While he was there the woman was burning papers and bloodstained sheets and towels. When the doctor asked why, she said she thought the man was going to die and, since she lived there, she'd be accused of murder. The pill-roller got away as soon as he could. They drove him back into the city – again going through all the back streets – until they finally dropped him near the Porte Guillaume. He took a taxi home from there.'

'Did he get the car number?'

'He says not.'

'They never do. All the same – ' Pel leaned forward ' – this is a break. Are you bringing him in?'

'Patron, I haven't got his name.'

Pel jerked back in his seat. 'You've got every other damned thing!' he snapped. 'Why not his name?'

'He wouldn't give it.'

'Couldn't you have interrupted him long enough to insist?'

'I tried, Patron, but he wasn't playing. In fact, I'd just persuaded him when he said "There's somebody coming. I'll have to go," and hung up.'

'Why didn't he telephone us immediately?'

'I think he's scared stiff. He said he'd read about the shootings and the explosion and thought the man was a terrorist and that was why he didn't want to go to hospital. He was afraid that if he put the police on to them, they'd come after him to silence him, or get at his family.'

'Couldn't you trace the call?'

'Martin tried but it was too late.'

Pel slammed his hand down on the desk. 'Had he no idea where it happened?'

'He said he thought the Montchapet area. And that would make sense because there are a lot of old houses and a lot of foreigners living there. We've had trouble there before.'

'Did he give a description?'

'He just said two-storey houses. Very old. He also noticed that there were unopened packets of bandage – broad bandage. The woman had made some attempt to bandage the man and because he was bleeding badly had given up and used the towels and sheets he saw.'

Pel frowned. 'We've got to find this damned doctor,' he said. He stared at his desk, his mind whirring. 'Any accent we could trace? North? South? Anything to go on?'

'Yes, Patron. He didn't seem able to sound his r's.'

'Then, in the name of God, let's find a doctor in the city who can't sound his r's.'

'We're already trying, Patron,' Darcy said gently. 'Claudie's telephoning the medical centres to see if they know anyone. Martin's telephoning the hospitals. After that, they're going through the whole medical list. We'll find him.'

'Right. Good. In the meantime, get on to Uniformed Branch and Traffic. Get the cars prowling round the Montchapet district. They're looking for a street with old two-storeyed houses. If they find one they've to ask at all the pharmacists in the district if anyone bought bandage and, if so, get a description. They can also ask if anyone saw an injured man brought home. If he was as bad as this damned doctor says he was then he wouldn't be easy to conceal.'

ten

The break came late in the afternoon. Nobody knew a doctor who couldn't sound his r's properly but then a nurse at the Ste Chantal Hospital mentioned that a certain Doctor Alexandre Lacoste had been accidentally hit in the mouth while in the hospital's recreation block and had since found it difficult to enunciate.

'Get the car, Darcy,' Pel snapped. 'Bring him in.'

Dr Lacoste was short, slight and dark and, despite his name, was an Algerian by birth. He had been in France for seven years and there was a large plaster over his upper lip. He looked terrified.

'Why have I been brought here?' he demanded.

'Questions,' Pel said. 'You might be able to help us. What happened to your lip?'

'I was hit by a squash racket,' Lacoste said. 'Two days ago. I had to have three stitches in it.'

Pel paused, then leaned forward. 'You the doctor who was called out to a man with a bullet in his back on the night of the 14th?' he asked bluntly.

Lacoste's eyes widened and he seemed to shrink into his chair. There was a long silence and a faint hospital smell of ether, cleanliness and floor polish seemed to come from him like the smell of fear. He was struggling to say something, but seemed unable to get it out, so Pel said it for him.

'It *was* you, wasn't it?'

Lacoste's head nodded slowly.

'Let's have it then. You guessed it was connected with the shootings in the city on that night, didn't you? Why did you try to hide it?'

Lacoste stared at Pel for a moment or two like a rabbit mesmerised by a snake, then he swallowed noisily and struggled again to speak. He had to have several tries. 'I did not try to hide it,' he managed at last in a thin uncertain voice. 'I felt I ought to inform the police but I did not want to be involved. I was afraid.'

'Why?'

'I decided the man who drove me was a North African like me. The papers next morning said the shootings were by terrorists. I have a wife and two children. France allowed me to come here and practise. I did not want to be sent away.'

'You'd have been less likely if you'd informed the police at once,' Darcy growled.

'You do not understand.' Lacoste's hands fluttered in an unhappy gesture. 'Why did they pick on me? There are other doctors. They must have known I was Algerian. They must have got my name from somewhere.'

'There are other Algerians working in the city hospital,' Darcy pointed out. 'It wouldn't be difficult. If these people are Algerians, too, they'd know of you.'

'I thought they might kill my children. I read of a boy being murdered also.'

'That may have nothing to do with this,' Pel snapped. 'Come on, let's have it! Where did you go?'

'I do not know.'

'You've got eyes. Did they blindfold you?'

'No. But I have not been in this city long. I do not know it well and they drove me round and round in circles. Deliberately, I think. To bewilder me.'

Pel glanced at Darcy. 'Have you no idea?' he asked.

'I think it was the Montchapet district of the city. But I cannot be certain.'

'What was it like?'

'It was old and dilapidated. The houses looked very broken down.'

'Anything else? Anything you noticed nearby? A cinema? A bar?'

'I saw a bar called the Bar Olivier – '

'Look it up, Darcy.'

As Darcy turned away, Pel leaned closer. 'Go on. Was it very near?'

'Not exactly. A few minutes away, I should say.'

'Anything else?'

'As I left I saw a street called the Rue Vendaduzzi.'

'That's in the Mareuil area,' Darcy said. 'I know it.'

'Same area as the bar?' Pel asked.

'No,' Lacoste said. 'The other way. They did not drive me back the way we had come and all the streets were different. I noticed the Rue St Josephe, though.'

Darcy's finger was on a map. With the other hand he was checking the directories.

'Got it,' he said. 'And the Bar Olivier. So where they took you must be somewhere in between. About here. It was a good guess, my friend. It might well have been the Mont-chapet district. Try again. We're getting closer. What else did you notice?'

'There was a supermarket. Super Flores, it was called. It was not really very big but that was its name. It was close by. I saw it almost as soon as they drove off.'

Darcy was turning through the leaves of the telephone directory. 'Rue Flores, Patron.'

'Was that the street?' Pel turned to Lacoste. 'Was it in the same street as the house where you went?'

'No.' The doctor's eyes were wide. 'The next street. Or perhaps the one after that. I am not sure.'

'What about this car they used? Why didn't you get the number?'

'I told you. I was frightened. I was afraid of being involved. I thought if they were part of this Libyan hit group that has been operating round Europe, I might be the next victim.'

'Didn't you even look?'

'No.'

'What about the colour?'

'I do not know. It was just dark. Black or blue perhaps.'

'How about the inside?'

'I do not know.'

'What about the people who drove you, the people who were there when you examined the wounded man?'

'I tried not to look at them. They were muffled up. It was clear they did not want me to see them.'

Pel stared at the doctor for a moment. His dark skin was grey with fright. Pel sighed and shrugged.

'Get on to Uniform and Traffic, Daniel,' he said. 'Tell them to look for our street in the area of the Rue Flores. When we find it, we'll take this type along in a police car and get him to identify it. In the meantime, he'd better make a statement. We'll need one.'

Lacoste was half-way through his statement when the telephone rang. It was Inspector Pomereu, of Traffic.

'One of my crews think they've found your street,' he said. 'Old, two-storeyed houses. Dilapidated. Rue Dubosc, two streets away from the Rue Flores. If you arrive from one end you pass the Bar Olivier. If you arrive from the other you pass the Rue Vendaduzzi and the Super Flores supermarket. We've made a few enquiries and we've found a pharmacist who was knocked up late on the night of the shootings by a woman asking for bandages. She said there'd been an accident. The pharmacist offered to go along and help but she wouldn't let him. She said it wasn't that important but she took away enough crêpe to bandage a horse.'

Pel frowned. 'Why has the damned man been sitting on this information all this time?' he growled. 'They're all doing it.'

'I asked him that,' Pomereu said. 'It's a rough district round there and people learn to mind their own business and keep their mouths shut.'

'Where are your people now?'

'They're parked in the Rue de la Justice just round the corner from the Bar Olivier end of the Rue Dubosc.'

Pel put the telephone down. 'Let's go,' he said.

Bundling Dr Lacoste into Darcy's car they roared away from the centre of the city, Lacoste cowering in the rear seat, terrified of being seen. The police car was waiting in the Rue de la Justice as Pomereu had said, the two men inside it trying to look as if they'd just stopped for a quick drag at a cigarette where they couldn't be seen.

As Pel's car halted alongside, the sergeant leaned over. 'Just round the corner, sir,' he said.

'Right.' Pel turned to Lacoste. 'Sit up and see if you can identify the place.'

Darcy's car cruised slowly down the Rue Dubosc, trying to look like any other car. It was a shabby area of peeling paint and torn posters, scraps of old newspaper fluttering in the gutter in the breeze.

'I think –' Lacoste spoke in a whisper as if terrified of being overheard ' – I think that's the place. That or the one next door.'

Pel glanced at Darcy. 'We'll try next door first,' he said.

As the car stopped, a man with a dark skin appeared in the doorway. He eyed them warily.

'We're looking for a man who was brought home here several nights ago,' Darcy said. 'He was hurt. Did you see anything?'

The man studied them for a moment. 'You Flics?'

'Yes.'

'I don't have to help you.'

'You don't,' Darcy said. 'But you'd better. He might have explosives and you might be the next one to go up.'

The man's eyes flickered then he gestured with a jerk of his head. 'Next door,' he said quietly. 'I heard the woman crying and looked out. They took him in there.'

'Who's there now? Do you know?'

'No idea. There was a woman and two men holding up another man. I thought he was drunk and the woman was his wife, and she was hysterical because he'd been beating her or something.'

'Know who they are?'

The man shook his head. 'People change too often round here for that.'

As they retreated to the car, the dark-skinned man vanished inside and returned a few moments later with several other men and women and a few children. Almost at once, doorways across the street began to fill with people.

Pel glared at them. 'They'd hang about with their mouths open if it were the last trump,' he growled to Darcy. 'Tell the sergeant from the car to get them back inside. Tell him to say there may be shooting. And there may well be. Got your gun?'

'Yes, Patron.'

'Radio in. We're not having another massacre. We'll try to be a bit more cautious than Goriot was. Tell Claudie to send out anybody who's around. They're to wait in the Rue de la Justice out of sight. You stay here to make sure nobody bolts.'

Pel had just walked back to the Rue de la Justice when a car screamed to a stop. It was Lagé, willing as ever. With him were Aimedieu, Brochard and Debray, blonde and pale like a pair of twins. A moment later Pomereu arrived with his sergeant.

'Thought you might be in need of a little help with the traffic,' he said.

Soon afterwards Inspector Nadauld of Uniformed Branch arrived, splendid in a uniform of black and sky blue, his képi outlined with silver braid. His sergeant already had the telephone in his hand ready to call for reinforcements.

The Chief arrived a few minutes later. 'Shouldn't we call in the CRS?' he asked. 'After all, they're the security forces. That's what they're for – to deal with rioting and terrorists.'

'I think we should handle it ourselves,' Pel advised. 'We'd look silly if it turned out to be gang warfare between the boys in Marseilles or a bunch of Corsican caids who've fallen out.' He shrugged. 'If it is, I suggest we leave them to it. I'm all for that lot shooting each other.'

While they were still deciding how to handle the business, Pel found himself facing a tall dark-haired young man wearing a smart Parisian suit. He held a microphone in one hand and behind him was a television cameraman with all his apparatus. He knew immediately who he was.

'I'm Robert Démon,' the young man explained.

Pel scowled. 'I've been wanting to meet you,' he said.

Démon smiled. 'I'm glad I'm so popular.'

'You're not,' Pel snapped. 'I'd like to know more about your sources of information. They might be of help to *us*.'

'Am I being interrogated?' Démon looked sardonic.

'You're being asked where you got all this information you disseminated in your television programme.'

Démon smiled again. 'I don't divulge sources.'

'That's a comfortable excuse to hide behind if your sources are dubious. And who are these people living in the area of the Impasse Tarien who've said there was something odd going on?'

'I can't give names.'

Pel glared. 'I suspect there are no names,' he snapped.

Démon shrugged. 'We have our contacts,' he said smoothly.

As they talked, Darcy arrived, pushing forward an old woman. She was loaded down with shopping.

'She lives opposite,' Darcy explained. 'She says there's nobody in there.'

'No, chéri,' the old woman agreed. 'There isn't. I know. There were four of them, two men and two women. I used to watch them from my window. It's right opposite and I can see in. There's not much else to do but watch when you're my age. I heard them come back late on the night of the shootings, but this time there were three men and one woman. One of the men was drunk. I saw two of the men leave later. I've seen nobody moving about this morning.'

Démon, who had been listening carefully, moved forward again. 'If there's nobody in there,' he said, 'isn't all this – ' his hand gestured at the police cars and the policemen standing in groups ' – rather a sledge-hammer to crack a nut?'

Pel was just wondering if he couldn't find a good reason to run him in when Lagé spoke excitedly.

'The old dear's wrong, Patron!' he said. 'There *is* somebody in there! The chimney's smoking!'

Every head jerked round and up. Lagé was right. A thin spiral of blue smoke was drifting up from one of the chimneys.

They went into a huddle again. Slowly, with the aid of the old woman and the dark-skinned man from next door, they managed to build up a picture of the interior of the house and the habits of its occupants. It seemed they spent most of their time upstairs and there was only a narrow staircase.

They looked at each other. A narrow staircase with a man at the top with a gun could be a death trap, and Pel had no wish for more butchery. They were still trying to decide what to do when Lacoste stepped forward. 'I will go in,' he said.

Pel looked at him. He was still clearly terrified but he seemed suddenly in control of himself.

'There might be a man in there with a gun,' Pel said. 'Perhaps more than one.'

'Never mind. I have caused much trouble and I owe France a great deal. I will take the risk. I have a perfectly legitimate reason. I was called to a desperately wounded man. I have only to say I was worried and wanted to know how he was.'

'What if they start shooting?'

Lacoste managed a twisted smile. 'Then I shall fling myself down,' he said, 'and wait for you to come and rescue me. First, though, I think I should have a medical bag to make my visit look more professional.'

Pel turned. 'Anybody know a doctor in this area?'

Brochard did. 'Doctor Garand,' he said. 'Rue Boromeo, just round the corner. Two of them run a surgery there. Him and Doctor Leclerc.'

'Go and borrow a medical bag. They must have a spare one between them. It doesn't have to have much in it.'

'It had better have *something*,' Lacoste said. 'In case they want me to identify myself.'

'All right.' Pel jerked his head at Brochard. 'You heard what he said. Tell him it's a matter of life and death.' He paused. 'It probably is,' he ended.

While Brochard disappeared to argue with the doctors in the Rue Boromeo, Pel organised his men. Debray and two of Nadauld's men went off with the old woman, making a circuitous route to the back of the Rue Dubosc, with instructions to watch from her window.

'There's to be no shooting,' Pel insisted. 'Not until you're told to shoot.' As he spoke, he looked firmly at Aimedieu, who still seemed on edge. Pel was afraid he might be after revenge for his dead comrades and decided to keep him close by where he could watch him.

He turned to Pomereu. 'Car at each end of the road,' he ordered. He looked at a street map and turned to Nadauld. 'Let's have men in the street which runs parallel,' he suggested. 'In case they've got an escape route.'

A dustcart was moving down the street as they talked and he remembered he'd seen dustbins on the pavement in the Rue Dubosc.

'Stop that cart, Lagé,' he said. 'You and Debray borrow overalls and move down either side of Rue Dubosc. Look as if you're getting the bins ready but warn everybody to get indoors. We don't want anybody hurt.'

As Lagé and Debray struggled into the blue overalls, Brochard returned, carrying a square medical bag. With him was another man also carrying a medical bag. He introduced himself as Doctor Garand.

'It sounded as if there might be trouble,' he said. 'If it's anything like the affair in the Impasse Tarien, I thought you might need an extra doctor. Would you like me to go in as well?'

Lacoste stiffened. It was as if now he'd decided to be a hero he wasn't going to share his heroism with anybody. 'I will go alone,' he insisted. 'They will know me.'

Grasping the handle of the medical bag, he headed for the Rue Dubosc. As he turned the corner and disappeared from sight, Darcy unbuttoned his jacket and felt for his gun. Aimedieu already had his gun in his hand.

'Put that away,' Pel snapped.

Faintly shamefaced, Aimedieu replaced the gun in its holster. Pel wasn't without sympathy. It wasn't easy for a man to see three of his colleagues shot dead.

They waited silently. The radio telephone in Nadauld's car was squawking. Its harsh tones jarred on the nerves.

'For the love of God,' Pel growled. 'Either answer it or turn it off.'

Nadauld's sergeant put the receiver to his ear, spoke briefly, and switched off.

'Lacoste's coming back,' Darcy said from the corner.

It seemed ages as they waited. Lacoste looked pale but relieved.

'Anybody in there?' Pel asked.

'The man I was called to,' Lacoste said. 'He's dead. There's also a woman. On the floor near the kitchen fireplace. She's probably dead, too.'

eleven

The house was shabby like most of the houses in the area. It had a diminutive hall with a staircase running up from it, a living room and a dining room – if they could be honoured by such names – containing sticks of furniture, threadbare carpets and one or two ugly pictures. The windows had no curtains, but shelves made by resting planks on bricks contained books by Marx, Engels, Nietszche and a few others, together with bundles of pamphlets – one, Darcy noticed immediately, like the ones he had seen at the home of Kiczmyrczik.

They edged through the rooms, two men moving out into the backyard to check a shed where there was a rusty bicycle frame and a few pieces of timber, and Darcy was just about to step into the back kitchen when he heard a heavy sigh. Beyond the kitchen table, lying on a rug beside the fireplace, was a girl. She was just stirring as if she'd been in an exhausted sleep, obviously the woman Lacoste thought was dead. As he entered, she sat up abruptly and, as her eyes fell on him, she immediately began grabbing papers and stuffing them on to the dying fire.

Bounding into the room, Darcy pushed her roughly aside and snatched the papers from the flames. As she struggled to stop him, Pel pulled her away, screaming, then Aimedieu hoisted her to her feet and thrust her into a corner, where she burst out sobbing, crouching against the wall, her hands over her face.

Darcy was staring at the papers he had rescued. 'Pamphlets,' he said. 'Revolutionary pamphlets.'

'For what?'

Darcy looked puzzled. 'Free Brittany. Free Gascony. Free Burgundy. They're all different, Patron. There's one here for the Friends of Libya, whoever they are, and another for Basque Freedom in France.'

Moving cautiously upstairs, they found a bathroom and three bedrooms, two of which were empty. From the door of the third, they saw a man lying on the bed. He was quite clearly dead, his face grey, his eyes sunken, a mandarin moustache surrounding his pale lips. He seemed to be in his middle twenties, black-haired, handsome in a starved sort of way, and his face was calm as if he had died quite peacefully. The bedsheets were stiff with dried blood and on the table beside the bed was a cap containing a few loose cartridges.

'Browning 9 mm,' Darcy said. 'Same as the ones that did for Randolfi and the others. There are a few rifle cartridges, too.'

'Have a look at him, Lacoste,' Pel said. 'We'll need to know he's dead.'

'He is dead all right.'

'You said the woman was dead but she isn't, is she?'

The two doctors exchanged glances then bent over the man on the bed.

'He's dead,' Garand said. 'He's been dead some time.'

'Get the woman down to headquarters,' Pel said to Darcy. 'See if you can get anything from her. Names chiefly. And let's have Doc Minet up here, together with Photography, the Lab and Fingerprints.'

'Patron!'

Aimedieu was indicating a jacket hanging on the door. Without removing it from the peg, he opened it out. There was a hole in the middle of the back, round which there was a dried stain of blood.

'It'll be his, I expect,' Pel said. 'Doc Minet will confirm it. Anything in the pockets?'

'Cartridges. Browning. 9-mill. again. They look the same as the ones in the cap.'

Pel turned to Lacoste. 'Is he the man you were called to?'

Lacoste nodded. 'Yes. You will find a bullet wound in his back.'

'Matching the one in the coat?'

'They had his coat off when I arrived, but I imagine it is in the same place.'

'Patron!' Aimedieu, who was still sniffing round the room, had lifted a corner of the mattress. 'There's a pistol under here.'

'What is it?'

'Browning 9-mill., 13-shot.'

'Leave it. Leguyader and the Lab boys will want it and we'll need photographs. It's probably his.'

'If it is,' Lacoste said. 'I do not think he put it there. He was in no state to think about hiding anything. As far as I can make out, he was pretty well unconscious when they got him home. Somebody else must have put it there.'

It made sense.

Aimedieu had come up with a few other finds, and was bending over a pile of papers, carefully fingering them by the corners. 'There's a lot of Communist literature here, Patron,' he said. 'Pamphlet here on how to make bombs and fuses, and a typed list of gun specifications. Things like that. There's also a letter from that type, Hogue, we picked up. One or two from allied groups, too.'

'We'll look at them when the Lab's seen them,' Pel decided. 'Any names?'

'None I can see.'

As they talked, Doc Minet appeared.

'Let's know all about him,' Pel said, indicating the body on the bed. 'These are Doctor Garand and Doctor Lacoste. They can probably tell you a lot.'

Leguyader arrived shortly afterwards, followed immediately by Grenier, of Photography, and Prélat, of Fingerprints.

'Names,' Pel informed them. 'We want names. This is the man who was helped from the Impasse Tarien, so I want his name. Knowing who *he* is will lead us to the others.'

The girl looked strained and anguished as she was brought into Pel's office. She was not an attractive girl, pale-haired, pale-eyed, pale-skinned, an anonymous sort of person who could well have been a sister to Brochard or Debray. She was hollow-eyed and wretched with weeping.

'Name?' Pel barked. He was totally devoid of sympathy.

Crime was crime and if women were involved in it, they had to accept the consequences.

'Huguette Debuillon,' Darcy said, reading from his notebook. 'Address, the house in the Rue Dubosc where we found her.'

'Anything known?'

'No, Patron.'

'Has she talked?'

'A little. It seems she's a Communist, but I think that's because her boy friend's a Communist.'

'And her boy friend?'

'The dead man we found: Name of Assad Kino. Probably Algerian by birth. They were living together at the address where we found him.'

'Go on. There's more. I can tell by your expression.'

Darcy permitted himself a small smile. 'He comes from Marseilles.'

'Of course.' All dissidents seemed to come from Marseilles.

'She's local, though, Patron. Daughter of Edouard and Renée Garthier, of Rue Talant. She calls herself Debuillon – '

' – because it's the practice of all dissidents to use a false name.' Pel waved his hand. 'I know. From now on, though, we'll call her by her real name – Huguette Garthier.'

'Born and brought up in the Rue Talant. Perfectly straightforward family. I've checked up on them. Brother serving in the 119th Regiment of Infantry. Father ex-sergeant-major of an alpine battalion.'

'And this one's the odd one?'

Darcy shrugged. 'She doesn't go with the rest of the family. Rebellious and not considered clever at school.'

'It fits.'

'Parents let's rooms. The dead man was one of their boarders. He was always talking politics and wasn't in the habit of working. She became his girl friend and six months ago went to live with him in the Rue Dubosc. She identifies one of his friends, Roger Hucbourg, believed to be Belgian, living in the Rue de Vignes. I'm having him brought in. Debray and Lagé radioed in to say he wasn't there but he was expected back. They'll collar him as soon as he turns up. She says she doesn't know Kiczmyrczik and doesn't appear ever to have been in his company.'

'What about the man who was with her when they fetched Dr Lacoste? The man who drove the car.'

'She says she doesn't know him. He was one of the men who brought Kino home on the night of the 14th. She says she didn't go out that night and wasn't the one who was seen as they were dragging him away. The neighbours verify that she was in when he was brought home – drunk as they thought.'

'Go on.'

'After they dumped him on the bed, she insisted on a doctor and Lacoste was fetched, but after that night she didn't see the others again and was left to look after him on her own. The others didn't come near her.'

'Which others? Doesn't she know their names?'

'She says not. She says she'd seen them when she'd been with Kino but, apart from Hucbourg, didn't know who they were, beyond that they were Kino's friends. I think she was involved, as she says, chiefly because she was in love with Kino, and that's about all.'

They tried to get more out of her but it was impossible and they finally had to accept that she was telling the truth. Hucbourg was in police custody by the afternoon, loudly protesting against his arrest and proclaiming his innocence.

'Of what?' Pel demanded. 'You haven't been accused of anything yet.'

Small, frightened-looking, like the dead Kino decorated with a mandarin moustache, Hucbourg rolled his eyes. 'Whatever it is you're accusing me of,' he said. 'I've always tried to be straightforward and honest. I've never done anything wrong.'

'Except fraud,' Darcy pointed out, opening a file he held in his hand. 'Last year. Fined. There was a case the year before, too, wasn't there? You were allowed free on that as a first offender.'

Hucbourg's eyes rolled again, but he didn't deny it.

'Know Tadeuz Kiczmyrczik?' Pel asked.

Hucbourg's eyes rolled again. 'No.'

'Anna Ripka?'

'No.'

'Jean-Jacques Hogue?'

'No.'

'Assad Kino?'

Hucbourg's head moved in a movement of negation.

'Huguette Garthier, known as Huguette Debuillon?'

'No.'

'She knows you. She says you're a friend of Assad Kino,
who was found dead this morning at an address in the Rue
Dubosc. You read the newspapers?'

'Of course.'

'Then you'll have read of the shootings and the explosion
in the Impasse Tarien. Three policemen and a passer-by dead,
two wounded. Kino's believed to have been there and to have
escaped with two other men. He was badly wounded and
was taken to the Rue Dubosc. Were you one of the other
men?'

'No.' Hucbourg's answer was a mere whisper.

The telephone rang. It was Claudie Darel speaking from
the office next door. 'Patron, Aimedieu's been on the
telephone. He's been going over Hucbourg's rooms. He says
there's a painting on the wall, signed by someone called La
Dette. There were addresses in a notebook in a drawer. One
was the Garthier girl's – her home address, her parents'
address. One was the dead man's in Marseilles. There was
another belonging to Bernadette Vaxsialades of the Rue
Vesolis. She could be La Dette.'

By evening they had four of them in custody – Jean-
Jacques Hogue, the driver; Huguette Debuillon, née Garthier; Roger Hucbourg, and Bernadette Vaxsialades.

The Vaxsialades girl was another like Huguette Garthier,
drably dressed with blonde hair which was now a streaky
brown.

'Which is the right colour?' Pel asked.

'Blonde,' she said sullenly.

'Who dyed it brown?'

'I did. Two days ago.'

'Why?'

'I was afraid.'

'What of? Were you a friend of Assad Kino?'

'I lived with him for a while. I thought they might think I
killed him.'

'Were you the one who was following him when he was helped away from the Impasse Tarien? There was a girl shouting "Go away, go away". Was that you?'

She nodded silently.

'Why did you shout that?'

'I didn't want anyone to follow us.'

'Why didn't you stay with Kino when he was taken to the Rue Dubosc?'

'He's not my man any more. He's Huguette Garthier's.'

'Who's *your* man?'

She stared at Pel with lacklustre eyes and didn't answer.

'Was it Hucbourg?'

'That idiot!'

'Why is he an idiot?'

'Because he's always afraid.'

'Then who *is* your man?'

Again she didn't answer.

'We shall find out,' Pel said.

She lifted her head and glared at him. 'Then find out,' she snapped.

In Leguyader's laboratory, Pel stood staring with Doctor Minet at the articles found in the rooms at the Rue Dubosc. There was a suitcase, a suit of clothing, marked with dried blood, a few coins, a few books and pamphlets, all of a revolutionary nature, seventeen assorted cartridges, and one Browning 9 millimetre, 13-shot pistol.

'Not his,' Leguyader said. 'The fingerprints on it don't match.'

'What about the bullets in it?'

'I was coming to that,' Leguyader said. He picked up a plastic envelope and, using a pair of tweezers, removed from it a small round-nosed bullet. 'That,' he explained, 'is what Doc Minet took from his chest.'

'It entered his back,' Minet said, 'touched a rib and moved upwards towards the heart. In touching the rib, it expanded and did a great deal of damage. He slowly bled to death. The girl made a great effort to staunch the bleeding but it didn't work. He literally slowly drained.'

Pel indicated the small piece of misshaped metal. 'And the pistol it came from?'

Leguyader moved forward another plastic bag containing the pistol they had found under the mattress. 'It came from this. That's the weapon that shot him. It's not his, as I've said, but it *is* one of the weapons that did the shooting at the Impasse Tarien. Bullets we took out of Randolfi, Desouches and the others came from this weapon. Whoever handled that weapon shot Randolfi and the others.'

'And him?' Pel said, indicating the clothes.

'Accident, as we thought,' Doc Minet said. 'He was hit in the scuffle and they put the pistol under the mattress hoping we'd think he'd shot himself.' He gave a twisted smile. 'Unfortunately, it's a bit difficult to shoot yourself in the middle of the back. I expect his friends thought that if they left him at the Impasse Tarien we'd pick him up and he'd give them away, so they grabbed him and rushed him to where Hogue was waiting with the car and he was taken finally to the Rue Dubosc.'

Pel was silent for a moment, then he gestured at the clothing. 'Does it tell us anything?'

'Nothing at all,' Leguyader said. 'Bought in Brussels. Date, uncertain. Price, cheap. Shoes, French, also cheap. Everything about this gentleman was cheap. He seems to be a North African – Tunisian, Algerian, Moroccan, Libyan, something like that – and he was clearly living a hand-to-mouth existence. He's undernourished. Probably here illegally.'

Pel opened the suitcase. It contained a set of dirty underclothes, a pair of socks and a dirty shirt.

'Probably all he possessed,' Leguyader said. 'In the habit of carrying his food around in it, too, it seems. There are crumbs in there as well.'

Two days later they had another stroke of luck. Fingerprints identified a set of dabs found in the Rue Dubosc as belonging to one Hamid Ben Afzul, a Tunisian with a record who was living near the Industrial Zone.

'Another foreigner,' Pel said. Like many Frenchmen, he tended to dislike foreigners because he was firmly convinced there were too many of them in France.

The Tunisian was missing but in his room were sheets of written music on which was found another name, Claude Raffet, who turned out to be a café pianist who ran a bar in the Chenove district. He was thin and pale-faced as if he were a night bird, but he had no dissident connections and had a good alibi for the night of the shootings, to say nothing of an excellent reference from the bar owner who employed him. He was helpful from the start.

'I knew them all,' he said. 'They came in my bar and they always sat together, even if they came in separately. There were two girls – '

'Huguette Garthier and Bernadette Vaxsialades?'

'Sounds like them. They were addressed as Huguette and La Dette. They often paid because they seemed to be working and the men weren't.'

'How many of them were there altogether?'

'I never saw them all together.'

'Well, work it out.'

Borrowing a pencil, Raffet wrote the names down on the back of an envelope.

'They aren't their real names,' he said. 'Just what I called them.'

116

After a lot of thought and adding up of ticks, he looked up. 'Eight,' he said. 'There were eight of them. At least, I think so. Perhaps nine.'

Pel produced pictures of the ones who'd already been brought in and Raffet studied them carefully. 'There were two others,' he said. 'One a type with red hair. They called him Tom. The other was a little guy. Bit like a ferret. There was also perhaps another woman. A mousy type.'

'They're *all* mousy types,' Darcy growled. Darcy was renowned for his taste in women.

Half an hour with a file containing pictures of known dissidents who lived in their diocese brought little that was fresh. The group they were investigating, it seemed, was a new one, intensely secretive, but amateur enough to have made enough blunders for almost all of them to have been roped in.

'This Ben Afzul?' Pel tried. 'The one who borrowed the music – '

'He was a bit of a musician. Played the guitar. He was trying to learn our music.' Raffet gestured. 'That is, *European* music, as distinct from North African music. You know what that's like. All half-notes and semi-tones. Never seems to end up where it sets out to go. He thought he might make a living if he could learn ours. I loaned him a few sheets of music.'

'What were they up to?'

'No good, I should think,' Raffet admitted. 'People who're within the law don't sit in tight groups whispering. They speak up. They laugh. This lot never laughed. Sometimes there'd be three of them. Sometimes six. I never saw the lot of them together.'

'Do you know Tadeuz Kiczmyrczik?'

'I've heard of him. I heard them mention him, too.'

'Did he ever turn up? Tall, shock of grey hair. Deeply-lined face.'

'Never noticed him.'

'Anna Ripka. Know her? She's Kiczmyrczik's woman.'

'I don't know her. On the other hand –' Raffet gestured ' – how could I? The place's full late at night. There's a lot of smoke. You're busy. I could easily have missed someone. The bar's L-shaped and you can't see round the corner. There are a couple of pin tables there, too. They seemed to like that corner. Perhaps the noise drowned what they were saying.'

Progress was still slow and time was beginning to run out. There weren't many days left to the President's visit and Pel was sure that the death of Kino and the arrest of the others would not have stopped what had been planned. Men prepared to murder for political ends were invariably ruthless and they would have made contingency plans for others to take over, if necessary, what they were intending – which, again, was something they hadn't yet found out.

They checked the houses around the Palais des Ducs where the President was to appear but turned up nothing, so they leaned once more on Hogue, Hucbourg and the two girls. They were all a little vague and Pel guessed they weren't the main participants, merely the helpers who prepared the scene while the perpetrators of what was in the wind could lie low. They knew Andoche, the student who had offered the police the support of the Free Burgundy movement and, while he clearly wasn't involved in the affair in the Impasse Tarien, they provided enough on him to involve him in a few other uproars.

Their aims were undoubtedly anarchistic and protesting. They objected to the way the world was run and had pledged themselves to replace all the bourgeois things they hated such as finance, government and order. But what they were intending to replace them with they didn't appear to know.

By means of intensive questioning in the Rue Dubosc and at the addresses they already had, they managed to come up with descriptions of the last two missing men. By this time, they had a feeling that they had the complete gang save for this last two. It was the view of Judge Brisard that they should take no chances but should also bring in Kiczmyrczik and Anna Ripka for questioning. Judge Polverari was inclined to wait a little longer.

'They'll probably tell us where these other two are,' Brisard argued.

Pel shrugged. 'I'm inclined to think Kiczmyrczik's beyond this sort of thing now. He's no longer young, and old revolutionaries usually manage no more than bitter memories.'

'He could have organised it,' Brisard insisted.

Pel shrugged again. He didn't like Brisard much and, to make things easy, Brisard didn't like Pel. They'd been enemies as long as Pel could remember, in fact, but it didn't disrupt the working of the department because Pel was tough enough, despite his size, to ride anything Brisard might do.

'He could,' he agreed. 'But it's my experience that young revolutionaries take the view that they've been let down as much by the old revolutionaries as they have by the capitalists. They feel they should have done more. In the end, this lot'll be the same, falling back on bitterness and memories, and the next generation will regard *them* in the same way.'

Polverari smiled. 'It's a hard life being a revolutionary,' he observed.

'It always was,' Pel said. 'It's an occupational hazard.'

twelve

Because of the greater urgency on the bigger case of the shot policemen, the reports of Leguyader and Doc Minet on the boy, Charles-Bernard Crébert, had inevitably been delayed.

Nosjean had plodded steadily forward, however, though so far his work had been a process of elimination rather than the building up of a dossier against a suspect. By a tremendous effort on the part of Uniformed Branch in the villages, he felt they had managed to trace every single individual who'd been dancing or drinking in Vieilly on Bastille Night. Every one of them had come from Vieilly or the neighbouring farms and, by a process of checking and cross-checking, alibis had been established for every one of them. According to the writers of detective stories, Nosjean thought bitterly, there ought to have been at least six who shouldn't have been able to verify where they'd been at the critical time but, in this case, because everybody knew everybody else, there wasn't a single one.

There had been a few surprises nevertheless. One or two men, it seemed, had disappeared into the shadows with women who weren't their wives and one man had actually been in a neighbour's bed. The fact that he had a black eye seemed to indicate that the neighbour had found out.

Because Vieilly was close to St Blaize, where the detonators had been stolen, and to Porsigny-le-Petit, where a woman had been wounded, it wasn't unreasonable to assume that the boy's death might have been because he had witnessed something; and Nosjean, never one to give up easily, climbed into the little red Renault he drove to have another go at his witnesses there.

'Didn't you see anyone?' he asked Madame Colbrun.

She shook her head. 'Only this car that came past.'

'Notice the number – or any part of it?'

'It was going too fast. I noticed one of the passengers, though. He was looking back the way he had come.'

'Which is something passengers don't normally do,' Nosjean admitted. 'Perhaps he was looking back to see if they were being followed. What did he look like?'

'It was dark.'

'Anything we could use to identify him? What was he wearing, for instance?'

'Just clothes. That's all. I wasn't really looking. I was sitting in the grass beginning to think I was dying.'

Lamorieux wasn't much more helpful. 'When they started shooting,' he said, 'I got down. Quick. I'm supposed to be a night watchman, not a cop.'

'Did you see what they looked like? What were they dressed in, for instance?'

The night watchman's description was the same as Madame Colbrun's. 'Just clothes,' he said. 'There were three of them. I noticed that. And they were all on the small side. That's why I thought they were kids. One had a thin face but it was too dark to see any more. One had red hair. I caught a glimpse of it in the glow of the car lights.'

'And the other?'

'I didn't really see him.'

Well – Nosjean was philosophical – they were making headway. One of the men seen at the quarry had red hair and the other had a thin face. They sounded as if they were the ones Hogue had mentioned and Raffet had seen in his bar, the man called Tom and the one with a face like a ferret.

Still, that was Pel's case, and you could hardly say the descriptions put them in hot pursuit of the killer of Charles-Bernard Crébert. In addition, there were those diazepam capsules found in the boy's pocket which needed explanation, especially as Doc Minet had pointed out that they couldn't be obtained except on prescription from a doctor.

On the way back to town, Nosjean decided to pay a call on Robert Delacolonge, Charles-Bernard's uncle. If Doctor Nisard had prescribed such pills for Charles-Bernard's mother, perhaps Delacolonge might know if he had stolen them from her. Unfortunately, Delacolonge was at work, and he had to be content with his wife.

Delphine Delacolonge was a thin-faced girl with a sly sideways manner of looking at him and pretensions to prettiness which, Nosjean suspected, would fade quickly as she grew older.

'My husband's at work,' she said. 'He can't afford to take time off.'

There were books and toys about the floor of the apartment and the dubious smell of baby clothes. Madame Delacolonge didn't seem much more efficient than her husband.

'He doesn't like working where he does,' she said. 'But he's too easy-going. But that's his life story, isn't it?'

There was a hint of contempt in her voice and Nosjean leaned forward. 'Is it?' he asked.

'Well, isn't it? His parents had money and his sister had a good education, but when it was *his* turn his father went bust and there was nothing left. He wasn't as clever as his sister either. She got into university. He didn't. It's always the same, isn't it? The one who needs it most has to go without.'

Nosjean said nothing and she went on. 'Then she married this type, Crébert, who's rolling in money, so she didn't even need her qualifications.' Madame Delacolonge sounded bitter now. 'She's a chemist by profession, you know. Worked in a pharmacy. But after her marriage she never did a stroke at it. It might have been better for her if she had. She wouldn't have had time to think so much about herself.'

'Does she think about herself?'

'She never does anything else, does she? She's a – what do you call them? – a manic depressive? That's what Robert says. Everything's against her. Everybody's ganging up against her – even her husband. She said he was always turning young Charles-Bernard against her.'

'Did you think he did?'

Madame Delacolonge pulled a face. 'She spoiled him. She'd been in St Saviour's herself, did you know? That's how Robert got the job, I think. He visited her a lot and they got to know him.'

'Your husband said he was a poet.'

Madame Delacolonge's mouth twisted. 'He'd like to be. He wrote a lot of poems. Free verse. Nothing rhymed.'

'Were they good?'

She gave him a sharp meaningful smile. 'I didn't understand them. It was like his painting and his sculpture. They never came to anything either.'

'What *is* he good at?'

'She gave him another of her sharp sly smiles. 'Nothing much. He always aimed too high. He wanted to show Crébert he could be noticed in the world, too. He didn't manage it.'

Nosjean looked about the apartment. A guitar hung on the wall and there was a bullfight poster from Spain. The records standing near the record player were the records of Piaf, Aznavour and Joan Baez. Alongside it stood a clarinet.

'Does he play that?'

'Not much. He once thought he might get a job in a group but he never did. It got him down at times.'

123

Nosjean moved about the room, his eyes alert. At the side of the fireplace was a newspaper cutting of two men fencing. One of them Nosjean recognised at once as Major Martinelle.

'You know him?' he asked.

Delphine Delacolonge smiled. 'He runs the gymnasium,' she said. 'I once ran Charles-Bernard there in the car. His bicycle was punctured so I took him. He's a fine-looking man, the major.'

It struck Nosjean that she was more than normally enthusiastic. He picked up a picture of Delacolonge with his wife. Delacolonge was wearing jeans and a heavy sweater with thick-soled plimsolls.

'Does he usually dress like that?'

'Mostly.'

'He was wearing a suit the day I saw him outside his sister's house.'

She smiled. 'He likes to impress his sister. He doesn't like them to think we haven't much money. He puts on a show.'

Nosjean paused, ready with the 64,000 dollar question. 'Has your husband ever expressed any interest in any dissident society?'

'Dissident society?' Madame Delacolonge looked blank.

'Is he a Communist?'

'Why?'

'I thought he might be.'

'Oh, no.'

'Fascist?'

'He just believes in law and order.'

'Ever talked about Free Burgundy? Or Free Corsica? Or Free Brittany?'

'Never.'

'Ever mentioned a man called Kiczmyrczik? Or Kino?'

'I've never heard him.'

'What did he feel about the shootings in the city the other day?'

'He was shocked.'

Nosjean, who had still vaguely hoped to connect young Crébert's murder with the shootings, was disappointed. Delacolonge had all the makings of a dissident, all the makings of someone who would turn to the Left because if there was one thing he didn't possess it was the makings of a capitalist. Yet he was right of centre, but not so far right as to believe the answer was fascism.

'Did he suffer from depression?' he asked as he left.

'Frustration would be a better word.'

'Did he take anti-depressant pills?'

'What sort of anti-depressant pills?'

'Diazepam.'

'I've never seen them.'

'Has he ever consulted a doctor about it?'

No, he hadn't consulted a doctor. When he was feeling low, Delacolonge went for a walk in the fresh air and always seemed to come back feeling better. But, if Nosjean wanted to check, his doctor's name was De Barante and he lived only just down the street.

Nosjean did want to check and what Madame Delacolonge said was correct. Delacolonge had never been to Doctor de Barante for depression, and the doctor had never prescribed pills for him beyond the usual things for coughs and colds, because Delacolonge was a normally healthy man. He was rather a sad sort of individual, the doctor thought, but that was because he wasn't very clever and he seemed to ride the problem all right. He had certainly never prescribed pills.

There was still the problem of where the diazepam capsules in the boy's pocket had come from and on his way back into the city, Nosjean stopped at the Créberts' house.

Fortunately, Madame Crébert was out and Nosjean found himself talking to her husband.

'Did you *know* your son was taking anti-depressants?' he asked.

Crébert looked angry. 'Was he?'

'Diazepam capsules were found in his pockets.'

'Doesn't mean he was taking them.'

Nosjean tried a new angle. 'Could you describe your son to me?' he asked. 'As honestly as you can. It might help.'

Crébert sighed. 'I don't know why he had these capsules in his pocket,' he said. 'He didn't get depressed. Just furious. He liked to put on an act – pretend to be ill, or fed up, that sort of thing – but it was usually to get his own way, that's all. He was inclined to be selfish. He'd been spoiled by his mother. He wasn't strong as a baby and she was over-protective. In fact, though, he grew up perfectly healthy and I gather he had the makings of a good gymnast, but she still did everything for him so that when he couldn't have his own way he sulked and did silly things.'

'Such as what?'

'Such as breaking my electric razor. Deliberately.'

'Had anyone ever prescribed diazepam for him? They're given to people who're depressed.'

'I know what they are,' Crébert said. 'My wife takes them. You've seen her. She's had more than one nervous breakdown. God knows why. There's nothing she lacks. I try to talk to her. I've had her to a psychiatrist. But it makes no difference. It never will, of course. The cure for that sort of ailment comes from inside, doesn't it?'

'Could the boy have stolen the capsules? From the medicine chest?'

Crébert sighed again. 'He could. I don't know. I insist on them being kept locked up, but my wife's careless – especially when she thinks things are against her.'

'Could *she* have given them?'

Crébert opened his mouth to speak and Nosjean got the impression he was about to say 'She's silly enough' but then he changed his mind.

'She might have done,' he admitted. 'Sometimes when she's down, she feels everybody else should share her unhappiness.'

Nosjean paused. 'I'm told you have a farmer friend at Vieilly, near where the boy was found, and that you were in the habit of shooting there.'

'That's right. He was at school with me. He's got a lot of land and he's a good farmer. I shoot pigeons with him occasionally.'

'Were you shooting pigeons on the night of the 14th?'

'What's the point of shooting pigeons on the night of anything? You need daylight.'

Nosjean agreed but it was a question he had to ask. 'What sort of gun do you use?'

'I have a rifle. A .303. But normally I use a shotgun. The game's pretty small round here and a rifle would be useless. Even if you hit anything, you'd ruin it with a .303.'

'Why do you have the .303 then?'

'I have a cousin who lives in Alsace. There are wild boar on his land. Occasionally, we kill one. They're no good for eating but they do a lot of damage.'

Meeting De Troquereau for a drink, Nosjean set out what he'd discovered.

'The boy *could* have got the diazepam from his mother, either by stealing them or because she gave them to him. She's been in St Saviour's.'

'Could any of the patients at that place have been out illegally the night the boy was killed?' De Troq' asked.

'They say prisoners can't get out of prison,' Nosjean pointed out. 'But some do. Found out any more about Martinelle?'

'He can give me no real proof of where he was that night. He says he was at the library and then at various bars. But nobody seems to have noticed him.'

'He might have been at Vieilly. Charles-Bernard was his star pupil. It wouldn't have been difficult to persuade him to go there.'

'It's my view,' De Troq' said, 'that he was with a woman.'

Nosjean remembered the picture of Martinelle in the Delacolonges' apartment. He finished his beer and jerked his head. 'Come on,' he said. 'We've got work to do.'

The Delacolonges' living room looked out on to a tree-lined square that was also overlooked by about forty-eight other living rooms, all belonging to the same block of flats and all exactly the same in size and shape. It was obvious at once that it would be very difficult to conduct anything at all unseemly without being seen.

'Visitors?' the woman in the flat directly opposite asked. 'What sort of visitors?'

'The sort,' Nosjean said, 'who visit when the husband's at work.'

She looked at Nosjean. 'Is it like that then?'

'It might be.'

'I always thought it was.' Delacolonge, it seemed, was no better as a husband than he was at anything else. 'I once saw a man go in.'

'Can you describe him?'

'Not very big. Walked on his toes a lot. Athletic.'

De Troq's questions in the flanking wing of the block brought an even clearer answer. 'Military man. Soldier. My husband calls him "the little corporal." He looks a bit like Napoleon.'

Several other neighbours had also spotted a short military figure – usually after dusk and usually when they knew

Delacolonge was on duty – but nobody had seen him on Bastille Night.

On the way back into the city, they stopped at Martinelle's gymnasium. Martinelle was sitting in the little room he used for an office, eating a sandwich and drinking a bottle of beer.

'Sorry I haven't any more,' he said. 'Ration myself. Keep fit.'

Nosjean came to the point at once. 'The night the Crébert boy died,' he said. 'Where were you?'

Martinelle looked up. 'I've told your friend here where I was.'

'Well, now *I'm* asking.'

'Surely you don't suspect me?'

'I don't suspect anyone,' Nosjean said. 'But everybody who hasn't an alibi's a suspect. *You* haven't an alibi. Were you with a woman?'

Martinelle's mouth curled. 'I suppose you have names.'

'I have one. Delphine Delacolonge. Her husband's an uncle of the Crébert boy. That's what makes it rather odd, don't you think? Bit of a coincidence.'

Martinelle said nothing. He had stiffened and was licking his lips. 'Don't know the woman,' he said. 'Never met her.'

'She says she knows you.'

Martinelle shrugged. 'A lot of people know me,' he said. 'But it doesn't mean I know her.'

'Never visited her flat?'

'Never.'

'I have reason to think you might have.'

Martinelle didn't even blink. 'Then you'd better think again,' he said.

thirteen

The newspapers were still having a field day and their headlines reflected the growing concern at the lack of progress. In the manner of most television commentators, Robert Démon concentrated less on concern than on criticism and even unearthed a number of terrorist sympathisers who appeared on his programme, hooded and masked and with their backs to the camera, to expound their opinions. His view seemed to be that in a country of free expression men should not only be allowed to plant bombs but that their friends should also be allowed to explain the reasons why over the air. His public increased enormously.

Free Burgundy, Free Brittany and Free Corsica were all brought into it in a way that made the men at police headquarters squirm, because they noticed that, while Démon appeared to show sympathy with terrorist attitudes, he had so far not uttered a single word of condolence for the families of the dead policemen.

Pel watched the broadcast with Darcy in the Bar Transvaal with a bitter look on his face. With people prepared to beat young policemen to death for kicks, Démon's comments seemed at times almost like encouragement.

'It's no wonder the crime rate goes up and never goes down,' Darcy growled. 'The great sporting public's more influenced by that rubbish than they are by the Church.'

During the following afternoon, however, something turned up which brought a little cheer. It wasn't much but it had possibilities. Darcy appeared in Pel's office with a small box which he opened on the table. It contained a few Marxist and anarchist pamphlets, two cartridge cases, a knife, a red badge showing a hammer and sickle, and a key bearing the number M138H.

'Belonged to Assad Kino,' he said. 'Brought in by the parents of the Garthier girl. As you know, he had a room in their apartment for a while and he left this in their keeping. Asked them to look after it very carefully. Those were his words: Very carefully.'

'Now why would he say that?' Pel asked. 'It looks harmless enough and it ought to be unimportant.'

They turned the box over once or twice. If things had turned out as they should have, it would have had a false bottom containing papers which would give the names of everybody involved in the killings and all the plans for the future, including the possible assassination of the President. Pel fingered it, half expecting a secret drawer to spring open. But, of course, it didn't.

'If it isn't the box,' he pointed out, 'then it must be what was in it.'

There seemed nothing odd about the pamphlets, the cartridge cases, the knife or the badge.

'So it must be the key,' he said.

He picked it up. 'It's a Brouard,' he said thoughtfully. 'And Brouards are good locks. Special locks. Locks for doors that people don't want opening.' He looked up at Darcy. 'Daniel, this is probably the key to a room that overlooks the Palais des Ducs. Some room from where they could get a shot at the President. Check it.'

By this time, Judge Polverari and Judge Brisard were working overtime preparing the dossiers on the people who'd been brought in. Despite the view of Pel and Judge Polverari, Brisard had also insisted on Kiczmyrczik being brought in for questioning, but he found he had bitten off more than he could chew. Kiczmyrczik was an old hand at dealing with juges d'instruction and he gave as good as he was handed out. When he didn't feel like answering, he simply sat mute, and in the end Brisard ordered him to be held until they felt they could change his views.

It didn't worry Kiczmyrczik in the slightest. He'd been in enough prisons during his career to regard them philosophically and there was probably quite as much comfort in them as in his spartan little apartment, while the food, according to Jaroslav Tyl, was probably better.

'Anna's a terrible cook,' he told Darcy. 'Her meals always look as if she'd picked them out of the pig bin.'

Darcy recited the names of the men and women they'd brought in. 'Know any of them?' he asked.

Tyl shook his head. 'Not one. But old Kiczmyrczik's a bit beyond this sort of thing these days, isn't he? Eyes are going. If he tried shooting at the police he'd probably hit one of his pals.'

'One of them did,' Darcy said dryly.

Tyl looked repentant. 'Yes, of course. I forgot that. If the Old Man had been active, I'd have said straight away, yes, he's the type but – ' he shook his head ' – the poor old bugger's long past it. Still – ' he grinned ' – with a week or two away from Anna's cooking, he'll probably come out a new man. You don't know what you're starting.'

Darcy smiled. 'How come someone so lacking in idealism as you are is always hanging round Kiczmyrczik's place?'

'I keep an eye on the Old Man, that's all. Soft-hearted.'

'I've never come across a soft-hearted revolutionary before.'

'We're not all the hard-nosed kind.' Tyl shrugged. 'Perhaps I'm not really a true worker for the cause. Perhaps I just fancy a good socialist country with fair shares for all – with a little extra for me on the side. I should hate to see blood flowing in the gutters. Too squeamish. I'm not that kind of revolutionary.' He grinned. 'I'm the insidious kind. I talk a lot and keep out of the way and let the others get picked up by the police.'

'It's probably cleverer,' Darcy agreed.

Tyl smiled. 'It's certainly safer,' he said.

They were beginning to recover their spirits a little by this time. Goriot was recovering slowly, but it would be months before he was on duty again, though Dunn was home, pale with pain and clutching his bandaged arm. It was even becoming hard to remember Randolfi, Lemadre and Desouches, but perhaps this was an inbuilt defence mechanism.

With the excitement dwindling, so was the number of reports. But also, so was the time at their disposal before the President arrived. There were still a few nutcases – sad people who needed notoriety to liven their dull existence – who claimed to have shot one or more of the three policemen. One claimed to have shot the lot – even Charles-Bernard Crébert. An elderly medium, though not claiming such an honour, said she knew exactly who *was* responsible and would be prepared to give the police all the help she could, while a woman in Paris insisted that the dead men hadn't been killed at all but had been flashed from earth by a death ray from Mars. Apart from the few they knew about, who confessed to every crime ever committed within the city boundaries, they had to check anything that sounded at all feasible.

They were all still at it flat out, working long days tramping the streets and asking questions. With the exception of Misset. Misset could always manage to dodge work and he had been itching ever since his trip to Paris to describe a voyage after dark through the Bois de Boulogne with a friend of his in the Paris force. It was the sort of story Misset always enjoyed.

'Girls,' he said. 'Round the area off the Cascade. Dozens of them. All wearing fur coats.'

'In summer?'

'They've got nothing on underneath. Not a stitch. They stand on the corners and when a car comes along and its headlights fall on them, they open the coats. That's how they get their customers. The police are always picking them up.'

By this time, they had learned the names of the two men Raffet had described. The detectives were still raiding the haunts of the shifty, the perverted, the dishonest, the violent, and the mean-minded, brooking no hindrance or delay, and a few people had squealed under pressure. Names and addresses turned up, new descriptions became available – even finally the two names, Tom Kotchkoff and Kasimir Hays.

Paris had heard of them and came up, not only with the information that they were dangerous, but with sound descriptions – even the startling information that Kotchkoff was known to have scars on his knees.

'You can forget that,' Pel growled. 'He won't be walking about without his trousers.'

He was certain by now that the people they had in custody were no more than fringe members of the group. While they could be charged as accessories before or after the fact they couldn't have been responsible for the murders.

'Not one of them,' he said. 'Kotchkoff and Hays are the ones we're looking for and they're the ones who got Kino away. Let's have another go at Hucbourg.'

Hucbourg was looking distinctly unhappy as he was brought into the office.

'I wasn't there,' he insisted at once.

'You were one of the gang,' Pel said. 'So you'd better tell us who they were.'

Hucbourg seemed on the verge of tears but he bit his lip and turned his head away.

'You realise that under Article 60 of the Penal Code you can be charged.'

'I made no bombs. I never possessed a pistol. I never even held anybody else's.'

'You gave comfort to these men.'

'No.'

'You discussed revolution.'

'Discussed. That's all.'

'Article 60 deals with accessories before and after the fact, those who – I quote – "by gifts, promises, threats, abuse of authority or power, machinations or culpable artifices, shall have provoked the act or given instructions for it to be committed." '

'I never suggested anything.'

'You have proof, of course?'

Hucbourg hadn't. He wasn't a strong character and he soon admitted he knew Kotchkoff and Hays.

'I only knew them as Le Rougeaud and La Belette. Rusty and Weasel. They always went about together.'

They tried the names on Raffet at his bar.

'They sound like the ones I called Tom and the Ferret,' he said. 'They came in here, but they didn't go about with the others much. They were always on their own and usually sat apart. They knew Kino though. I remember that.'

Pel studied the shabby bar. 'I think we ought to have a watch put on this place,' he said.

Raffet grinned. 'Do you think I'm going to kill someone?'

'No,' Pel said. 'But I think someone might be going to kill you.'

It was late when Pel left the Hôtel de Police for home. As he climbed into his car, he looked at his watch. All normal people with good sense and a degree of honesty were in their homes now, and probably in bed. He longed to pick up the telephone and ring Madame Faivre-Perret's number. But, like everyone else, she, too, would be in bed by this time. The thought depressed him. One day, perhaps, he thought, he might even be in it with her.

When he reached home, be sat in his car for a while, staring at his house. It looked a wreck, while inside it seemed to be furnished entirely in brown. Even before he entered he could hear the television going but the minute he put his key in the lock it stopped. The silence was the sort of silence you get when you're in an aeroplane and someone switches off the engine.

Madame Routy was just rising from the 'confort anglais', which was the only worthwhile chair in the house. She had a sour look on her face. 'I'm off to bed,' she said.

Pel watched her disappear, suddenly realising that not only he and Darcy and the rest of them were affected by the butchery in the Impasse Tarien; it had affected Madame Routy too, and she'd decided it was wiser not to get on the wrong side of him.

He poured himself a whisky and sat down in the 'confort anglais', a little startled by the discovery that for once, through no doing of his, he had the upper hand. He was still absorbed by the thought when the telephone rang. To his surprise it was Madame Faivre-Perret.

'Geneviève!'

Her voice was gentle and consoling. 'I took the liberty of telephoning the Hôtel de Police to see if you'd left. They told me you'd gone home. I thought you might like to know I haven't forgotten you.'

Oh, wonderful woman! What on earth would they do without women? Where could man ever find the comfort and the solace that was needed in a world full of violence?

'I'm very touched,' Pel said.

'How are things going?'

He knew she wasn't really interested because he'd discovered long since that the harsh facts of crime appalled her and she preferred not to think about them. Which made the enquiry all the more warm.

'Not very well,' he admitted. 'We move forward but not very quickly.'

'You and I, Evariste, seem fated.'

That was what Pel had often thought.

'How long will it be before it will be over?'

'It could be a week, or a fortnight, or a month. Or forever.' There was a shocked silence and he tried to explain. 'The file on this thing will never be closed until we get the murderers but there'll come a time when it will seem pointless to continue. The President's due in ten days. It'll die down a little then, I suppose – provided nothing happens.'

The silence continued, then Pel heard a faint sigh. 'I'll telephone you as soon as it seems possible,' he said.

He put the telephone down slowly, poured himself another whisky and sat with it in his hand for a long time. The Chief was married. Goriot was married. Misset was married. He wondered how they managed. In Misset's case, perhaps he didn't, because it was obvious Misset's marriage had become a burden to him. His eyes – and his hands – had begun to wander and there were a few of the secretaries in the Hôtel de Police, Pel had heard, who had had occasion to fend him off.

Lagé seemed happily married, however. Perhaps his success sprang from his perpetual good-temper and his everlasting willingness to do someone else's work. Perhaps he'd developed a nice line in washing up.

Pel slept badly that night. He liked to think he slept badly most nights. When things were on his mind, he did sleep badly but, because he believed he needed his sleep, he usually went to bed far too early and, since he could manage – and had proved it often by still being on his feet when everybody else round him was wilting – on three or four hours a night, he was invariably expecting too much of himself.

Nosjean was waiting for him when he arrived at his office the following morning. He outlined everything he and De Troq' had done. He then fished in his brief case and brought out a bundle of papers, all ruled and covered with unformed writing.

'I don't want reports,' Pel said. 'I'm too busy. If you have anything for me to see, let me have it on one sheet.'

'It's not a report, Patron,' Nosjean said. 'It's a set of essays. School kids' essays.' He went on to explain what he'd done. 'Most of them contain nothing at all. Just the usual things. A car with a flat tyre. A man with a red nose. A woman standing in a bedroom window undressing. He's going to be a voyeur, that one. But there are two here – friends. Both of them knew Charles-Bernard Crébert. They say they saw him getting into a car just after dark by the Porte Guillaume, the evening he died.'

Pel leaned forward. 'Go on, mon brave.'

'I asked them what sort of car. They couldn't be certain – Peugeot. Renault. British Ford. German Volkswagen – only that it was a small hatchback. It was some distance away, but they knew it was Crébert because he was wearing a red, white and blue jersey. The one he was wearing when he was found.'

'Did they see who was with him?'

'Whoever was inside the car was in shadow.'

'Did they notice the number or the colour of the car?'

'Not the number. They said the colour was grey or fawn.'

'Are they sure about that?'

'They each confirmed the other, and neither of them knew what the other had written until I told them. Moreover, they didn't discuss seeing Crébert get into the car at the time, because they both knew him and they knew he sometimes went off with that uncle of his. It didn't even occur to them that it was odd until they were asked to write an essay about anything odd they'd seen and then they only considered it odd because the boy had been found dead.'

'What about the uncle?'

'Renault,' Nosjean said. 'Bright red. Like mine. There's no way it could be considered grey or fawn.'

'Where was he? Have you checked?'

'Yes, Chief. He was at his sister's. She said he was there. Her husband was away and he went to cheer her up. They're very close. It was his night off-duty and she telephoned his wife who said she'd send him round.'

'Everybody's very concerned with Madame Crébert.'

'I think Madame Delacolonge is more concerned with Madame Delacolonge.' Nosjean smiled. 'Martinelle was probably with her. The nights her husband was out she often had a visitor.'

'Was he there that night?'

'That's something I haven't been able to establish yet.'

'Is he married?'

'Yes.'

'Interested in boys?'

'He runs a gymnasium for them. And he's served in the East. A lot of men who served out there picked up the habit of pederasty.'

Pel frowned. 'I think you'd better check up on his car.'

'I have, Patron. Silver Volkswagen. Could look grey.'

'What about the man himself? Any reason to suspect he was connected with Kiczmyczik or any of the others?'

'None at all, Patron. In fact, I think now it was pure coincidence that young Crébert was murdered at Vieilly on the night of the shootings here.'

The following day, Judge Brisard had the Créberts brought in for questioning.

'Do they have anything they can add?' Pel asked.

'I don't think they had anything to do with it,' Brisard said. 'Beyond the fact that it was probably the mother's fault that the boy made friends where he shouldn't.'

How right he was, was proved that afternoon when Pomereu appeared with one of his men.

'This is Sous-Brigadier Floc,' he said. 'He has something to tell you.'

Pel stared at Pomereu. 'Then let him get on with it,' he snapped.

Floc nodded, about turned and disappeared. Pel looked at Pomereu. 'That is it?' he said. 'He has become an expert at doing the vanishing trick?'

'Wait a moment,' Pomereu said and, sure enough, two seconds later Floc reappeared, pushing in front of him a small man with glasses. 'This is Monsieur Bailly. He found a note under the windscreen wiper of his car after leaving it parked in the square opposite the Palais de Ducs.' He jabbed Bailly in the kidneys. 'Produce your evidence,' he said.

Bailly fished in his pocket and solemnly produced a slip of paper. On it were the words, 'I killed Crébert.' It was signed with three crosses.

Pel stared at it. It was printed carefully on a piece of paper torn from an exercise book. 'This is evidence?' he said slowly.

Bailly indicated Floc. '*He* said it was.'

Pel studied Floc coldly. 'Haven't you yet discovered that every crime since Cain killed Abel brings in its wake all the usual nutcases who claim to be part of it for the simple reason that they wish to enjoy a little notoriety. Up to now, I would say we've had about three million of these.' He glared. 'To me, it's just another hoax. Get rid of him, Pomereu.'

fourteen

Despite his contempt for Sous-Brigadier Floc's witness, when Nosjean brought in another note later in the day, Pel began to wonder if he'd have to eat his words. This time, the note was addressed to Delacolonge, was signed 'The Strangler,' and described exactly how Charles-Bernard Crébert had been killed. Since no details had been released to the press on this point, it was enough to make Pel sit up and take notice.

'Fingerprints?' he asked.

Nosjean shook his head. 'None, Patron. Prélat's boys have been over it. There's nothing at all. But that doesn't mean a thing. Everybody's read the books these days. They know to wear gloves. Delacolonge thinks it must have been pushed through his door because there was no stamp on it.'

The following day another note arrived, brought in by Doctor Nisard, once more claiming responsibility for Charles-Bernard's murder, and then they began to come in at a rate of one or two every morning and afternoon from a variety of addresses. Another for Doctor Nisard, two more for Delacolonge. One from the newspaper, *Le Bien Public*. One from St Saviour's.

'There's a pattern emerging,' Nosjean said, as he bent over a map with De Troquereau. 'They all seem to be addresses in the area around the home of the Créberts. That is, with the exception of the St Saviour's one and the one sent to the newspaper.'

'Think they're genuine?' De Troq' asked.

'He's got the details right. And nobody knows them but us.'

'Then,' De Troq' said, 'we must be dealing with a nut.'

'I'm sure we are,' Nosjean said. He produced the note which had arrived some time before, complaining about the lack of notice taken of the case in the newspapers. It was on the same sort of paper. 'He hadn't expected the police shootings when he killed the boy and he feels other people are getting more publicity than he is.'

The following day a new note arrived, brought in by one of the Créberts' neighbours. It was again signed 'The Strangler'. 'I shall strike again,' it said. 'This is the crime of the century.'

'He's beginning to get hysterical,' De Troq' said.

The Post Office was asked to look out for letters addressed to the area round the Créberts' home with a view to recognising the writing, but it was a case of closing the stable door after the horse had escaped. Several were handed over from the sorting office but they told them no more than they knew already, and the letters were now being addressed further afield. There was one to Radio Diffusion Française, demanding that the story be told over the air, one to *Le Figaro* in Paris, saying there would be more murders unless the case was given full coverage in the newspapers, on the radio and on the television – inevitably it was – and one even sent to England, addressed to the editor of *The Times* in London.

The climax came when Claudie Darel appeared with Pel's mail. She held out a brown envelope showing the lower half of a figure dressed in jeans, one hand holding a revolver. The photograph, which had been cut off just below the head, was signed 'The Strangler.'

Pel looked up. 'Is it male?' he asked. 'Or female?'

Claudie shrugged. 'Hard to tell, Patron. It's not a good photograph. It could be either.'

'Tell Nosjean I want to see him.'

Nosjean arrived almost at once. He silently laid another note on Pel's desk. 'From the Chief,' he said. 'Arrived in his office this morning.'

The message had been printed in the sort of letters used by computers. It had been carefully done so there should be no identification and it described in detail how the boy had died, how the blood had pulsed in the carotid artery. 'I knew it would be easier with the thumbs in front,' it said. 'But it took almost five minutes and even then he tried to crawl away. In the end, it was much simpler than I realised. I pushed his face into the soft soil and he suffocated.'

Pel read the note and looked up. On the faces of all three of them was a look of horror and distaste. 'What sort of a lunatic would write this sort of stuff?' he demanded. He came to life abruptly. 'Find out where the picture was printed. It was certainly done somewhere. Check your suspects. See if any of them go in for photography. And keep on your toes, mes braves. The man's obsessed. He thinks he's committed the perfect crime. He's done something nobody else could do. He may have another go.'

When Nosjean had gone, Pel paced up and down, frowning. On the table at the other side of the room from his desk were all the articles which had been brought from the house where Kino had been found dead. Pel stared at them. He had studied them again and again – the clothing Kino had worn, the pistol recovered from under the mattress, the letters and pamphlets found on the floor by the fireplace which the Garthier girl had been trying to destroy, the suitcase which had contained his few items of clothing.

He glanced at the calendar. Time was growing short. Only five days were left before the President arrived. What were the terrorists up to? What were they planning? He was due in the Chief's office in half an hour to talk the thing over.

There was a tap on the door and Darcy appeared.

'No luck with the key, Patron,' he said. 'We've checked all apartments overlooking the courtyard of the Palais des Ducs. None of them has a Brouard lock. I've also checked what the President will do. He'll lunch with the city officials – Brisard and Polverari and the Chief and a few more will be there. That's in the great hall. Then he'll talk with them for a while in the Maire's apartment. Aperitifs will be taken in the Blue Salon. Afterwards, of course, he goes to the exhibition of Burgundian art in the Musée des Beaux-Arts. I've checked all apartments overlooking the windows of all those rooms. No Brouard locks.'

Pel's eyes narrowed as he pushed his spectacles up on his forehead.

'People don't fit Brouard locks unless they want to keep something safe,' he said. 'It must have some significance. Try Brouards themselves. See if they can help.'

Frowning, as Darcy left he moved across to the table and picked up the coat with the hole in the back. It told him nothing. Leguyader had been able to produce no new facts. The labels had been removed, because people like Kino and his friends liked to be dramatic and would remove them as a matter of course, and it was impossible to trace where it had been bought. Like the rest of the dead man's clothes, it had doubtless come from a supermarket where the turnover was so brisk it was unlikely that customers could be identified. The suitcase was the same. It was cheap and scuffed and had originally been bought, he suspected, at somewhere like the Nouvelles Galeries.

He stared at it for a moment, frowning, fingering the scuff-marks as if he expected them to tell him something, then he flicked the catches and opened the lid. Inside was the usual old fluff that went with someone who was inclined to be indifferent about his habits, together with one or two pins, a cigarette end, several matches, and a few tiny particles he'd seen before which he assumed were crumbs. For a moment, he stared at them. The fluff, the pins, even perhaps the cigarette ends and matches, had a reason for being there. But not many people carried food in a suitcase. It was possible in this case, though, because Kino would inevitably have moved about a lot contacting friends and sympathisers and, like them no doubt, he had lived a hand-to-mouth existence, so that any journey he made would be made in the cheapest possible way, and that would mean taking his own food to eat en route.

He picked up one or two of the tiny particles, rubbing them between finger and thumb. Were they crumbs? Crumbs became as hard as lead pellets after a while but these weren't and they didn't crumble.

As he peered at the minute fragments in his fingers he noticed that one of them had a red fleck on it and, abruptly, he remembered Didier Darras' description when they'd been fishing – months ago now, it seemed – of Louise Bray, his girl friend, who as a child had had novelty flowers at her parties that opened when placed in water.

He peered closer at the 'crumb' and on an impulse he turned to the intercom on his desk and pressed the switch. 'Claudie,' he said. 'Bring me a glass of water.'

She appeared, looking puzzled, because it was Pel's habit to consider water only of use to wash the glasses he drank wine out of. He indicated the suitcase. 'A small experiment,' he said, placing one of the crumbs in the glass.

For a while they watched it, then Pel saw a faint movement. 'It's not a crumb,' he said.

He peered more closely, thinking warmly of his good friend Didier, now doubtless languishing in Brittany far from the charms of Louise Bray.

'It's paper,' Claudie pointed out. 'It's uncurling.'

Fascinated, they stared as the tiny piece of paper began to take shape until they could see colour, a distinct red and black.

'What is it, Patron?'

'It looks as if it might be part of a label. Put the rest in.'

Carefully, Claudie picked the remaining 'crumbs' from the suitcase and placed them in the glass, watching them uncurl.

As Pel tried to pick one of them out, Claudie stopped.

'Just a minute, Patron,' she said. 'For this we need tweezers.'

'And these you have?'

'For the eyebrows, Patron.'

Carefully, using the eyebrow tweezers, they picked out the minute fragments. They were all printed in red and black on white paper. By the time they had finished they had enough paper to cover an area of about four square centimetres. Some of the pieces had curved edges.

'It's a label,' Claudie said.

Pel gestured. 'It's also a jigsaw puzzle,' he pointed out. 'Sit down over there, and put it together. I have to see the Chief. Perhaps by the time I return you'll know what it was a label *for*.'

The conference in the Chief's office was a grim one. So far they had made only a little progress in either of the two cases which were involving them, and Paris was beginning to be difficult, with the Minister asking awkward questions. What were they doing to allow three policemen to be murdered, and why hadn't they found the murderers yet? The sort of questions that were always asked by people who had no idea what went on, but it didn't make things a lot easier and the Chief was understandably short-tempered.

'I've had the mother of the boy brought in again for more questioning,' Judge Brisard said. 'I think she knows more than she says.'

Judge Polverari sighed. 'I make *no* progress,' he said. 'All I know for certain is that the people we're holding didn't shoot Randolfi and the others.'

'Can Goriot or Durin contribute anything yet?' the Chief asked.

'Nothing,' Pel said. 'The only man they saw properly was the one we found dead – Kino – and Goriot swears that Kino did not have a weapon. The shots came from the back of the house.'

'That would be my opinion, too,' Doc Minet agreed.

'We know who they are now,' Pel said. 'We've even managed to identify them. Kasimir Hays and Tom Kotchkoff. It's believed they're Serbians who changed their names and that their families came to France because they objected to the Tito régime in Jugoslavia, which forced Serbians, Montenegrins, Slovenes and Croatians to accept a single nationality known as Jugoslav. There were many who preferred to keep their original nationality and many fled. It's thought in Paris that the resentment of Hays and Kotchkoff eventually became anarchical and they were prepared to join any and all protest movements. They're experienced at the game and offer their knowledge to any movement in need of it. Their names and descriptions have gone to all forces.'

The Chief frowned. 'What about the key we're trying to identify?'

'Brouards don't keep a list of where individual locks are sold.'

'Can't the people we have in custody be made to talk?'

'They know nothing. They were only on the fringe of the organisation, the women simply because they were living with the men. Hucbourg was little more than a passenger and Hogue was only the driver. Hays, Kotchkoff and perhaps others seem to have been the active part of the organisation, with Kino as the go-between. There may be a third man who's the leader, but so far we have no hint who he is. It's my opinion we shan't find him until we find Hays and Kotchkoff.'

'And are we likely to find Hays and Kotchkoff?' the Chief asked quietly.

'It's just possible,' Pel said cautiously, thinking of Claudie Darel in his office, 'that we might be nearer today than we were yesterday.'

When he returned to his office, Claudie had pulled up a chair and was working at his desk. Carefully, she had placed all the small pieces of coloured paper on a fresh sheet of white typing paper.

'There are one or two pieces missing, Patron,' she said. 'But nothing very important. I suppose they got caught up when the clothes were removed from the case. I've searched all the cracks but I can't find any more. All the same, I think we have enough to make an exhibit for the court and enough to identify what it is.'

'Inform me.'

'It's a label, Patron. I think it came off that hammer we found at the Impasse Tarien.'

Pel bent over the label with her. 'Quincaillerie Madon,' it said. '—e Pasteur.'

'The bit that's missing,' Claudie pointed out, 'seems to be the number and the first part of the word "rue." Unfortunately, practically every town and city in France has a Rue Pasteur.'

'Not all of them with an ironmongers in it, though. Try Dôle, Besançon, Beaune, Chalon, Autun, Vesoul. Even Auxerre and Avallon. If they had enough sense to scrape off the label, they probably also had enough sense not to buy the hammer in this area.'

Half an hour later, Claudie was back, holding a directory in her hand. 'There's a Rue Pasteur in Dôle, Patron. Pasteur was born in Dôle. I've been in touch with the police. There's an ironmongers there by the name of Madon. Number Seventeen.'

Pel smiled at her. He didn't often smile at the members of his team but Claudie was different. Everybody smiled at Claudie.

'You busy?' he asked.

'I'll have to organise someone to watch the phone.'

'Organise it. We're going to Dôle.'

Dôle's narrow streets were hot in the rays of the midday sunshine. They found the ironmongers in the Rue Pasteur not very far from where Pasteur was born. It was a large shop filled with garden furniture, motor mowers, tools, and shelves containing boxes of nails, screws and bolts. Out of the heat, it was cool and pleasant.

Pel produced the hammer. The man behind the counter looked at it as if he thought Pel had brought it back with a complaint and wanted it exchanged.

'This one of yours?'

'It's a line we carry.' The man reached behind him and produced a replica, carrying the red, white and black label they were seeking. Pel produced his identity card with its tricolour strip. 'Police Judiciaire,' he said. 'We're searching for the man who bought this one. Would you know?'

The man stared at the hammer. 'Was it used to kill someone?' he asked. 'That case in Metz? They used a hammer in that, didn't they?'

'This isn't the case in Metz,' Pel said coldly. 'It's more serious than that.'

'More serious than murder? What's more serious than murder?'

'Four murders.'

The man's eyes flickered over Pel and Claudie. 'Well,' he said, 'we don't sell hammers very much. People seem to inherit them. Father to son. That sort of thing. Mostly the new ones go to apprentices or people setting up as carpenters

149

or something like that. I didn't sell it myself but my wife might have.'

The proprietor's wife came in from the back of the shop in a waft of cooking. 'I sold the hammer, she said. 'It's the only hammer we've sold in three or four months.'

'How did he pay? By cheque?'

It was a wild hope and it didn't come off.

'For a hammer?'

'Prices are high these days. A lot of people do.'

'This one didn't.'

'Any way you could identify him?'

'None.'

'There must be something. Do you remember him?'

'Yes.'

'Then what did he look like?'

'Just ordinary.'

Pel drew Claudie to one side. 'Talk to her,' he said. 'I don't think she likes men. She might remember for you. I'll wait in the car.'

An hour later, Claudie appeared. She looked pleased with herself.

'She doesn't like policemen,' she said. 'One once pinched her behind when they were called in to investigate a burglary. I bought a hammer so we have a replica for the court. It persuaded her to talk.'

'And?'

'Small. Round. Fat. Glasses. Slight foreign accent. Big smile.'

'Tyl,' Pel said at once.

But when they went round to Tyl's apartment, they found his sister looking puzzled. 'He's gone,' she said. 'He hasn't been home for two days. He's run off with the Ripka woman.'

fifteen

A watch was put on Tyl's apartment at once and a request was sent out to all police forces, stations, ports and airports, to keep a look out for him.

The disappearance with Anna Ripka seemed well in character. Tyl had spent a lot of his time at the Kiczmyrczik flat. Doubtless he and Anna Ripka had got to know each other rather better than Kiczmyrczik had suspected – after all, they were of an age and looked alike in the way that husbands and wives often grew to look like each other. But Pel was under no delusion that Tyl had disappeared because of a love affair and he was firmly of the opinion that he was still somewhere in the city.

He had no real reason for thinking this, but it was a hunch and he had a feeling it was a good one. Though detective work was based largely on attention to detail, there was still a lot of room for a good hunch.

Which was exactly how Nosjean was thinking. The notes about the Crébert boy were still arriving and, while an idea had been building up in Nosjean's mind for a long time, somehow things didn't fit together. The boy had been seen to get into a car just before he had finally disappeared. Whose car was it? Madame Crébert's? Despite the fact that it was highly improbable, Nosjean still wasn't satisfied that she wouldn't have killed her own son, and the family's second car was a small blue Peugeot hatchback that could easily have been mistaken for grey. And what about Martinelle?

151

They still hadn't been able to pin down just where his silver Volkswagen had been. Deciding it was time to talk a little more to Solange Caillaux, he explained to Pel what was in his mind and made a date for lunch.

'De Troq' will look after things,' he said. 'And I'll leave my telephone number.'

Pel eyed Nosjean shrewdly. After the early days when he'd spent much of his time bleating about the lack of nights off, Nosjean had developed into a shrewd and imaginative detective.

'You think something might come of this meeting, mon brave?' he asked.

'I don't know, Patron.' Nosjean was painstakingly honest and never tried to mislead. 'But we've got nowhere with the photograph. We've tried everybody in the city who prints pictures but they don't look at them properly, of course, and there are no names in their receipts that ring a bell. We're also checking the labs that do that sort of work, but so far we've drawn blanks. They don't keep the receipts. I thought Solange Caillaux might just recall something she'd forgotten.'

'Is she pretty?'

Nosjean managed to blush. 'Yes, Patron.' Even in this, Nosjean couldn't dissemble.

'And how is your heart these days, mon brave?'

Nosjean frowned. 'Perhaps Odile Chenandier was right to get herself engaged to someone else,' he said. 'Perhaps I'm too involved with the job.'

'It's a failing in good policemen. Very well, off you go. You've deserved your night off. Had it been Misset – ' Pel left the sentence unfinished and gestured towards the door.

Solange Caillaux appeared for the date in a neat flowered dress that went with the warmth of her smile.

'I made it myself,' she said.

'It looks most professional,' Nosjean admitted.

'Anyone can become professional if they work at it. My mother did sewing to help out the family funds. I watched her. You can pick up a lot just by watching. That's how I learned to become a teacher.'

'It is?' Nosjean was suitably impressed.

'I decided when I was still at school that I wanted to teach, so in the last two years there I started watching the teachers. I was so absorbed in picking up their little tricks I forgot to listen.' She smiled. 'I became good at teaching but my examination results were abysmal.'

While Nosjean was discussing the habits of Charles-Bernard Crébert with Solange Caillaux the report from Brouards arrived.

Darcy tossed it on to Pel's desk with a sigh. 'They say there are hundreds of their locks about,' he said. 'But only three places in this area where they're sold. Tincals, Brandt Ironmongery in the Rue Sembac, and Marshals, the builders' suppliers in the Rue Billette. Nobody else will stock them because they're so expensive. I've checked, of course. Marshals say that, judging by the number of the key we have, M138H, the lock must have been sold several months or so ago, and they have no record whom to.'

'Put it on the radio,' Pel suggested. 'Ask if anyone has a Brouard lock with that number. Make it important.'

The day ended with Pel beginning to grow concerned. The President's visit was close enough now to be worrying, and when Darcy offered to buy him a beer at the Bar Transvaal, he suggested Raffet's bar instead, to check on Raffet's guard and whether he had heard any more of Kino's friends.

Misset was at the counter with a beer, looking bored, and he jumped as he saw Pel's small frame alongside him.

'I hope you're remembering that you weren't placed here merely to fill yourself with that,' Pel growled.

'No, Patron! Not at all! He gave it to me!' Misset indicated Raffet. 'Took pity on me. It's a boring job, this.'

'You could always talk to the customers,' Pel said. 'You could even help with pouring drinks, so long as you didn't pour too many for yourself.' He turned to Raffet, his eyes questioning, and Raffet shrugged.

'I think you've frightened them off,' he said. 'I expect they're over the border by now or hiding out in Paris or Marseilles.'

'Don't be too sure.' Pel was never one to take chances.

'I'll be glad when Lagé comes to relieve me,' Misset said. 'You get sick of standing around.'

'Try sitting down,' Pel growled. 'It might help.'

They had their drink then Darcy headed for his car. He had a date with a girl.

'You're growing too senior to have dates,' Pel warned.

Darcy smiled. 'And you're growing too senior,' he said, 'not to. People will begin to think there's something odd about you.'

Pel wondered if there were. He drove home gloomily, his mind occupied half by Madame Faivre-Perret and half by the thought of the families of Randolfi, Desouches and Lemadre. He had been that afternoon to see Goriot, who still looked pale and was obviously in pain.

Madame Routy was watching the television when he arrived. It seemed to be a bird-watching programme but she had the volume control turned up so loud it sounded more like a riot. Glancing quickly at Pel, she turned it down at once.

'There's something in the oven,' she said.

'I don't need it,' Pel said.

She gave him a sour look and he decided to push his success a little further.

'I need to work,' he said. 'I shall need some quiet.'

She gave him another sour look and switched off the television. 'I'll go and see my sister,' she said.

As she disappeared, Pel took off his shoes, poured himself a whisky and settled himself in the 'confort anglais'.

He was feeling weary but he consoled himself that he probably wasn't half as weary as some of the men still making house-to-house enquiries. By this time, he suspected some of them were beginning to curse the day they decided to become policemen and were wondering why they hadn't become sewage workers instead.

There were still teams of them going round with clipboards. Did you see this? Did you hear that? Any strange neighbours? Any strange noises in the night? Any strange smells? That one usually baffled the people they spoke to but they didn't know that some explosives had strange smells – strange enough, in fact, to give you a headache if you got too much of them.

If only they could get a lead. If only – !

He came to life with a jerk as the telephone rang. He hadn't been aware how tired he was and he'd dropped off to sleep, still clutching his glass. He slammed it down on the table and reached for the telephone.

It was Darcy. 'I think you'd better come down, Patron,' he said.

'What now?'

'They called me in. Somebody's just shot Raffet.'

'What!'

'He'd just closed the bar and stepped outside for a cigarette when this car came roaring past and someone stuck a gun in his face and pulled the trigger. Twice. He's dead.'

Raffet's body was still lying in the gutter with a canvas screen round it. Leguyader's men were already measuring tracks left in the road by the car as it had swerved past. They didn't tell them much and it was very much just a formality that had to be gone through. Misset and Lagé were watching them, looking worried.

Doc Minet was angry. He wasn't a young man and the shootings seemed to have got under his skin. 'Why him?' he asked.

'Information,' Pel growled. 'He'd been helping us.'

'You'll not get anyone else to help you.'

Pel said nothing. Minet was right. But at least they knew it couldn't be any of the people they'd brought in. Which left the three they hadn't yet put their fingers on. Hays, Kotchkoff or Tyl.

'Any witnesses?' he asked Darcy.

'Nobody. The street was empty. Raffet told his wife he was going outside for his usual breath of fresh air. It was something he did every night when they pulled the shutters down.'

'Did his wife see anything?'

'She only heard it. She heard him call out then she heard a car start up. She thinks it was waiting along the street. Then she heard it accelerate and suddenly decided something was wrong. She didn't know why. Instinct perhaps. She was running from the kitchen to the bar as she heard the shots, then Raffet staggered and fell at her feet. He was already dead.'

'Did he manage to say anything?'

'No. Nothing.'

'Did she see anyone in the car?'

'She thought there were three of them. Two in the front and one in the back who had the gun. It was over in a matter of seconds.'

'What about the car? Any description?'

'She thought a big Citroën. She saw no number. One could hardly expect her to. Raffet fell against her and almost knocked her down. When she recovered her senses, it was just disappearing round the corner.'

Pomereu of Traffic appeared. 'We've got the car,' he said. 'We found it near the Cours de Gaulle. It's obviously been abandoned in a hurry. It was standing at forty-five degrees to the curb, the doors open and the engine warm. One of our crews stopped alongside it, thinking something was wrong, and reported it by radio. They hadn't heard of the shooting. We've just learned it was stolen yesterday at Chatillon. Belongs to a solicitor. We're having it checked for fingerprints.'

Minet was just straightening up and flash bulbs were going off as Photography did their stuff.

'Two bullets,' Minet said. 'One entered his right eye and came out at the back of his head. The other hit him in the throat and came out through his neck just under the left ear. Either would have killed him.'

'Make sure all roads out of the city are stopped,' Pel snapped to Pomereu. 'They're still here, so let's make sure we keep them here.' He stared savagely at Darcy. 'We had a guard on the damn' place,' he said. He looked at his watch. 'It was Lagé. Where was he?'

'Having trouble with his car, Patron. It wasn't his fault and he was only four minutes late arriving, but you know what Misset's like. Always slow at relieving other people but if anyone's late relieving *him* he goes up the wall. He was in the bar, telephoning Lagé's home to find out where he was.'

Pel's eyes were hot. 'I want him in my office at eleven o'clock tomorrow morning,' he snarled. 'By twelve o'clock he'll be back in uniform patrolling the Porte Guillaume.'

sixteen

As it happened, it didn't work out that way.

The next day was one of surprises. The first even as Pel sat down in his office.

There were three days left before the President arrived. The Chief was working himself up to a heart attack over the arrangements and chivvying Pel to get a move on. Once more he had tried to get the visit put off and received a second flea in his ear from an official at the Elysée Palace, who had told him that the President of France didn't put off visits because of threats.

The tension was becoming electric and Pel was watching everybody he passed in the streets for outward signs of anarchic tendencies or for the hostility he felt the city – stirred up by the television and despite the recent sympathy over the murders – was beginning to feel for the police. He hadn't eaten a proper meal for days, subsisting largely on beer and sandwiches at the Bar Transvaal, and he couldn't remember when he last had a good night's sleep. Raffet's murder had provided just one more night when he hadn't even been to bed.

The rings under his eyes like the circles left by sloppy wine glasses, unshaven, his clothes rumpled, he was staring bitterly at the new pile of reports concerning Raffet's murder when Claudie Darel appeared. Despite the pressure of work she looked as pretty as ever, her black hair neat and shining.

'Can I have a word with you, Patron?' she asked.

'I'm busy. What's it about?'

'Robert Démon.'

Pel scowled. 'Robert Démon's no friend of mine.'

'He's no friend of mine, either, Patron.'

'Then what's the trouble?'

Claudie gestured. 'He rather fancies himself with the girls. He passed me in the car park last night and followed me to ask me out for a drink.'

'And you went?'

'I thought it might be useful, Patron. Now I'm sure it is. I was in plain clothes, of course, and I think he thought I'd come to report a lost dog or something.'

Pel leaned forward. This pretty girl who looked like Mireille Mathieu obviously had hidden depths.

'There wasn't much happening last night,' she went on. 'At least not before the Raffet shooting. He took me to St Symphorien. We had a meal. Then we drove back to the city. By a roundabout route, of course, and we stopped on the way. They all do.'

Pel frowned. There had been a time once when he had, too. 'Go on,' he growled.

'He talked a lot. Mostly about himself. He has a high opinion of Robert Démon and Robert Démon's spot on the television. I had a pocket tape recorder in my handbag and I switched it on. You'd be surprised what I heard.'

'What did you hear?'

'Well, I encouraged him a bit, I have to admit. But he was hardly discreet. Would you like to hear what he said?'

She placed a small tape recorder on the desk. The voice that came from it was thin and reedy but it was quite clear and was quite obviously Démon's voice. For a few minutes, Pel listened to a lot of chat about Démon's work. He was obviously struck by Claudie and was trying to impress her. Then Claudie gestured to him to pay attention.

'It's rubbish, of course,' the voice went on. 'I know it's rubbish, but it sells. It's what people want.'

'Is it wise to give it them, though?' The voice now was Claudie's.

'Does it matter?' Démon's voice continued. 'We all have to make our way in this world and I'm making mine very nicely, thank you.'

Claudie leaned forward as the voice paused and switched off. 'This is the relevant bit, Patron,' she said.

As she switched on the tape again, Démon's voice came again. 'I'm going to demand on my programme that the Security Police are called in. Make a proper job of it.'

'Isn't it better to take it quietly?' The voice was Claudie's once more. 'Less people get hurt that way.'

There was the sound of a chuckle then Démon's voice came. 'What does that matter? It makes better viewing to see people helped away with blood on them. Especially if they're Flics. I've more than once persuaded kids to heave bottles at them to get a better story. That business at Castel, for instance. You remember that? I had my cameras with the kids and a few francs here and there, a petrol bomb or two, and away you go. Everybody wondered how I got the pictures.'

Claudie switched it off and looked at Pel. 'There's more of the same sort, Patron. But that's the best, I think.'

'Through his tiredness, Pel was impressed not only by her skill and cleverness but also by her loyalty.

'And the quiet moment in the car?' he asked.

She gave a twisted smile. 'If you look at him carefully, Patron,' she said. 'You'll see a long scratch on his right cheek. We could probably get him for assaulting a police officer. He'd plead that he didn't know I was a police officer, of course, but there you are, you can't have everything. The tape recorder was still going and, if nothing else, he was pressing his attentions on me when I was objecting. I have evidence. You could call it molesting.'

It was late when they finished but even as Pel reached for his hat, the telephone rang.

It was Darcy. 'Better come in here, Patron,' he said excitedly. 'We've got a lead, and I think it might be good.'

In Darcy's office was a middle-aged man with a moustache and glasses. His clothes were shabby and he wore a checked cap with a red pompom.

'We might,' Darcy said ' – we just *might* – have found out where they are.' He gestured at the man in the cap. 'This is Patrice Dennis, Patron. He runs a grocery store in the Rue Balam. Go on, Monsieur Dennis. This is Inspector Pel. Tell him what you told me.'

Dennis glanced at Pel and swallowed hard. 'Well,' he said, 'I've read all the newspapers about the shootings and the rewards for information. All those appeals for anyone to come forward who might know where they are. I've had the police in my shop asking if any of my customers have been behaving oddly.'

'And have they?'

'Well, I don't know.' Dennis swallowed again. He looked scared to death. 'There's one who might be.'

'Name?' Pel said.

'Got it, Patron,' Darcy said. 'Liliane Lefèvre. Apartment C, Top floor, 97, Rue Daubenon. Montchapet district again. Aged about thirty-one. Single.'

'Go on.'

'She lives alone,' Dennis said. 'She always has. Well – ' he paused ' – sometimes there's a man there. She's not fussy, you know. We always know by the amount of groceries she buys. Half a kilo of butter becomes a kilo. A kilo of apples becomes two kilos. We can always tell how many there are in a family.'

Pel was listening quietly, not interrupting. 'When she has a man there, what she buys always goes up. Double. Sometimes a bit more.' Dennis tried a nervous smile. 'Depends on whether they're big eaters, I suppose.'

'And you think she has someone there now?'

'Not one. Three, I think.'

'You've seen them?'

'No. Just worked it out. My wife said to me "I see Liliane's got a boy friend in again" but I didn't take much notice at first because she's like that. It often happens. Then my wife said. "He's a big eater, this one. Eats enough for two. Perhaps even three." '

Pel glanced at Darcy, lit a cigarette and passed the packet to Dennis who helped himself gratefully.

'Well, when she said that,' he went on, 'I remembered what I'd seen in the papers. Police looking for three men and all that. I started wondering. When she came in again, I made a careful note of everything she bought.' He fished in his pocket and produced a torn scrap of brown wrapping paper. 'That's it. There's a lot of groceries there for one.'

'Perhaps she buys for long periods,' Pel suggested.

'She's not that organised. Buys by the day. Almost by the meal. Comes in during the morning for the midday meal, about six o'clock for the evening meal. Except Mondays when we close. Then she goes round the corner to Barnardi's place. His vegetables are terrible.'

'Is this her usual practice? Twice a day?'

'Without fail. She's on the knock, of course, and sometimes she's short of cash and just buys what she can afford.'

Pel interrupted, gesturing at the scrap of brown paper. 'She doesn't seem to have been short of cash on this occasion. Was it for one meal?'

'If it's the usual method,' Dennis said. 'Yesterday morning she bought eggs for lunch. She said she was going to make an omelette.'

'How many eggs?'

'Twenty.'

'For one omelette? For one woman?'

'That's what she said. She came in again last night and bought some more.'

'Anything else?'

'Tomatoes. Bread. Wine. And a large bottle of Scotch. That was unusual. She doesn't usually afford that sort of thing.'

Pel glanced at Darcy. 'She was buying them Dutch courage,' he murmured. 'Before they set out to fix Raffet. I think we'd better look into this. First, though, let's have Monsieur Dennis taken home.'

'Is it safe to go home?' Dennis asked.

'Is your wife there?'

'Looking after the shop. It's closed, of course. That's why I was late coming. You can't afford to miss a customer these days.'

'I think you'd better get back to her,' Pel said. 'Behave quite normally. Say nothing to anyone. Don't tell anyone where you've been.'

'Not on your life. I've read about that lot. There was a new one last night, I heard.'

'Have you ever seen anyone going in to this Liliane Lefèvre's rooms?' Pel asked.

'No, sir. My shop isn't in the Rue Daubenon. It's round the corner.'

'Never mind. We'll find out. Off you go. You were right to come in.'

When Dennis had gone, Pel began to make his plans. 'Every available man,' he said to Darcy. 'No mistakes. Better to look silly by finding nothing than have them get away again.'

'What about Misset?'

'Misset too,' Pel snapped. 'He might get shot. We shall need binoculars and rifles. We shall also need marksmen, barricades, loud-hailers, walkie-talkies. Everything. Inform Pomereu – there'll need to be traffic control. And Nadauld – we'll probably have to draw on his men, and we'll certainly require a few uniforms to keep back the crowds. They're always willing to get shot for the sake of seeing someone bleed to death on the pavement. But they're to keep out of sight and no one's to move until I give the word. I don't want our friends frightening away.'

Pel's manoeuvre moved like clockwork. People in the houses in the Rue Mozart facing the back of 97, Rue Daubenon, who were known to be friendly to the police, had been knocked up, and now their rear rooms were filled with policemen dripping weapons, their feet stamping dirt from the wet street across best carpets. From the rear windows, they could see Number Ninety-Seven plainly. It was a narrow-gutted, four-storey house with a yard backing on to a builders' premises that stretched across to the houses in the Rue Mozart. The streets around remained silent and still except for an occasional prowling cat. Standing in Dennis' shop, Pel discussed with Darcy and Inspector Nadauld how they should get at the men believed to be in Liliane Lefèvre's rooms.

While they talked, the Chief arrived, his car coming to a stop with a quiet squeak of brakes. Polverari was with him and they closed the doors gently.

'They called me,' the Chief said.

'It might be as well,' Pel observed. 'A few tricky decisions are going to have to be taken.'

Round the corner, where the Chief's car was halted, four police cars blocked the road. Though the inhabitants weren't yet aware of it, all the other streets in the neighbourhood were also blocked and a headquarters had been set up in a shed at the back of Dennis' shop. Dennis was none too keen but there seemed to be nowhere else until daylight and the idea of collecting the reward consoled him.

Among the fruit and vegetable boxes, they pored over a plan of the area obtained from the department of the City Engineer, one of whose minions had been dragged from his bed and taken down to his office to root through his drawers for it.

'If it's our friends,' Polverari said, 'then we can expect shooting.'

'We've got the answer to that one,' Pel said. 'There are men at the opposite side of the Rue Daubenon, overlooking the windows. We also have men at the back to keep heads down at that side.'

'There are people in Number Ninety-Seven, though,' he went on, drawing on what Dennis had told them. 'At least three families, the owner on the first floor. We have all their names. We ought to get them out. To say nothing of the woman herself. She's probably not putting them up willingly and we've got to give her the chance to get clear.'

Eventually they decided to try the ground floor apartment first, and De Troquereau, who was considered the most persuasive, was sent to bring the family out. As he knocked on the door, a small thin woman appeared, her expression hostile.

'You Madame Treville?'

'Yes.'

When De Troq' explained that they needed someone to go up to Liliane Lefèvre's flat to persuade her to come down, she refused at once.

'Not me,' she said. 'I'm on my own with three children, one sick. My husband's on nights. He's permanently on nights. If you want Liliane, you'll have to get her yourself.'

'Is she in?' De Troq' asked.

'I heard her go up earlier and I haven't heard her come down.'

'How about us getting a Policewoman to look after the kids so you can go up and tell her to come down?'

'Not for fifty thousand francs! I don't like her that much. Besides we're not on speaking terms. She'd know there was something funny going on.'

'We need her out of there.'

'Well, you'll have to get her out yourselves. Nobody round here would go and fetch her out in the middle of the night. She's got a tongue like a viper. Especially if she's got a man in there.' Madame Treville hitched at her housecoat. 'And now, if you'll shift yourself, I'd like to shut this door and go back to bed. My youngest girl's got a cough. Listen.' From the back of the apartment De Troq' could hear the persistent coughing of a child.

As she tried to close the door, De Troq' put his knee against it. 'How long has your child been ill?' he asked patiently.

'A week now.'

'Would Liliane Lefèvre hear the coughing?'

'Everybody can hear it. You can hear it in the next street.'

'Look, go up to the top flat and tell her your child's very ill and your husband's at work and you need help.'

She studied him suspiciously. 'I don't see why I should help the police,' she said. 'They've never done anything for me.'

De Troq' refrained from pointing out that they only kept the streets safe in a day and age which would rapidly descend into anarchy without them, and that they were helping her now by trying to catch three dangerous men who had shot and killed three cops, wounded two others, killed a woman and a bar proprietor, and would just as easily shoot anybody else who got in their way, including Madame Treville.

'Look,' he tried. 'Your children could be in danger. So could everybody else in this building. If she sees a woman at the door, she'll not suspect anything.'

'Can't you get a policewoman?'

'She needs to recognise you.'

Eventually, Madame Treville agreed to go but she was worried about her children so Claudie Darel was smuggled in to sit with the children. Her calm demeanour immediately soothed Madame Treville's fears.

'All right,' she said. 'I'll go up now.'

As she vanished, De Troq' and Nosjean heard her knock on a door above their heads, then a low conversation, and finally the sound of footsteps descending the stairs.

'There are two of them,' Nosjean murmured. 'We've got her.'

They took up positions behind the door and, as Madame Treville entered the room, followed by the woman from upstairs, De Troq' closed the door quietly.

Liliane Lefèvre was a tall, well-built woman with untidy blonde hair and she was in her slip. 'What's this?' she demanded.

'Police,' Nosjean said. He jerked his head at Claudie. 'Get the Patron.'

'What's going on?'

'Just be quiet. We want to talk to you.'

'I'm in a fine state to talk to anybody. Half-undressed.'

'Can you lend her a coat?' Nosjean asked Madame Treville.

Madame Treville sniffed but she produced an old coat of her husband's and the Lefèvre woman shrugged herself into it. As she was buttoning it, the door opened and Pel appeared.

'We're looking for three men,' he said. 'Jaroslav Tyl, Kasimir Hays and Sergei Toom Kotchkoff, also known as Tom Kotchkoff. There's possibly a fourth also, Hamid Ben Afzul. We have reason to believe they're hiding in your flat.'

She tossed her head. 'I'm a single girl. I don't have men in my flat.'

Madame Treville sniffed again. Pel continued in the same cold voice.

'These men are suspected murderers,' he said. 'We want them for questioning in connection with the deaths of three policemen and a woman in the Impasse Tarien on July 14th and the murder of a bar owner, Claude Raffet, last night.'

Her eyes narrowed but she said nothing.

'We know there are people in your apartment beside yourself.'

'It's a lie!'

'Very well,' Pel said. 'I'd better go up. If I'm shot dead then you'll be charged under Article 60 of the Penal Code. You could get several years.'

Liliane Lefèvre's eyes swept across Pel, De Troq' and Nosjean like those of a trapped animal. Then she nodded.

'Yes,' she said. 'They're there.'

'Names?'

'I don't know their names. Not their proper names. I've met them in bars. One of them's called Jaro, one's called the Russian and one's called Weasel. None of 'em's very old.'

'Old enough,' Pel said. 'Are they awake or asleep?'

She sighed. 'One of them's always awake.'

Pel glanced at the stairs. They were narrow and curving; he couldn't see any attack being made up them without someone being hurt, and he had no intention of chancing that. Policemen's lives were as sacred as anybody else's.

He gestured at Nosjean. 'All right, mon brave. Take her away. She'll be charged with harbouring known criminals, knowing them to be guilty of criminal offences.'

As the Lefèvre woman vanished, Pel gestured. 'Let's have everybody out,' he said. 'We need a clear field.'

It was easier said than done. It was raining, the drops splashing on the windows in an unexpected noisy shower, and Madame Treville had no wish to leave her warm apartment.

'I've got a sick child,' she pointed out.

'She can be wrapped in blankets,' Pel said. 'We'll see she's taken to where she can be properly looked after.'

It was De Troq', using all his charm, who finally persuaded her it might be dangerous to remain.

'Is there going to be shooting?' she asked.

'We hope to do what we have to do without that, but it may come to it.'

The thought that she might be missing something changed Madame Treville's mind again. 'We'll go across the street,' she said. 'To my sister's. We'll see better from there.'

'Nobody's crossing the street,' De Troq' explained. 'Any movement that's taking place is taking place on this side, hard up against the wall, so it can't be seen. Have you any friends on this side?'

She hadn't and changed her mind once more, coming to the conclusion that she might see better from her own front window. It took another quarter of an hour of tortuous arguing, conducted in whispers, before she agreed to move.

They got them out at last, hurriedly dressed, the sleepy children in the arms of policemen. The landlady followed, equally unwillingly, from the first floor, then a whining old man from the second floor.

'Go away,' he said, as they tapped at his door. 'I don't know you.'

'We're police officers.'

'I don't want anything to do with you.'

They eventually managed to get inside and told him he would have to leave.

'This is my home,' he wailed. 'Why am I being evicted?'

'You're not being evicted,' De Troq' explained. 'We've just got to clear the place.'

'I don't want to go. It's my home!'

'Well, we all love our homes,' De Troq' said patiently. 'Most of us have nice homes and wives and kids – '

The old man sniffed. 'Home's all right,' he said. 'I was never very keen on the wife and kids. Besides, I like to keep quiet. At my age, people die. If I keep quiet, I might not be noticed. Anyway, I can't manage the stairs. I get vertigo. I'd fall. I'm ninety-one. I fought at Verdun in the first war before you were even thought of.'

De Troq' decided to try the problem on Pel.

Pel scowled. 'We can't bring in an ambulance crew,' he said. 'Can he be carried down on someone's back?'

'Not on mine, Patron,' De Troq' said. 'He's big and looks heavy.'

'Misset,' Pel said maliciously. 'Get Misset.'

Misset, who had been keeping well out of Pel's way, came forward sheepishly. 'There's a man in the second floor flat,' Pel said. 'He needs carrying down the stairs. Go and do it. If you drop him, I'll have you shot.'

Eager to reinstate himself, Misset hurried off. The old man was still sitting on his bed, whining, but Nosjean had managed to get him into trousers and an overcoat and had wrapped him up with a scarf and placed a cap on his head.

It wasn't easy getting him on to Misset's back but they managed it in the end, Misset's face red with the effort. The noise they made going down the stairs seemed enough to wake the dead.

'Name of God!' Misset panted. 'The old bastard's heavy! What's he been eating? Lead shot?'

They got the old man into the street at last but as Misset put him down, he immediately started whining about the cold.

'Pick him up, Misset,' Pel said. 'We want him safely out of sight.'

Misset gave him an anguished expression and, hoisting the old man on his back again, tottered off, reeling from side to side, until he vanished round the corner.

Pel looked at the Chief. 'That's the lot,' he said. 'The place's empty now except for our little friends in the top apartment.'

'What do you propose now?'

Pel frowned. 'We wait,' he said.

seventeen

Daylight came with the sky rapidly filling with heavy black clouds which soon started to increase into a brewing storm. The eerie light made the wet pavements shine.

The street remained empty of traffic. If anyone made a run for it, Pel wasn't having any obstacles in the way of the police marksmen. Nevertheless, nothing was done to prevent people going to work, because he wished everything to look as natural as possible. Not that he thought the men in the top floor flat had missed much. By this time they must be well aware, from the very absence of noise, that the rest of the house was empty.

The first workers – the market employees and people who did their jobs before the rest of the world woke up – began to move off towards their places of employment and it didn't take them long to spot the police cars waiting round the corner and the policemen in doorways and behind windows in neighbouring streets. Obviously something was happening and, as the word got round, the district began to fill with people whom the police had to keep moving and out of sight.

By now Pel was well aware that the men they were after must be conscious that their time had come. You didn't have to see the policemen: Just the people in windows all staring towards Number Ninety-Seven, all aware that something unusual was about to happen and determined not to miss it.

Barricades were erected out of sight round the corners and the crowd immediately assumed they'd been put there to enable them to see better. They pushed up to them, like spectators at a football match, youngsters sitting on them to get a better view, some actually climbing over, only to be driven back by the policemen.

'All right, les gars! Back you go!'

For the most part the police were still good-tempered but they were ready, if any one argued, to come down hard. One teenager who tried a slanging match was yanked out of the crowd at once and waltzed off to a police car whose crew rushed him down to headquarters to charge him with obstruction. Memories of Randolfi, Desouches and Lemadre were still strong in the minds of the police and they were in no mood to play games.

Pel was checking the last details. 'Darcy, inform the electricity, gas and water people that I want everything turned off.'

Darcy vanished. After a while, he returned. 'It's not possible, Patron,' he said. 'The water cock for Number Ninety-Seven's in the yard at the back.'

'How about electricity?'

'They can turn *that* off, but gas is a problem. It has to be done from the road. Right in front of the house.'

'Right!' Pel made up his mind at once. 'Warn everybody what's happening and turn it off for the whole area. Arrange for water to be supplied. Hot meals had also better be available. Get in touch with the emergency services.'

By this time, the rain had stopped but it had grown stuffy, dark and threatening, and occasionally there was an ominous roll of thunder as the storm that had been gathering in the hills for over a week drew nearer. The heavy atmosphere seemed even more oppressive as Pel thought of the narrow staircase and how to deal with it.

'If it comes to an all-out attack,' the Chief said, 'we shall have to ask for volunteers from among the unmarried men.'

'Let's hope it doesn't come to that,' Pel growled.

He finished his cigarette as if it were to be his last, dragging the smoke down until he coughed. The besieged house was still silent, the shutters on the ground floor closed. His eyes watering, he tossed the cigarette end away and gestured for a loud hailer. It was time to start the ball rolling.

'Jaroslav Tyl,' he called and the iron voice boomed round the narrow street. 'Kasimir Hays. Sergei Toom Kotchkoff. We know you're there. The house's surrounded. There's no escape. You'd better come out and give yourselves up.'

There was no response and it was impossible to see what was going on inside. The ground floor windows were shuttered and the windows on the upper floors were blank, their curtains still drawn. Then Pel saw a curtain twitch in the top apartment and knew he'd been heard.

'We have plenty of time,' he went on. 'We can wait as long as necessary. Eventually, you'll run out of food. I've had the water, electricity and gas turned off. You'll be unable to eat and drink very shortly, and you'll have no light when it grows dark.'

The curtain twitched again and he could just imagine the men in Number Ninety-Seven hurrying about the apartment, trying the taps. But there was no response.

By afternoon there was still none and by this time a few tempers were growing ragged and the Chief was being nagged by the hordes of newspapermen to hold a press conference. It was clear they'd have to give way eventually because the newspapermen were beginning to get in everybody's hair; Sarrazin, the freelance, had been warned that if he didn't get out from under Pel's feet he'd be arrested for obstructing the police in the performance of their duty.

Television and radio vans helped to complete the confusion, the crews wandering about with their apparatus, hoping for a shot of something happening and, when it didn't, having to fall back on pictures of policemen looking round corners, something they were more than willing to do so long as it wasn't a corner that mattered, even putting on tense expressions for the occasion in case their families or girl friends happened to be watching.

Because everybody wanted to see some action, the absence of it began to get on the nerves.

'There are a lot of complaints,' the Chief pointed out to Pel. 'Don't you think we should move in?'

'No,' Pel said.

'People want to go about their business. The Press – '

'Damn the Press!'

The Chief's voice grew harsher. 'We've got to give them *something*,' he said. 'We depend on them as much as they do on us.'

Pel scowled but the Chief was right and eventually they agreed to meet the pressmen in a nearby school. Démon was there, smooth, immaculate and handsome, the scratch Claudie Darel had put on his cheek clearly visible. Pel glared at him. Remembering Madame Routy, he had always known he would dislike television personalities in the flesh.

There were the usual questions about their intentions. 'We wait,' Pel said.

Then Démon got in on the act and Pel could see the cameras directed on him. 'Wouldn't you say you have rather a lot of men on the job, sir?' Démon asked politely. 'After all, there are only three men in there.'

Pel frowned. 'We would welcome the offer of anyone prepared to go in there to talk to them,' he replied silkily. 'Are *you* offering?'

As Démon searched for a reply, Pel went on. 'Let's have no sentimental nonsense about it,' he said firmly. 'These men have killed three policemen and two other people, and wounded several others. They're ruthless and prepared to kill again. I'd rather have *them* rotting in gaol than my men rotting on the pavement.'

'Aren't they the result of the system, sir?' Démon was still smoothly polite but his questions were pointed. 'Haven't these types been created by aggressive policing?'

'The state exists for the benefit of the decent citizen,' Pel snapped. 'Any criminal who thinks he's being harshly treated has only to stop being a criminal.'

'Isn't there something in all men, though, sir, that should be sought and brought out? Wouldn't closer contact with the criminal classes help?'

'You should open your eyes,' Pel snorted. 'It's the decent citizen not the criminal who finds himself being ambushed and beaten up. I've no room for men who make war on society. Because it *is* war, and war's conducted in cold blood.'

'Nevertheless, sir – '

Pel glared. 'I was brought here,' he snarled, 'to give the Press a report on what we're doing, not to take part in a chat show. As far as I'm concerned, I've given it.'

There wasn't much of Pel but he could make his views felt and, as he stalked out of the schoolroom, it was left to the Chief to sort out what was left.

The interview was on the early evening show an hour later and Pel watched it on a portable set the Chief had brought along. Pel's words had not been changed but Démon had inserted a new lot of questions and comments and they made Pel sound aggressive, unsympathetic and harsh, and the police as mindless thugs eager to kill.

Still nothing happened, despite Pel's repeated requests on the loud-hailer, until abruptly two window panes fell out, one at the front, one at the back. They all knew what it meant. They'd been knocked out by weapons so that the men behind them could fire more easily.

'How long are we going to wait?' the Chief asked.

'All week, if necessary' Pel said. 'They have no hostages because we've got everybody clear. We starve them out. It's better than trying to rush them up those stairs.'

By this time, lights had been brought up ready so that the whole street could be flooded with an ice-white glare when darkness came and there was a lot of grumbling by house-holders unable to get to their homes. With the exception of those with people sick in bed, most of them had been evacuated, while the sick had been moved to rooms at the back where they were safe. Schoolrooms had been taken over and, while parents were complaining, the children were enjoying themselves. The emergency services providing water, meals and bedding were treating it as an exercise. So far it was working well, and despite the drama that was taking place life in the streets around was continuing quite normally. Bakers and grocers and bars were operating, and a pop group, which had been rehearsing in a disused garage round the corner, had enlivened the hours with the thumping rhythm of their music. Despite the objections, they had refused to stop. 'We've got a new number to work out,' they insisted.

Pel's temper was mounting. Eventually there would be a demand for action but he was frightened by Number Ninety-Seven's narrow stairs. There was still no sound from the apartment, however, and Pel even began to wonder if the men who'd been there had escaped. The policemen watching from top storey windows overlooking the back and front of the house, and the men in the neighbouring houses, in case an attempt was made to break through the walls or roof, assured him that nothing had changed.

'We can hear them,' Darcy reported from next door.

They were still anxious to know exactly how many men were in the house. They could be anywhere now, but the general opinion was that there were two on the top floor – one watching the front, one watching the back – and the third watching the stairs. Three different voices had been heard, low and gruff as the besieged group discussed what was happening, and the Lefèvre woman had also insisted there *were* only three men.

There were policemen clinging to the chimneys and in every window fronting the silent house. There were rifles with telescopic sights, submachine guns, concussion grenades, tear gas, everything that was needed. What places of vantage weren't occupied by the police were occupied by the citizenry who, if someone was going to die, wanted to be in the front seats. But, because there were so many police about, a considerable amount of sympathy for the besieged men was running as an undercurrent to the indignation against the killers. It was a David and Goliath situation and sympathy in such cases was invariably with the underdog.

They tried the loud-hailer again. 'You three in there!' This time it was the Chief who was at the microphone. 'Can you hear me?'

There was no reply and he went on slowly, enunciating carefully so no one could suggest the warning hadn't been clear.

'This street and the streets around are blocked and we have men with guns in every window and on every rooftop, front and rear. You're trapped. Is that clear?' There was still no answer. 'Are you coming out or do we have to come in and get you?'

The curtain twitched once more but there was no sound from the empty apartment. There was another long silence while the crowd held its breath. The Chief turned to Inspector Nadauld.

'Very well' he said. 'Let them have the tear gas.'

Tear gas bombs shattered glass but cupboards and wardrobes had been pushed up against the windows behind the curtains and the bombs bounced back to the pavement to fill the street with smoke. Carried on a slight breeze, it began to drift towards the crowd and a wail went up as those who caught a whiff of it stumbled away, cursing and crying. Pel scowled. Somewhere in the background he could hear Démon's voice gleefully informing his viewers of yet another police manoeuvre that had gone wrong.

As it happened, the weather came to their aid. The storm which had been threatening for some time arrived suddenly and unexpectedly. There was a flash of lightning and a tremendous crash of thunder, then the rain came down like stair rods, huge drops bouncing off the roadway and lashing at the men sheltering in the doorways. It washed away the gas and thinned the crowd but it didn't drive them away. They were there to see blood and they were determined to see it. Instead, the men sent their wives off for umbrellas and raincoats and kept their vigil, determined not to be cheated.

They were still wondering what to do next when suddenly, quite unexpectedly, a figure appeared in the doorway of the besieged house. It was as though the men inside had decided to take advantage of the storm, and those policemen who hadn't turned their heads away from the downpour found themselves staring at a solitary gunman, hardly able to believe their eyes. They had long since come to the conclusion that nobody was coming out and for a second they all stared, frozen. The man had a weapon in each hand and was looking for someone to fire at. As he pointed the guns towards the crowd, hoping in the confusion of a new killing to escape, one of the watching policemen lifted his rifle and fired quickly.

The figure in the doorway reeled back, then lunged forward, firing with both weapons. At once, now that the spell had been broken, every weapon in the area started hammering and the bullets began to chip chunks out of the brickwork. Caught in a crossfire, the man by the doorway staggered to the right, only to be blasted back by the shooting from that side. For a second he clutched the doorpost then struggled forward again, head down, red splotches already on his clothing. This time the firing seemed to lift him clean off his feet and dropped him on his back near the door.

A policeman, with more courage than sense, stepped forward to see if he was dead and, as he did so, a hail of bullets, the first that had been fired from inside the house, struck the pavement about him and he bolted for cover, the bullets ricochetting and whining over the heads of the screaming, ducking onlookers.

Taking advantage of the panic, policemen started to barge at the crowd. 'Now, in the name of God, will you get away from here to where it's safe?'

A few decided it might be safer inside their own homes but, as the firing died down, the rest elected to see it out. The man on the pavement lay on his back, his knees up, his arms spread wide, blood flowing from chest, throat, face and legs.

'Who is it?' Sarrazin asked.

'Well, it's not Tyl,' Pel said. 'And, since he hasn't got red hair, I'd judge that it's Hays, the one they call the Weasel.'

'Is he dead?'

'You're welcome to go and see for yourself.'

Sarrazin declined the offer and for a long time there was silence except for an excited murmur from the crowd as everybody craned their necks to see the dead man. The firing had stopped completely now, both from the house and from the street.

'Can we get him in?' the Chief asked from his vantage point at the end of the street.

'I'm sending none of my men out there,' Pel said sharply.

Inspector Nadauld gestured. 'It's not important, anyway,' he said. 'The important thing is that there are now only *two* of them. One at the back and one at the front. There can't be anyone watching the stairs. If we rush the place we're bound to make it.'

The Chief looked at Pel. It was still Pel's view that they should wait but it was clearly becoming more difficult, and eventually the Chief overruled him. Conferring with Brisard and Polverari, he decided that a group of Nadauld's men should make the rush.

'We've *got* to make the attempt,' he said. 'The Palais des Ducs wants to know what's happening.'

'Tell them we're waiting,' Pel growled.

The Chief shrugged and it was finally decided to make the attempt with volunteers from the unmarried men.

'Two groups to keep their heads down front and rear,' Nadauld said. 'Another to rush the door and go up the stairs.'

'There's a builder's yard at the back,' Judge Brisard pointed out. 'With a garage backing up against the wall of the yard of Number Ninety-Seven. With ladders, we could get men over the garage roof and in through the back door.'

'You'll be leading them, of course?' Pel asked, his eye running over Brisard's plump figure.

'That isn't my job,' Brisard said stiffly.

'Neither is tackling criminals,' Pel snapped.

Brisard disappeared with a flea in his ear but his idea had taken root and a fourth group was organised to go over the roof of the garage to the back door.

Pel didn't like it at all but he had no option. 'Divide your men,' he told Darcy. 'One lot with each group. If they're going in, we'll need our people in there before Nadauld's lot destroys every scrap of evidence with their great boots.'

As the policemen hitched at their belts and checked their weapons, Darcy moved among them. 'The rear party goes first,' he was saying. 'It's going to be harder for them. They've got to clear the wall and get to the back door. The front party moves as soon as firing starts.'

The rear party hurried off, their heads down against the rain, and a few minutes later a radio message came that they were in position. Almost immediately, they heard the out-break of firing from the houses in the Rue Mozart overlooking the back windows of Number Ninety-Seven as the marksmen there tried to keep the gunmen's heads down.

'Stand by!'

As firing started at the front, the group of uniformed and plain clothes men gathered against the wall. Firing came from the upper windows every time a policeman raised his head to shoot and they received a message by radio that the rear windows of the house were similarly guarded.

'They're both fully occupied now,' Nadauld said. 'Go!'

There was a yell and the clatter of boots as the policemen rushed for the door. Immediately, they heard firing inside the house and a second later one of the policemen burst out and crouched against the wall outside, just out of range of the upper front windows. He lifted his head and yelled to the watching officers across the street.

'There are still *three* of the cons!' he yelled. 'There was one on the stairs! They hit the man in front of me!'

'So much for Brisard's splendid plan!' Pel growled.

There were a few more shots then Nadauld's men reappeared, their heads down, and crouched against the wall by the doorway, before bolting for shelter. There was a derisive cheer from the crowd and Pel scowled as he heard Démon's voice, surprisingly loud over the chatter, describing what had happened. 'Despite the numbers,' he was saying, 'the attack ended in a failure.' It made them sound incompetent idiots.

The firing went on sporadically as they waited, and they were all deep in conference again behind Dennis' shop when Darcy, who had been directing the operations at the rear of the house, appeared.

'Misset's been hit,' he said.

Pel rounded on him in a fury. 'It would be Misset!' he snarled. 'What was *he* doing there? It was supposed to be the unmarried men.'

'I think he was trying to save a bit of face. He must have slipped in.'

Pel scowled, then his natural concern for his men broke through. 'Is he badly hurt?'

'Not if we can get him away. He was just behind De Troq' who was leading the rush with Aimedieu. The bullets missed them and hit Misset. One of Nadauld's men was also hit but not seriously. Misset's different. He seems in a bad way, but I can't really tell because every time I stick my head up they start firing. De Troq' shouted that they're all crowded in the kitchen at the back of the house. We can't get up the stairs and they can't get down. He says it was the Ripka woman who got Misset.'

'*She's* with them?' Brisard said.

Pel gave him a glare and, as he backed away, Pel sighed. He had been trying all the time to save people from being hurt, but now there was nothing more he could do. He was being forced on to the offensive. They all were. As Ney had said at Jena, the wine was poured and they'd have to drink it.

'I'll come,' he said.

eighteen

The builder's yard was full of policemen. They were crouching among the piles of timber and tiles, and Nosjean and a group of plain clothes men were huddled with the man from the City Engineer's Department against a steep-roofed garage that backed on to the wall which separated the area from the narrow yard at the rear of Number Ninety-Seven. Two ladders reared up against the side of the garage to show where the rear party had scrambled over.

Darcy gestured. 'They went up the ladders, up the roof and down the other side. The wall of the yard of Ninety-Seven lifts about half a metre above the guttering at that side. We're all right on this side – at least, we are up against the garage there, where we're in dead ground out of their fire. We're also all right on the roof but you have to go over the ridge double-quick and down to the wall. That's when they could get you. You've got a bit of shelter by the wall, which is just high enough to protect you, so if they start shooting, lie down behind it in the gutter. When you reach the gutter, you have to roll over the wall double-quick and drop into the yard. It's about three metres down.'

'Just enough to break a leg or two,' Pel growled.

A few shots were still being fired but the men inside the house were lying low now, though they didn't seem to be running out of ammunition.

Darcy peered out from behind the timber. 'When you're ready, Patron,' he said, 'we'll make a dash for the ladders.

The boys here'll keep their heads down, and as soon as they start firing, the guys in the Rue Mozart will open up, too. Right?'

'Right!'

'Let's go!'

As the firing started, Pel and Darcy made a zigzag dash bent double across the yard. Out of the corner of his eye, Pel saw splinters fly from a dismantled door leaning against an old van without tyres, then he was with Darcy hard up against the garage wall alongside Nosjean, panting after the run. Darcy grinned.

'Made it,' he said.

'So far!'

Darcy's grin died. 'So far,' he agreed soberly. He jerked a thumb upwards. 'We go up the ladders, then up the roof. Take it slowly, Patron, then when you get near the peak, make it fast. Over the ridge, down the other side and over the wall into the yard. The guys in the houses behind can see us and they'll keep up the fire on the windows.' He looked round him, frowning. 'We've got to do something soon,' he pointed out. 'The people in those houses back there are growing restive. Their windows have been broken and their walls and furniture chipped. A child's also been hit in the hand. Nothing serious, thank God, but they're beginning to think it's been going on too long.'

He took his cigarette from his mouth and tossed it aside. The stuffy heat had gone now and the rain was coming in a downpour that saturated their clothes.

'We've asked for a doctor,' he said. 'A volunteer. Someone young. Doc Minet's a bit old and fat for scrambling up ladders under fire. Nosjean here will explain what he's to do. We have to communicate by shouting from the back door. But they can't hit anybody there and they can't hit anybody here, so long as we're close to the wall. You ready?'

Pel nodded and, as Darcy gestured, began to climb one of the ladders with his head well down, while Darcy climbed the other. At the top they paused as firing started from the other side of the builder's yard. Glass broke and shots came back from the upper windows of the house.

'Ready, Patron? Now!'

Reaching for the top of the ladder, Pel scrambled up the last few steps. Missing his footing, so that he scraped his shin agonisingly on a rung, as he clung to the top of the ladder wanting to howl at the pain, Darcy called out.

'We go up the roof together, Patron. It's better that way.'

Firing from the house started again as they sprawled on the grubby tiles of the garage roof and glass tinkled to the ground. Bullets chinked off the walls and Pel could hear them whining away, some of them uncomfortably close.

'Now!' Darcy yelled.

Scrambling up the roof, Pel rolled over the ridge and down the other side until he was brought up sharp against a wall that rose beyond the guttering. A tile not far away shattered as a bullet struck it then the firing from the houses across the builder's yard increased.

'Over, Patron!' Darcy yelled.

Scrambling over the wall, Pel dropped down into the backyard of Number Ninety-Seven where De Troq' dragged him to his feet and shoved him unceremoniously through the back door.

Misset was lying on a stained mattress, propped up with coats. As Pel appeared he opened his eyes.

'I think I'm dying, Patron,' he said hollowly.

Pel glanced at De Troq' who shook his head. 'Shock,' he said quietly. 'It's bad but not *that* bad.'

'I was doing my duty, Patron,' Misset groaned.

Pel frowned. It *would* be the most difficult and intractable member of his squad who'd been hurt – Misset, who'd been due to face the Chief and translation back to uniform. Pel

could hardly do that to him now, but it was also typical of
Misset, who was always more than willing to avoid both
work and responsibility, to make a song and dance about
doing his duty. Pel looked down at the fleshy handsome face.
Misset had drunk too many beers and sat on his behind too
much over the years and was running to seed. In another few
years, the good looks would be gone and he would be just a
podgy, too-fat man. All the same, he was badly hurt, spitting
blood and in a state of collapse, and the least Pel could do for
him was offer a few words of comfort.

'Don't worry,' he said. 'We'll get you to the hospital.'

'It's going to be damn' difficult, Patron,' De Troq' pointed
out. 'We can't take him out by the front door because the
woman's watching the stairs and she shoots as soon as
anybody puts his head into the hall.'

'It's all right,' Misset moaned. 'I can die here.'

Self-sympathy, Pel thought, killed almost as many as
bullets did. He turned his head sharply.

'Don't talk rubbish,' he snapped. 'It's an offence against
the police code to die when people are trying to rescue you.
You ought to know that.'

It so startled Misset he stopped moaning and lay quietly,
his eyes on Pel, frightened, in pain, but no longer full of self-
sympathy.

'We'll get you to hospital,' Pel went on gruffly. 'We're
getting a doctor to you. He'll fix you up here and then we'll
strap you to a stretcher and get you out somehow. Never
fear.'

This time Misset even managed to look grateful and brave.

Pel glanced round. The wounded uniformed man was
sitting in a corner, his back against the wall. De Troq' and
Aimedieu had bandaged his arm with handkerchiefs, and
though he looked pale and shaken, he was quite rational.

'You all right?' Pel asked.

'Yes, Patron. I'm all right. It hurts but I can use it after a fashion.'

Pel patted his shoulder and drew Darcy, De Troq' and Aimedieu to one side.

'He'll have to go over the wall,' Darcy said.

'How about *through* the wall?' Pel asked. 'Can't we knock a hole in it?'

'I thought of that one, Patron,' Darcy said. 'But the City Engineer type in the builder's yard said the wall's too old and if you removed so much as a couple of bricks, the whole lot would come down on us.'

Pel stared up at the wall. 'Very well,' he said. 'We'll get him out the way he came in. I'll go back and organise it. I'll need a shove up. Then we'll get ladders over with men on the roof. We can back up a van to the garage wall and get him down that way. Getting him up from here's going to be the most difficult part, but we'll double the numbers of marksmen in the windows opposite to keep their heads down till we're clear.'

As they made their plans, the firing increased again and they heard someone scrambling across the roof and the thump of feet as a man dropped into the yard. It was Doctor Lacoste. His face was grey with fear and his dark eyes were huge. A policeman, crouching behind the low wall against the roof, lifted himself long enough to drop the doctor's bag to him, then ducked down again as tiles jumped and danced under the firing from the windows above their heads. Then, as the covering fire from the Rue Mozart blazed up, he jumped to his feet, scrambled up the roof and rolled over the other side.

Lacoste, who had caught the bag like a rugby ball, was leaning against the wall, trying to get back both his breath and his nerve.

'What do you want?' Pel snapped.

'They called for a volunteer.'

Considering how terrified he'd been when he'd first seen him and clearly still was, Pel couldn't help feeling admiration for him. He gestured at Misset, and Lacoste bent over him. After a while he rose to his feet, wiping the blood from his hands on a handkerchief.

'The bullet has entered his chest,' he said. 'It struck a rib, glanced along it and came out at his side. He's bleeding internally. We need to get him to a hospital.'

'And if we don't?'

Lacoste shrugged.

Pel glanced at Misset who was lying back, almost seeming to enjoy the attention he was receiving.

'We'll get him to the hospital,' Pel said, 'if you can patch him up to make him fit to go. He's going to have a nasty trip over that roof.'

Lacoste looked startled. 'Isn't he going out through the front door?'

'Try that,' Darcy said, 'and you and another two or three'll probably end up like him.' He jerked a thumb at the wall opposite the back door. 'That's the only way.'

Lacoste frowned. 'It's dangerous,' he said.

'Do you think we don't know that?'

'I mean, it'll be dangerous for him.'

'Doc,' Darcy said, 'it'll be dangerous for all of us.'

'I'm going to organise more marksmen to cover the windows,' Pel said. 'I'll also bring up more ladders and get a stretcher over. Then we hoist him up here and down the other side of the roof. Think he can survive that sort of treatment?'

Lacoste frowned. 'I'll make it so he can,' he said. 'We shall have to be quick, and handle him carefully but I'll stay with him all the way.'

'You don't have to, once he's patched up.'

'I'm a doctor,' Lacoste said stiffly.

'Very well.' Pel nodded. 'Right, you get on with your job. I'll get on with mine.' He looked at Darcy. 'Is it possible to organise radio contact?'

'Not from here,' Darcy said. 'The houses block off the signals. But Nosjean'll hear if we shout loud enough.'

'So will everybody else,' Pel said dryly. 'Right, then you'd better give me a push up.'

'Make it fast, Patron,' Darcy advised. 'It doesn't pay to stand around whistling and playing the piano.'

Aimedieu, Darcy and Pel edged outside the door, and stood hard up against the wall of the house. 'Right,' Pel said. 'Now!'

He ran to the wall opposite and stood facing it, his arms raised. As Aimedieu and Darcy grabbed his feet and heaved, he went up with a rush that landed him across the top of the wall with all the breath knocked out of his body. Scrambling to his feet, he scuttled up the sagging roof of the old garage with its broken tiles, to roll over the top and down the other side. He was going so fast, he took a length of ancient guttering with him and went straight over the edge to fall into the builder's yard without any further effort. Fortunately, his fall was broken by a policeman and the two of them sagged in a heap against the wall of the garage.

'More ladders,' Pel panted, as Nosjean dragged him to his feet. 'Plenty of ladders. Two up the roof on this side. Two for down the other side. And two to drop into the yard. Then we need a stretcher and a van backed up against the garage here. That's the only way we can do it. Get on with it, mon brave.'

The policeman standing by the entrance to the apartments in the Rue Mozart overlooking the builder's yard and the back of Number Ninety-Seven gestured as Pel appeared. The owners of the apartments were standing outside in an agitated group and as they saw him they surrounded him at once.

'When's it all going to finish?' one man yelled at him. 'My windows have been shot out and my furniture's full of holes. It's time someone did something!'

Pel rounded on him coldly. 'If you care to come back with me over those roofs, volunteers are very welcome.'

The man edged away hurriedly, and Pel began to climb the stairs.

What he'd been told was correct. Windows had been broken and the plaster inside the rooms facing the besieged house had had chunks shot out of it. The police marksmen standing by the windows gave him a grim look.

'They seem to move about between the two upper windows,' one of them said. 'Sometimes they come down a storey to the second floor.'

As he spoke, there was a flurry of shots and the policeman gave Pel a shove. As he reeled away, glass fell out and there was a solid thump as a bullet hit the opposite wall, gouging out plaster in a shower.

'Pays to keep your head down,' the policeman said.

'I'm sending you reinforcements,' Pel said. 'I want the firing from that house smothered. We've got a badly wounded man in there and we're going to try to get him out over the roof.' He pointed to Nosjean in the builder's yard. 'The type with the light jacket there will wave a handkerchief when things are happening on the other side. When you see that, give it everything you've got.'

Heading back to the Rue Daubenon, he conferred with the Chief.

'We've got all the ammunition you'll need,' the Chief said. 'I've got more men, too. Take as many as you need.'

By the time Pel returned to the builder's yard, Nosjean had collected the ladders, which were lying on the ground hard up alongside the garage. Pel explained his plan.

Ten minutes later they were ready. As firing started from the Rue Mozart, chunks of brick leapt from the walls of

Number Ninety-Seven and splinters flew from the furniture the besieged men had propped against the windows. The fact that they were still there and full of life was clear from the shots that came back at them.

As the firing swelled, Pel nodded and policemen swarmed up ladders to the wet roof, dragging more ladders with them. Lying flat, they edged the ladders to the apex until they overbalanced and slid down the other side. More ladders were pushed up to them and over the ridge.

Lying on the blind side of the roof in the pouring rain, Pel explained again what he wanted. 'Two ladders a metre apart,' he said. 'So we can drag the stretcher up between them. Two more, the same, at this side. Then two over the wall into the yard. We'll place them in position from there.'

He looked at the tempestuous sky and spat rainwater from his lips. 'I wish to God this rain would stop,' he complained. 'Where's the stretcher?'

'Ready, Patron,' Nosjean said. 'We'll pass it up when you're ready. I've got a van round the corner. We'll back it up to the garage as soon as you're clear.'

'Right. Let's go.'

Despite the covering fire, shots kept coming from the windows of the besieged house as the ladders were pushed into position beyond the roof peak. Scrambling down them to the raised wall, uniformed men slid two more ladders down to the yard. As the stretcher was hurried forward, Pel waved away the men on the roof.

'Get under cover!' he yelled. 'Wait for orders!'

There was a rush to the safe side of the roof, then Pel slipped over the peak, slid down to the projecting wall and rolled over it into the puddled yard of Number Ninety-Seven. Once again, De Troq' dragged him to safety.

For a moment, drenched and gasping, he sat just inside the kitchen door, trying to get his breath back. For some reason, he thought of Madame Faivre-Perret. Doubtless, he decided, she'd hear eventually what they'd been up to. It might even do him some good – unless of course, it wasn't enough to put her off policemen for the rest of her life.

nineteen

Doctor Lacoste had done a good job on Misset. The doctor seemed quite calm now, his fear gone as he had become absorbed in his work. Misset was silent, his eyes closed.

'I've killed the pain,' Lacoste said. 'And the wound's well padded and bandaged. I'll be there to keep an eye on him.'

As they strapped Misset to the stretcher, Pel studied the men with him – Darcy, De Troq', Aimedieu, two uniformed men, Lacoste and the man who'd been hit in the arm. Lacoste would be fully occupied with Misset, so De Troq', who was the smallest, had to go up first with the lightly wounded man. Darcy, Aimedieu and the uniformed men could do the lifting, because they were the strongest, and he would bring up the rear himself.

'It's got to be fast,' he pointed out.

'We'll make it fast,' Darcy promised grimly.

As they talked, the storm seemed to roll round again. The sky crackled with lightning and thunder shook the windows, then the rain came again, as if the skies had opened.

'It'll probably help us, Patron,' Darcy observed. 'Blur things a bit.'

There was a pause of a second or two then the covering fire started again. As it reached a peak of intensity, competing with the thunder for the attention, they pushed the ladders into position against the wall. They clearly hadn't been seen because the heavy firing from the Rue Mozart was keeping heads down above them.

'Let's go,' Pel said.

The lightly wounded man went first, climbing awkwardly with his bandaged arm. De Troq' was behind him, pushing hard. Scrambling over the wall, he half dragged the wounded man to the ridge of the roof and pushed him over. There was a call from the other side.

'We've got him!'

Scrambling back, De Troq' reached down for the stretcher. Darcy and Aimedieu went up the ladders with the head, while the two uniformed men and Pel pushed from behind. Reaching down, De Troq' eased it over the wall to the roof, as the two uniformed men scrambled up the ladders.

Drenched with rain, blinking water from his eyelids and spitting it from his lips, Pel scrambled after them. The uniformed men, De Troq', Darcy, Aimedieu and Doctor Lacoste were still struggling up the slope of the roof with the stretcher and so far the terrorists seemed to be fully occupied with shooting at the house opposite, and they had gone unobserved. But, as they reached the peak of the roof where they were in full view, a uniformed man stuck his head up and asked if he could help.

'Get back, you damn' fool!' Darcy snarled.

But it was too late. The shout had attracted attention and shots began to smash down on the wet and slippery tiles. Doctor Lacoste, astride the ridge directing operations, staggered and fell to his knees, and Pel saw there was a red weal across his forehead where a bullet had grazed his skull. As he sat down abruptly on the roof peak, a dazed look on his face, blood beginning to trickle over his eyes, Pel yelled.

'Get him out of sight!' he screamed.

Aimedieu began to scramble towards the doctor, but the tiles were wet and he slipped and cannoned against him, so that they both overbalanced and disappeared over the other side. Nosjean's head popped up.

'Stay where you are!' Pel yelled, and, scrambling over the ridge, the bullets pecking at the tiles and the whine of ricochets in their ears, they got the stretcher to the ridge.

Then one of the uniformed men slipped and vanished and as Pel, Darcy, De Troq' and the other uniformed man struggled to lift the stretcher over the angle of the roof, the handle jammed under the end of the ladder and they couldn't swing it round. For what seemed ages they fought to get it clear.

'Patron!'

Blinking away rainwater Pel realised Misset's eyes were open.

'Unstrap me,' he whispered.

'Don't be a damn fool!'

'Unstrap me, Patron, and I can roll over.'

For a moment, blinking in the hissing rain, the bullets whacking into the broken tiles, Pel, Darcy and De Troq' stared at each other, then Pel made up his mind quickly.

'Unstrap him,' he agreed.

They started working on the straps with clumsy fingers and pushed Misset to the peak of the roof. Darcy and De Troq' scrambled after him to help, while Pel pushed from behind until, abruptly, Misset vanished from sight, carrying Darcy and De Troq' with him.

Giving the uniformed man a shove so that he also vanished from sight, Pel was just about to follow when a bullet struck the heel of his shoe. It felt as though his foot had been kicked from under him and he fell heavily and rolled back down the roof on the wrong side until he fetched up against the wall that rose from the backyard. Scrambling to his knees, he was about to set off up the roof again when a shot snatched at his sleeve and he flung himself down once more.

For a moment, he wondered where the bullet had come from, because up to that moment the shots from the besieged house had only been troublesome as they reached the peak of the roof. Then it dawned on him that the people in the house had realised the besiegers had left the kitchen and one of them had run down the stairs and was shooting from the kitchen doorway which was protected from the houses opposite by the wall and the garage. It seemed very much that he was stuck.

For a long time, he lay flat in the gutter that ran along the angle made by the sloping roof and the wall. He could hear Darcy's voice coming from the builder's yard.

'Patron? You hit?'

'I'm all right. They can't get at me.'

'We've got Misset inside the timber store and Lacoste's plugging him up again because he opened his wound when he rolled down the roof. The ambulance's on its way. The doc's got a headache he'll feel for a week. What about you, Patron?'

'One of them's in the kitchen now so anybody who puts his head over the peak of the roof's a target. I'm all right, so long as I lie still.'

There was silence at the other side of the roof then, over the roar of the rain, Pel heard the sound of the ambulance arriving and eventually the siren as it moved off. He was soaked to the skin now, the rain pounding down on him and running off the roof to fill the gutter where he lay. It was like lying in a stream and he felt the water was running in through his trouser legs and out through the neck of his shirt. There were times, he decided, when it wasn't much fun being a policeman. Saturated and cold, he tried to shift his position but a shot from the kitchen door made him throw himself flat again.

He was still thinking of Misset. What he had done wasn't far short of heroic. There was more to men than one ever realised. It would bring a commendation inevitably and that

it should go to Misset of all people was a source of
wonderment to Pel. But that was the way it often was. Men
who did their duty faithfully and well got nothing, while the
fool who showed spontaneous courage got the awards. Perhaps he'd have to think again about Misset. One thing was
certain, there'd be no demotion now. He'd still have to go
before the Chief because the report on the shooting of Raffet
had already gone in, but inevitably the Chief would go easy
on him. A wound and a show of heroism did wonders. The
reprimand would be a mild one and Misset would stay in
Pel's squad.

As he lay with the rain soaking through to his skin, Pel
hoped Doctor Lacoste would get a commendation of some
kind, too. Undoubtedly he deserved it. And Evariste Clovis
Désiré Pel? What about him? Until a few weeks ago, Pel had
considered his affairs were making very good progress, had
even been considering buying a house with a garden at
Plombières, and perhaps a dog so he could walk out in the
evening, a true countryman, married to a woman of sub-
stance. Madame Faivre-Perret had favoured living in the
house she owned at the top of the hill to the north of the city.
Perhaps she knew Pel better than he knew himself and was
aware that he'd soon tire of the country because the city was
his life and his burden at the same time. First though – he
jerked back to the present – he had to get out of this farcical
predicament before he perished of cold, drowning, pneumon-
ia or shotgun wounds, because he wouldn't be much good to
Madame Faivre-Perret dead or crippled.

Shivering, his nose within an inch of the rainswept tiles, he
began to wonder how long it could go on. Probably all night
and into the next day. He was just about to utter a groan of
frustration when he found himself staring at the tiles under
his nose. Of course! There was an escape route! He couldn't
imagine why he hadn't thought of it before.

Working feverishly, his hands bleeding as they were torn by the nails in the roof, he began to work one of the tiles loose. It wasn't easy and he was covered by black mud caused by the rainwater on the grime of years that lay beneath. Eventually, he got it free, and then a second. As he pushed it aside, he saw the tile next to it move under his nose and a second later it was pushed aside and, through a hole in the laths and crumbling plaster beneath, he saw Nosjean's face peering up at him.

'Seems we both got the same idea at the same time, Patron,' he said.

Slowly they made the hole bigger and – head-first because he didn't dare lift himself above the low protecting wall – Pel squirmed through, tearing the sleeve of his jacket as he went. In the garage below, standing on the roof of a dust-covered vehicle which clearly hadn't been used for years, Nosjean helped him down and five minutes later he was in the builder's yard.

He was just trying to brush off the plaster and the dirt from his clothes when Darcy appeared alongside him, his face excited.

'Patron,' he said, 'I think we've found the owner of the Brouard key! A woman called Tremolet just telephoned and young Martin radioed through. She says her mother has a top floor room she lets out cheaply to students. She's deaf so she didn't hear the broadcast and it was only because she and her daughter were discussing the room that it cropped up. The last tenant was a man called Trentignant who said he was a medical student, but he sounds as if he could have been Kino. He said he had a lot of valuable equipment – microscopes and so on – and could he put a new lock on the door because other students were in the habit of "borrowing" things and sometimes forgot to return them? It was fitted two months ago.'

Pel was still knocking dirt from his clothes. 'Where is this apartment?'

'Alongside the station, overlooking the exit where the President will appear when he leaves the platform. God knows why. They can't take a potshot at him from there with all the crowds and bodyguards there'll be. I'm going down there now to take a look at the place.'

'Does this Madame Tremolet have a key?'

'No, Patron.' Darcy grinned. 'But *we* do. Kino's.'

Filthy and in a vile temper, Pel appeared before the Chief. Brisard and Polverari were with him, together with a horde of pressmen, including Démon who stood with a microphone in his hand while one of his helpers sheltered him with an umbrella.

'Good God,' Brisard said. 'What have you been up to?'

'You might well ask,' Pel snarled.

Polverari silently handed over a brandy flask and Pel took a grateful swig from it.

Sarrazin, the freelance, grabbed at Pel's arm. 'How about telling us what happened?' he said.

Pel brushed him off. 'Later,' he said. 'There are things to do.'

'They want a truce,' the Chief said. 'They've put out a white sheet. They say there's a woman in there and they want to get her out.'

'So do I,' Pel snapped. 'She's the one who shot Misset.'

Half an hour later, with the rain still pounding down, Anna Ripka appeared at the street entrance, holding a white towel. Aimedieu and De Troq' were waiting on either side of the door, pressed against the walls where they couldn't be seen from the upper windows, and, as she stumbled out, peering shortsightedly about her, they each grabbed an arm. As they hurried her away, she missed her footing but they didn't stop and went on running towards the schoolroom

200

where the headquarters had been set up, her feet dragging behind.

The press appeared as they forced their way through the crowd, camera flashes going off in their faces. Above the hubbub, Pel could hear Démon's voice, slow, precise and damning.

'...bundled roughly away. She looked exhausted but the police are showing no mercy today...'

'His mother must have been frightened by a traffic cop,' Aimedieu snarled.

Brushing the newspapermen aside, Pel pushed his way through the crowd. They still seemed determined to get themselves killed and it was all Nadauld's men could do to keep them out of range. They seemed to regard the affair as a cross between a circus and a television drama, and certainly the cameras were taking it all in. Mounted on huge vans, they had pictured the arrest and doubtless within minutes it would be going out over the air with a breezy commentary from Démon.

As Pel reached the schoolroom, Darcy appeared. He was smiling.

'Patron, I've been in that apartment! The damned place's an arsenal. Two Armalite rifles, three 9 mm pistols, half a dozen Garands and a Russian-made rocket launcher. They aren't going to take a potshot at the President. They're going to fire a rocket. With one of those, they don't have to worry about anyone getting in the way. It would polish the lot off.'

'Why wasn't it found?' Pel snapped. 'Everything along the President's route was supposed to have been searched by the security boys.'

'It was, Patron. The key was even left with the caretaker so it could be. But it wasn't in the flat. It was all in the roof space. There's a loft with a trapdoor in the bathroom. It was all up there. I've got two of Nadauld's boys guarding it.'

'Even the jelly? Was that there?'

'What's left of it. In a couple of drums part-connected to an alarm clock and tucked under the eaves. After they'd fired the rocket all they had to do was finish connecting the alarm clock, give themselves five minutes and run. It would have brought the wall and roof down on the crowds watching the uproar after the rocket and given them a chance to escape.'

'They'd never have got away.'

Darcy's face was grim. 'Martyrdom's part of the creed, Patron,' he said. 'Perhaps they didn't want to.'

As the Ripka woman was brought before Pel, he glanced at Aimedieu.

'Has she been searched?'

'Not yet, Patron.'

'Get Claudie Darel on the job.'

Ten minutes later, Claudie appeared. 'Not much, Patron. A few coins in her pockets, a fifty-franc note, and this.' She held up a key. 'It's a Brouard, Patron, Number M138H. It's the twin of the one in Kino's box. They always supply two. This is the other. I think she's hoping to slip it to someone. I think that's why she gave herself up. After all, she's doing no good holed up in Number Ninety-Seven.'

'I think you're right,' Pel said. 'Well, she doesn't know we've already found their weapons, so give her everything back and watch who appears. Pick him up as she tries to hand it over.'

They were still conferring in the schoolroom, their ears full of the sound of the rain, the murmur of the crowd and the muttering of tired policemen, when a shout lifted heads.

'The place's on fire!'

There was a wail from the crowd that gave way to what sounded like a sigh as they realised they had reached the grand finale of the drama. Hurrying outside, Pel saw a wisp of smoke curling out of the upper windows of Number Ninety-Seven.

That the men inside the house had not given up, however, was proved a moment later as the fire brigade arrived and began to run out their equipment. A shot rang out and the fireman leading the rush stopped dead and stared with surprise at the spray of water that leapt from his hose. As the police began to push the firemen back, it almost led to a fist fight.

'We're here to put a fire out!' the fire officer yelled.

'And we're here to stop you getting killed doing it,' Nadauld yelled back.

As the fireman hesitated, the smoke increased. The rain had stopped again and a squally wind began to get up, swirling the smoke away.

'With a little pressure now,' Brisard said, 'they're bound to surrender.'

Pel scowled at him. It might be better for everybody, he thought, if Brisard kept his mouth shut.

Occasional shots still came from the house and every time the firemen tried to move forward, they were driven back. Eventually the Chief intervened.

'Let it burn,' he ordered. 'Save the houses on either side. We're having no one else hurt.'

The firing had died down completely when a figure appeared on a second floor balcony. He was a slightly built man with red hair in long locks over his face. There was a gasp from the crowd.

'Kotchkoff,' Darcy said.

'He's going to jump,' one of the firemen gasped and a ladder was edged forward. But the man on the balcony had no wish to be helped. As he lifted his hand and pointed a pistol, Darcy raised his own gun and fired quickly, twice. The first shot kicked red brick dust from the wall. The second one hit Kotchkoff in the chest and sent him staggering back. For a moment he stood spreadeagled against the wall then he took a few staggering steps forward until he came up against the balcony rail where he wilted, slowly bending forward as if making a bow, before overbalancing and crashing into the street. Two uniformed men ran forward, grabbed his arms and dragged him away.

The roof of Number Ninety-Seven was alight now, the flames roaring through the windows. As they watched, the roof collapsed and they had just come to the conclusion that there could no longer be anyone alive inside when they heard a flurry of shots from the back of the house. Hurrying round to the Rue Mozart, Pel found a policeman just coming out of the builder's yard to look for him.

'We've got the last one, sir,' he burst out.

It was Tyl. He was lying on his back, a bullet wound in his shoulder, a great weal on his head, a pair of broken glasses by his side.

'He came up the ladders, over the roof and started shooting,' Nosjean explained. 'Lagé shot him in the shoulder and he fell off the roof. But he was still firing as he got to his feet. De Troq' brought him down with a piece of timber. He's not badly hurt.'

'Then, mon brave,' Pel said slowly, 'you'd better get the handcuffs on him before he does anyone any more damage.'

twenty

The barricades were coming down and the crowds had disappeared except for the last few soaked and dogged watchers determined to wrest the last ounce of drama from the siege. Firemen and police stood in groups clearing up the last details. Misset was in hospital but the wounded uniformed man and Doctor Lacoste had been allowed to go home. The dead had been carted away and were now lying silent and still at the mortuary where they'd been joined by a last unexpected victim; as the firemen had entered the burnt-out house, a wall had collapsed and buried one of them.

Pel was in a bitter mood as he watched the pressmen trying to get eye-witness accounts to go with their stories, Démon prominent among them, immaculate and handsome, a microphone in his hand.

'There'll be a press conference at headquarters at midnight,' he said abruptly.

Darcy's head jerked round. 'Bit soon, isn't it, Patron?' he asked.

'No,' Pel snapped. 'I'm not having any martyrs made out of this business. They're going to know this time how the thing was done.'

Darcy looked sideways at his chief. Pel was never one to crow at a triumph, any more than he was one to whine when things went wrong. But he was in a strange mood.

'For once,' he said, 'they're going to get it right. They do a lot of talking but they never bother to listen much, and you can learn a lot by listening. This time they'll make no mistakes. Three policemen are dead and four are wounded. I want you to set the facts down, Daniel, for a statement and I want it ready for when they arrive. Nosjean, let the press know.'

But Nosjean wasn't listening. Or at least he was listening to something in his own head that Pel's words had stirred up, something which had nothing to do with what Pel was saying, and he knew suddenly what it was that had troubled him about Madame Crébert.

'Nosjean!'

Nosjean's head turned. 'Patron,' he said slowly. 'Could you give the job to someone else?'

Pel's eyes narrowed. He never liked people dodging duties. But it was unlike Nosjean to beg off. 'Inform me,' he said.

'I've just had an idea, Patron.'

'This is a funny time to have ideas.'

'It was something you said, Patron. Things clicked together. It isn't a hunch. It all fits. I think I know who killed the Crébert boy. I'd like to go and sort it out.'

Pel eyed him, blank-faced. Nosjean's hunches were sometimes right, and Pel believed in hunches. His mind slipped back to the night of July 14th, and the dark woods outside Vieilly, even to Madame Faivre-Perret being driven home in a police car when Pel had hoped to have that privilege himself.

'I'll need de Troq', Patron,' Nosjean said.

'Would you also perhaps like Lagé and Darcy and Aimedieu? Perhaps also myself and Inspector Nadauld. Perhaps, even, you'd like Inspector Pomereu, of Traffic, to set up a few diversions?'

Nosjean blushed. 'No, Patron,' he said. 'Just De Troq'. I think we can clear it up between us. An hour or so will be long enough. We can be back for the press conference.'

Pel was silent for a second then he gestured. 'Very well,' he said. 'Tell Lagé to tell the press.'

Nosjean hurried away to make a telephone call and find De Troquereau. Pel's words had started up an idea in his mind: You can learn a lot by watching and listening. The words echoed Solange Caillaux's sentiments and seemed to fill in the gaps that had been worrying him.

Away from the Rue Daubenon the city was functioning normally. People were going about their business, heading homewards in the darkness. Considering what had been happening, the place looked remarkably placid.

The lights in the Delacolonges' apartment were all out save one which they assumed was the bedroom.

'Reading in bed,' De Troq' said.

'Doing something in bed at any rate,' Nosjean agreed. 'Her husband's not at home. He's on night duty. I checked with St Saviour's.'

He looked up at the flat. It was on the first floor, its balcony roughly twelve feet above the ground. 'You stay here,' he said. 'You ought to have some fun.'

The apartment block was silent as Nosjean mounted the short flight of stairs. As he rang the bell, he heard voices beyond the door. For a long time he waited, then he knocked and rang the bell again. The bolts were already being drawn as he walked slowly back down the stairs. As he reached the entrance to the block, he heard a cry and, as he went outside, he saw De Troq' holding a man in the shadows.

'You were right,' he said cheerfully. 'A *lot* of fun. He came through the window and over the balcony.'

He pushed forward the man he was holding. It was Martinelle. He looked a great deal tougher than De Troq' but De Troq' had his arm and his hand was up near the back of his head, so that his face was twisted with pain.

As they pushed him up the stairs, Madame Delacolonge was looking out of the door. She was wearing a housecoat and didn't appear to have much on underneath. When she saw Martinelle, her face fell.

'Oh, my God,' she groaned.

'Look,' Martinelle said, as they thrust him into the flat. 'It isn't what it seems.'

'Isn't it?' Nosjean said blandly. 'What is it then?'

'She's frightened of being alone when her husband's on nights.'

'And you come to hold her hand?' Nosjean gestured at the settee and as Martinelle and Madame Delacolonge sat together he looked at them coldly. 'How long has it been going on?' he asked.

'A few months,' Martinelle admitted eventually. 'We got to know each other when she brought the boy to the gymnasium when his bicycle was punctured.'

Nosjean looked at Madame Delacolonge. 'Regularly?' he asked. 'When your husband's on night duty.'

She nodded silently.

'Does he know?'

'No.' She paused. 'He wouldn't object, anyway. He's so pathetic.' She gave a weary gesture. 'He was about as good at that as he was at everything else.'

Nosjean broke in. 'I have a question,' he said. 'You can both answer it, if you like. Were you here together the night young Crébert was murdered?'

They glanced at each other then decided there was no point in denying the matter.

'And your husband?'

'He went to see his sister,' Madame Delacolonge snapped. 'He was always going. They wept on each other's shoulders. They were a perfect pair.'

Doctor Bazin, the director of St Saviour's, was none too pleased to be disturbed when off duty.

'Of course it's possible for a patient to get out,' he said. 'Nothing in this world can be considered perfect.'

'Then,' Nosjean asked, 'how do you know he *didn't* get out?'

'I can only take the word of my staff.'

'This staff: Are they at hand when the doctors do their rounds?'

'Of course.'

'Do they make notes?'

'Some do. It depends on their skill or their enthusiasm.'

'Could they learn from what they hear? Could they learn symptoms?'

Bazin sniffed. 'Some are even able to diagnose and several are quite capable of prescribing. They don't, of course, and only the sister in charge is able to obtain drugs.'

'Never the nurses?'

'Never!'

'Never?'

Bazin hesitated. This, he recognised, was a dangerous question. 'We try not to make mistakes, of course,' he said, 'but this place is staffed by human beings.'

Neither Nosjean nor De Troq' spoke as they drove back into the city.

The Créberts' door was opened by Crébert himself. 'Good God,' he said, when he saw them. 'At this time of night?'

'I'm afraid so,' Nosjean said. 'We'd like to see your wife.'

'She's gone to bed.'

'Then I'd be grateful if you'd ask her to come downstairs, Monsieur.'

Crébert frowned. 'Is it absolutely essential?'

'I'm afraid it is.'

'You realise what this will do to her, don't you? She's just beginning to get over the thing.'

'Monsieur,' Nosjean said stiffly, 'we're trying to bring the murderer of your son to justice.'

Crébert studied them for a long time then he shrugged. 'Very well,' he said.

Madame Crébert came down the stairs nervously. Nosjean said nothing until she was sitting down and Crébert had placed a brandy in her hand. Nosjean watched her carefully. He understood now the feeling he'd had about her being torn between two loyalties.

'I'd be grateful if you'd make it as quick as possible,' Crébert said.

'We'll do our best,' Nosjean promised as Madame Crébert watched him warily. 'It consists really of just one question. On the night of your son's death, Madame, you said your husband was away on business and that, because you were feeling low in spirits, your brother, Robert Delacolonge, came to keep you company.' Nosjean paused. 'Was that true?'

Crébert gestured. 'If my wife says so, then it must be.'

'I have to make sure, Monsieur. Was it, Madame?'

Madame Crébert lifted a pale beautiful face towards her husband, then she looked at Nosjean again and inexplicably burst into tears.

'Damn you!' Crébert snarled at Nosjean. 'Now look what you've done. You'd better go.'

'I haven't yet had an answer,' Nosjean persisted.

'You can see – '

'I have to insist, Monsieur.' Nosjean's voice grew harder. 'Much as I dislike distressing your wife.'

Crébert turned to his wife. 'In the name of God, Régine, answer them!'

She gazed at her husband, the tears streaming down her cheeks. Crébert turned to a drawer, took out a tablet and handed it to her. She swallowed it quickly and took a sip of her drink. Nosjean suspected she wasn't as distressed as she appeared to be, that she'd become skilful like her son at putting on an act to get her own way and that she was playing for time, hoping that by appearing distressed she'd put them off and they'd go.

'Well, Madame?' he said. 'Was your brother here that night or not?'

Still she didn't answer and Crébert gestured at the door. 'You'd better go,' he said.

'I must insist on an answer,' Nosjean said stiffly. 'If I can't get one, then I shall have to ask your wife to come to headquarters where, doubtless, the juge d'instruction will be able to persuade her.'

Crébert looked angrily at them, then back at his wife. 'You heard what he said, Régine,' he said harshly. 'For God's sake say "yes" or "no" and let's be rid of them.'

Her eyes were huge and swimming with tears. Nosjean steeled himself. 'Well, Madame?' he said. 'Was he or was he not?'

She looked at him for a moment and then she seemed to throw back her head and howl like a dog. 'No-o-o-o!'

Nosjean and De Troq' escaped as fast as they could. Crébert was still staring, shocked, at his wife as they let themselves out.

De Troq' was deep in thought. 'There's still one thing we can't get round,' he said slowly. 'The boy was seen to get into a *grey* car. Was it hers?'

'It was at the Porte Guillaume,' Nosjean pointed out. 'A roundabout. And like all roundabouts it's lit with sodium lights.'

He headed for the Porte Guillaume and drove the little red Renault round it slowly, giving De Troq' time to take a good long look.

'It's grey!' De Troq' said.

'Exactly,' Nosjean agreed. 'What those boys saw as a grey car was a red car. The colour had been changed by the lights.' He drew a deep breath. 'She knew,' he went on. 'She knew what her brother suffered from. She knew, because it was the same thing *she* suffered from. The same thing her elder son, her parents, her whole family suffered from: Mental instability. She guessed where he really was but she couldn't say because he was the only one who could get her out of her moods. Only an unbalanced woman could have entertained such a division of loyalties for a minute.'

'God help her husband,' De Troq' said. 'It's funny the people you can find you've married.'

'Yes,' Nosjean agreed, remembering Odile Chenandier. As he considered her, he realised he hadn't thought of her for days. It had been easier than he had imagined. A month before he'd been wondering whether to join the Foreign Legion.

twenty-one

Nosjean and De Troq' got back to the Hôtel de Police just as the press conference was about to start, and by that time, it had all been cleared up.

As they'd expected, Anna Ripka had insisted on a lawyer and to nobody's surprise he appeared within half an hour and turned out to be a man of an Arab cast of countenance and of Libyan descent by the name of Sorudz Rassaud. It was to him that she attempted to pass the key and he was stopped as he left.

He was of less stern metal than Anna Ripka and, with his help, they had picked up at his flat three more men – one of them the missing Hamid Ben Afzul – all from North African countries, who though they firmly denied it, were clearly intending to use the store of arms and explosives hidden in the room near the station. Their aims were vague but they seemed to be hoping to influence through terrorism France's attitude to Libya.

Faced with their evidence, Anna Ripka had also thrown in the sponge. The original intention had been to plant gelignite in a sewer near the station entrance and detonate it by remote control but, with the police alert, it had proved too difficult and, when they learned that the sewers were to be searched, they had decided to use the rocket launcher and placed the gelignite in the roof Another few corpses more or less were easy enough to accept.

As they got the last of it down on paper, Pel felt satisfied. He had no need to pull any punches with the press now. Despite the slanging they'd received, they'd done the job. Only just, but they had.

Stretching, Pel looked at the clock and dragged his jacket straight. It was the same jacket he had worn throughout the siege, battered, soaked, torn and wrinkled. His face was grey with fatigue.

'I think I'd better go home and change,' he said. 'It'll soon be time for the press boys.'

'Why not stay as you are, Patron?' Darcy suggested slowly. 'Démon will be there, looking clean and pretty. Let him see what the men he criticises so much have to look like.'

'It's an idea, Daniel.'

'It's even worth developing,' Darcy said. 'I'll get hold of all the boys who were involved and have them in, too, still covered with blood and snot. I'll also get the type who was hit in the arm. A bit of bandage and a sling might make that smooth bastard think a bit.'

As they rose, Nosjean and De Troq' appeared. They looked flushed and excited and Pel stopped and managed a smile.

'Inform me,' he said. 'Were you right?'

'Yes, Patron,' Nosjean said. 'We've got him. It was Delacolonge. He confessed. He said first that his car had been stolen on the night of the murder, then that it had been taken by the Strangler to carry the corpse of a Marseilles gangster who'd been shot, to be buried in the woods. He even showed us a letter to that effect, signed with his own name. Then he denied his confession and said he'd been on duty. The roster at the hospital said different. He was a failure at everything he did and, though he didn't show it, he suffered from depressions and took tranquillisers. The capsules in the boy's pocket came from him. He stole them from his sister and from the drugs cabinet at St Saviour's.'

'It seems to slot together,' Pel observed mildly.

Nosjean nodded. 'He knew how to treat depression, of course, because it was his job to accompany the doctors at St Saviour's on their rounds and he knew all about diazepam. When the boy couldn't talk to his father and found his mother's black moods worse than his own, he went to Delacolonge.'

'And Delacolonge's a nut?' Darcy asked.

'He's a nut all right. He's never done anything successful in his life and that was the point of all those notes, for the demands that there should be more publicity about the case. He wanted to be noticed. He felt he'd committed the perfect crime and was furious when he found he'd been squeezed off the front page by the killings in the Impasse Tarien. We found the revolver he was holding when he took the picture of himself in the telephone booth. It doesn't work. The firing pin's missing. The head-shrinkers are having a session with him now. I think they'll decide he isn't fit to stand trial. The only thing in his mind was that his memoirs would be worth a fortune.'

Pel nodded his satisfaction. 'One more club to hammer the press with,' he said. 'Let's go and get it over.'

The lecture room was crowded with pressmen, and chairs and tables had been arranged on the raised dais. Permission had been granted to the television crews to assemble arc lights so they could get their pictures, and Démon was there, dominating the scene, smooth, confident and immaculate. As Pel took his seat, with him to make it fully official were the Chief, Judge Polverari and Judge Brisard.

The statement Darcy had prepared, giving all the facts, was handed out. It stated in neat columns just who'd been killed and just who'd been wounded. Alongside were the

215

names of the dead terrorists – one of them shot accidentally by his friends – and of those under arrest. It was a formidable array, but the dead and injured on the side of terrorism were well outnumbered by the dead and injured on the side of law and order.

The details about the attempt to assassinate the President set up gasps among the unsuspecting journalists and one or two of them even began to edge towards the doors and the street where the telephones were.

'Don't hurry,' the Chief advised. 'They've been locked and you haven't got all the facts yet.'

Pel gave them the facts, the weapons that had been found, the last arrests, the room overlooking the station, the rocket launcher. The pressmen wrote furiously.

'So let's have no martyrs,' Pel said coldly. 'This is why this conference has been called. These men are terrorists and they don't hesitate to shoot – even, you'll remember, at the Holy Father in Rome. There have been lots of demands for an investigation into the methods of the police who, in carrying out their duties, have even been subjected to a marked campaign to discredit them.' He paused and looked over the journalists. 'It's conveniently overlooked by some of those critics,' he went on slowly, 'not only that policemen risk their lives so that the people who criticise them can sleep safely in their beds, but also that they're assaulted by petrol bombs, nail bombs, blast bombs, hand grenades and a variety of other more sophisticated weapons. Do these critics who want an enquiry into police methods also wish an enquiry into the use of these things by terrorists?'

There was a long silence during which the pressmen eyed the locked doors again, wondering if they could manage when the time came to be first out with their information, then a confused hubbub of questions rose from the body of the hall. Above them came the voice of Démon, clear, sharp and imperious.

216

'Enquiries,' he observed calmly, arrogantly certain that all the other journalists were behind him, 'can produce the most extraordinary facts.'

Pel gestured at Darcy who began handing out bundles of pictures – of the men in custody, the dead men, the scenes inside the besieged house and the house where Kino had been found. Photography had worked fast and the newspapermen grabbed them eagerly.

Démon studied them. 'The details you've given about this organisation you claim to have smashed,' he said, his manner faintly disbelieving. 'How were they acquired?'

'The woman, Anna Ripka, talked.'

'Was she persuaded?'

'She didn't have to be,' Pel snapped. 'It was all over and she knew it.'

There were few questions. The intelligent ones among the pressmen accepted that there had been a rebuke in Pel's words because there *had* been a lot of irresponsible criticism. As Pel sat down the Chief rose.

'It should be made clear,' he said, 'that the police cannot and will not permit terrorists to take control of the streets and that the police will always use firearms when there's a grave threat to life. Inevitably, fatalities will occur occasionally but it should be remembered that the police would have no need for weapons if there were no violence.'

As he spoke, the newspapermen were busy writing, glancing occasionally at Démon. As the Chief sat down, Démon rose. He looked pink but still smooth and very confident, as if he relied on his reputation to carry him through.

'I feel,' he said, 'that I must reply to the vague accusations which have been made against the press, sir. There's a feeling among us that these complaints are uncalled for – '

'Not with me,' Sarrazin said sharply.

The interruption seemed to startle Démon but he pressed on. 'I feel the finger has been pointed at us and that we should be able to reply, because we're being accused of a lack of integrity – '

Sitting frozen-faced on the dais, Pel interrupted to indicate a loudspeaker which had been set up alongside him. 'I think,' he pointed out, 'that before we accept any recrimination for what's been said here, we should hear a tape made the other evening by one of my officers.'

He gestured at Claudie Darel who had slipped quietly into the room to stand near Darcy and he saw Démon's jaw drop. As he nodded, she pressed the switch and Démon's voice came from the loudspeaker, overlaid with crackling but quite clearly the voice that was known over the whole of France.

'...It's rubbish, of course. I know it's rubbish, but it sells. It's what people want... We all have to make our way in this world and I'm making mine very nicely, thank you...'

Sarrazin started scribbling furiously. Fiabon, who'd been sitting open-mouthed, saw him and started, too.

'...It makes better viewing to see people helped away with blood all over them. Especially if they're Flics. I've more than once persuaded kids to heave bottles at them to get a better story...'

As the voice came to a stop, Démon's face went pale. 'I demand an explanation,' he said. 'That tape was taken without my knowledge.'

'I can hardly imagine,' Pel said stonily, 'that you would have said those things if you'd known they would be made public.'

'I have a right – !'

Sarrazin looked up, his wrinkled face cynical. 'I think, my friend,' he growled, 'that you'd be wiser to sit down and shut up.'

For a moment Démon stared round him, studying the hostile faces of the other journalists then, snatching up his coat, he turned and strode to the door. Finding it still locked, he was obliged to wait in humiliated embarrassment until someone let him out.

Pel was staring at Sarrazin, bewildered. Everybody seemed to be behaving in an extraordinary fashion today. First Doctor Lacoste and Misset being heroes. Now Sarrazin, his most ardent critic, appearing on his side. As the room began to empty, Brisard touched his shoulder.

'Well done, Inspector,' he said. 'That was clever. I imagine that one's been shut up for a long time.'

Pel stared after him as he hurried away. Good God, he thought. Brisard, too! The whole world was acting out of character! He stopped, warmed by the gesture, then signed to Darcy. 'Come on, Daniel,' he said. 'Let's wind up the paper work.'

'Leave that to me, Patron,' Darcy said. 'That's what I'm here for.'

Pel hesitated, then he nodded. 'Very well,' he agreed. 'I'll go home.'

'Not just yet, Patron,' Darcy said. 'There's someone in your office wants to see you.'

Pel's head turned. 'The Chief?'

'No.'

'Judge Polverari?'

'No, Patron. Turned up just before the conference. I said you'd be rather a long time.'

'I don't want to see anyone just now,' Pel snapped. 'I've seen everybody I want to see today.'

Darcy didn't move, blocking the doorway so that Pel couldn't pass, and in the end he sighed and headed for his office. He still wore his ruined suit, his feet dragged and he felt stiff and weary, and was quite certain that he'd be in bed for the next six months before retiring prematurely, his health ruined.

As he pushed the door open, he saw Madame Faivre-Perret sitting by his desk. She wasn't doing anything, just sitting quietly, waiting. Her mackintosh was soaked and her umbrella had dripped a pool of water at her feet.

As he entered, she rose, pale and anxious, and Pel stood in the doorway, touched and feeling a little like tears. 'I'm in no state to be seen by anyone,' he muttered. 'I haven't changed. I'm filthy.'

She smiled uncertainly. 'Evariste,' she said. 'Do you think that matters?'

MARK HEBDEN

DEATH SET TO MUSIC

The severely battered body of a murder victim turns up in provincial France and the sharp-tongued Chief Inspector Pel must use all his Gallic guile to understand the pile of clues building up around him, until a further murder and one small boy make the elusive truth all too apparent.

THE ERRANT KNIGHTS

Hector and Hetty Bartlelott go to Spain for a holiday, along with their nephew Alec and his wife Sibley. All is well under a Spanish sun until Hetty befriends a Spanish boy on the run from the police and passionate Spanish Anarchists. What follows is a hard-and-fast race across Spain, hot-tailed by the police and the anarchists, some light indulging in the Semana Santa festivities of Seville to throw off the pursuers, and a near miss in Toledo where the young Spanish fugitive is almost caught.

MARK HEBDEN

PEL AND THE PARIS MOB

In his beloved Burgundy, Chief Inspector Pel finds himself
incensed by interference from Paris, but it isn't the flocking
descent of rival policemen that makes Pel's blood boil –
crimes are being committed by violent gangs from Paris and
Marseilles. Pel unravels the riddle of the robbery on the road
to Dijon airport as well as the mysterious shootings in an
iron foundry. If that weren't enough, the Chief Inspector
must deal with the misadventures of the delightfully
handsome Sergeant Misset and his red-haired lover.

"…written with downbeat humour and some delightful
dialogue which leaven the violence." *Financial Times*

PEL AND THE PREDATORS

There has been a spate of sudden murders around Burgundy
where Pel has just been promoted to Chief Inspector. The
irascible policeman receives a letter bomb, and these
combined events threaten to overturn Pel's plans to marry
Mme Faivre-Perret. Can Pel keep his life, his love and his
career by solving the murder mysteries? Can Pel stave off the
predators?

'…impeccable French provincial ambience.' *The Times*

Mark Hebden

Pel Under Pressure

The irascible Chief Inspector Pel is hot on the trail of a crime syndicate in this fast-paced, gritty crime novel, following leads on the mysterious death of a student and the discovery of a corpse in the boot of a car. Pel uncovers a drug-smuggling ring within the walls of Burgundy's university, and more murders guide the Chief Inspector to Innsbruck where the mistress of a professor awaits him.

Portrait in a Dusty Frame

The sudden popularity of the poet, Christina Moray Tait, seventy years after her death, gives her great-grandson, Tennyson Moray Tait, a new-found notoriety. When approached by a man claiming he could reveal the true circumstances surrounding Christina's mysterious death, Tennyson decides to join him in Peru, facing the dark green extremes of the Amazon, a reluctant American freelance photographer, and a suspicious native guide.

TITLES BY MARK HEBDEN AVAILABLE DIRECT
FROM HOUSE OF STRATUS

Quantity		£	$(US)	$(CAN)	€
☐	THE DARK SIDE OF THE ISLAND	6.99	11.50	15.99	11.50
☐	DEATH SET TO MUSIC	6.99	11.50	15.99	11.50
☐	THE ERRANT KNIGHTS	6.99	11.50	15.99	11.50
☐	EYE WITNESS	6.99	11.50	15.99	11.50
☐	A KILLER FOR THE CHAIRMAN	6.99	11.50	15.99	11.50
☐	LEAGUE OF EIGHTY NINE	6.99	11.50	15.99	11.50
☐	MASK OF VIOLENCE	6.99	11.50	15.99	11.50
☐	PEL AMONG THE PUEBLOS	6.99	11.50	15.99	11.50
☐	PEL AND THE TOUCH OF PITCH	6.99	11.50	15.99	11.50
☐	PEL AND THE FACELESS CORPSE	6.99	11.50	15.99	11.50
☐	PEL AND THE MISSING PERSONS	6.99	11.50	15.99	11.50
☐	PEL AND THE PARIS MOB	6.99	11.50	15.99	11.50
☐	PEL AND THE PARTY SPIRIT	6.99	11.50	15.99	11.50

ALL HOUSE OF STRATUS BOOKS ARE AVAILABLE FROM GOOD BOOKSHOPS
OR DIRECT FROM THE PUBLISHER:

Internet: www.houseofstratus.com including author interviews, reviews, features.

Email: sales@houseofstratus.com please quote author, title and credit card details.

TITLES BY MARK HEBDEN AVAILABLE DIRECT
FROM HOUSE OF STRATUS

Quantity	£	$(US)	$(CAN)	€
☐ PEL AND THE PICTURE OF INNOCENCE	6.99	11.50	15.99	11.50
☐ PEL AND THE PIRATES	6.99	11.50	15.99	11.50
☐ PEL AND THE PREDATORS	6.99	11.50	15.99	11.50
☐ PEL AND THE PROMISED LAND	6.99	11.50	15.99	11.50
☐ PEL AND THE PROWLER	6.99	11.50	15.99	11.50
☐ PEL AND THE SEPULCHRE JOB	6.99	11.50	15.99	11.50
☐ PEL AND THE STAG HOUND	6.99	11.50	15.99	11.50
☐ PEL IS PUZZLED	6.99	11.50	15.99	11.50
☐ PEL UNDER PRESSURE	6.99	11.50	15.99	11.50
☐ PORTRAIT IN A DUSTY FRAME	6.99	11.50	15.99	11.50
☐ A PRIDE OF DOLPHINS	6.99	11.50	15.99	11.50
☐ WHAT CHANGED CHARLEY FARTHING	6.99	11.50	15.99	11.50

ALL HOUSE OF STRATUS BOOKS ARE AVAILABLE FROM GOOD BOOKSHOPS
OR DIRECT FROM THE PUBLISHER:

Hotline: UK ONLY: **0800 169 1780**, please quote author, title and credit card details.
INTERNATIONAL: **+44 (0) 20 7494 6400**, please quote author, title, and credit card details.

Send to: **House of Stratus Sales Department**
24c Old Burlington Street
London
W1X 1RL
UK

Please allow for postage costs charged per order plus an amount per book as set out in the tables below:

	£(Sterling)	$(US)	$(CAN)	€(Euros)
Cost per order				
UK	2.00	3.00	4.50	3.30
Europe	3.00	4.50	6.75	5.00
North America	3.00	4.50	6.75	5.00
Rest of World	3.00	4.50	6.75	5.00
Additional cost per book				
UK	0.50	0.75	1.15	0.85
Europe	1.00	1.50	2.30	1.70
North America	2.00	3.00	4.60	3.40
Rest of World	2.50	3.75	5.75	4.25

PLEASE SEND CHEQUE, POSTAL ORDER (STERLING ONLY), EUROCHEQUE, OR INTERNATIONAL MONEY
ORDER (PLEASE CIRCLE METHOD OF PAYMENT YOU WISH TO USE)
MAKE PAYABLE TO: STRATUS HOLDINGS plc

Cost of book(s):———————— Example: 3 x books at £6.99 each: £20.97

Cost of order:———————— Example: £2.00 (Delivery to UK address)

Additional cost per book:———————— Example: 3 x £0.50: £1.50

Order total including postage:———————— Example: £24.47

Please tick currency you wish to use and add total amount of order:

☐ £ (Sterling)   ☐ $ (US)   ☐ $ (CAN)   ☐ € (EUROS)

VISA, MASTERCARD, SWITCH, AMEX, SOLO, JCB:

☐ ☐ ☐ ☐ ☐ ☐ ☐ ☐ ☐ ☐ ☐ ☐ ☐ ☐ ☐ ☐ ☐ ☐ ☐ ☐

Issue number (Switch only):

☐ ☐ ☐

Start Date: **Expiry Date:**

☐ ☐ / ☐ ☐   ☐ ☐ / ☐ ☐

Signature: _____

NAME: _____

ADDRESS: _____

_____

POSTCODE: _____

Please allow 28 days for delivery.

Prices subject to change without notice.
Please tick box if you do not wish to receive any additional information. ☐

House of Stratus publishes many other titles in this genre; please check our
website (**www.houseofstratus.com**) for more details.